ARCHANGEL EVOLUTION

Book Three of the

Evolution Trilogy

David Estes

Copyright © 2011 David Estes

All rights reserved.

ISBN-10: 1466422939
ISBN-13: 978-1466422933

Jacket concept by Adele Estes
Jacket art by Phatpuppy Art
Jacket design by Winkipop Design

This book is dedicated to my readers,

past, present, and future.

You are the reason I write.

PART I

"Everyone's running from something
But we don't know when it's coming
So we keep running and running gotta

Now I'm looking up the bible tryna find a loophole
Yeah I'm living for revival dying for a new soul
Now there's no light to guide me on my way home
Now there's no time to shine my rusty halo

Now I'm running for the light in the tunnel but it's just the train
Yeah I'm looking for the right type of pleasure but all I find is pain
Now there's no light to guide me on my way home
Now there's no time to shine my rusty halo"

The Script- "Rusty Halo"
From the album *The Script (2008)*

One

Shining liquid streamed down her arm. Blood. Angel blood. But not hers.

Someone's.

She cradled his head in her arms. She was glowing. He was bleeding. Gabriel was bleeding. It seemed as if his entire body was covered in the gleaming milk. She needed to find the wound…to heal him. Fast. He was dying—that much she knew.

He was wearing a white tunic. *Strange*, she thought. It could be replaced. She tore it off him, revealing the horror beneath.

There was a softball-sized hole in his chest. From the hole streamed the glowing blood. In the hole was his beating heart. Thud, thud. Thud, thud. Thud……..thud. The beating was slowing—he was dying. His heart—not red or pink, but white—had been attacked: two round puncture wounds marred its fleshy surface. The marks were familiar somehow.

She thrust her hand in the open wound, clutched the heart, and whispered words long forgotten. Her hand glowed as energy was transferred to him. She felt the heart squeeze out a final beat, heard the sucking of air as his lungs took a final gasping breath, and then nothing. Nothing. She had failed him.

What Evil? she thought. What Evil would do such a thing to her? Would take the love of her life? Would take her reason for living, her water, her air? Wanting revenge, she whirled around, seeking the Evil. It found her first.

The enormous ink-black snake latched onto her chest with vice-like jaws, twisting, squeezing, tearing, ripping. Intent on one thing: piercing her heart. Like it had Gabriel's.

At first she struggled, attempting to pry it from her skin, but eventually she realized the futility of her efforts and succumbed to its desires. After all, she had nothing left to live for. Because he was dead, too.

The snake torqued its head back violently and she felt her chest open. She collapsed to the cold, hard ground. Rearing above her, the serpent reveled in its victory. It held something in its mouth; the thing was dripping bright, white liquid. It was her heart—also white, like Gabriel's; an angel's heart. The snake's face transformed from a scaly serpent to something humanlike. A face she had hoped never to see again. A face she both hated and feared equally.

Dionysus laughed, and in doing so dropped her heart, allowing gravity to carry it towards her face.

Taylor screamed. She stopped when a hand was thrust in front of her eyes, catching the heart in mid-fall. Lolling her head to the side, she gasped when she saw the piercing eyes that met hers. He was alive.

Two

Dionysus's eyes sparked open as he was released from the trance. He had entered the girl's dream only to monger fear. For fun, really. While it was within his power to infiltrate the dreams of angels, demons, and humans alike, he was unable to cause any real damage by this method. The damage would have to be done in person. He was glad about that.

He longed to close his hands around her filthy neck, to ring the life out of her. His hands almost itched at the thought. While revenge would surely be sweet, it was not his main goal. If only he could be so foolish, so impulsive. In another time, maybe he would have charged off in a fit of rage, seeking to satiate his growing bloodlust. But not now. Now he was a man of self-control, mature and calculated in his meticulous planning and scheming. The leader of his people. Loved and respected.

For a week he had meditated on what had happened, taking his meals while sitting cross-legged on the floor. At times he dozed, and his dreams were filled with flashbacks of the girl ruining everything: her unexpected and seemingly fortuitous appearance on the Warrior's Plateau, her willingness to bargain for Gabriel and his family, and her miraculous transformation into an angel.

Well, more than an angel, really.

When he wasn't sleeping, he was thinking. For the last decade he had focused on carrying out The Plan. Despite its genius, The Plan was a simple concept: destroy the demons, enslave the humans, and harvest their bodies.

Ten years ago while travelling the earth, Dionysus had learned that he could inhabit the body of any human he chose. This was valuable because despite the many superhuman capabilities that angels had been endowed with, immortality was not one of them. Unfortunately, Dionysus could not outlive his body. His only option was to replace it.

Now he was in his early fifties, but had the body of someone in their early thirties. He fondly remembered the day he had added decades to his life expectancy:

He had just finished a day of futile and frantic experimenting. The eight expended human corpses were heaped in a pile. There was no messy cleanup—not one drop of blood had been shed. All he had left to do was burn the bodies.

The last subject was chained to the wall, cowering, like a child afraid of the boogeyman. Dionysus would have almost pitied him if he hadn't hated him so much. The twenty-five-year-old was not bad looking, handsome even by human standards, but he was still a human, and therefore, pathetic, weak.

Despite his frustrations, Dionysus had managed to meditate for a few minutes, blocking out the sobbing whimpering of the last test rat. Concentrating hard, he remembered each failed experiment and tried to pinpoint what had gone wrong.

In each case, Dionysus had attempted to harness the aura, or the inner light, of each human subject and convert the aura into energy to power his own abilities. They were the humans with the largest auras he could find, and yet they broke under his influence; shattered beyond repair, their internal organs had imploded upon themselves, causing instant death. Locking on to their auras, his powers had increased by twenty to thirty percent, a small gain that was a far cry from what he had hoped for.

During each failed experiment there was a point where something…strange had happened. At the point where he could feel his own powers beginning to magnify, he could also sense that the human was dying. He felt a pull from within him. Not a physical pull, but a pull that could only be described as spiritual. It was as if his soul, if he even had one, was trying to escape his body. He could sense this pull, feel it, and it scared him. So he simply sucked even more of the humans' auras from them, killing them, and releasing the strange pull.

As he dwelled on the phenomenon, he wondered if the pull was really dangerous. Perhaps it was just a part of the process required to harness the human aura. Or perhaps it would kill him. Either way, it was a risk he might have to take. All great scientists were forced to take risks to further their knowledge. Maybe this was his great risk. His kite in the lightning storm, so to speak.

Dionysus had boldly delved into the final subject, the one with the largest aura, and began harvesting the power within him. The man had screamed—oh how he had screamed; his shrill cry was deliciously full of fear and pain and weakness. At the point of no return, the point where he felt the pull on his very being—his soul?—he had allowed the process to continue, had allowed the subject to live, albeit in great pain.

It was then that he had an out of body experience.

He could see his body, glowing, glowing, and then going dark like an extinguished candle. While his spirit, or something like it, hovered in the air, his body crumpled to the floor; what was full of life became suddenly lifeless.

He turned his attention to the subject, who was still screaming, screaming, and whose aura was glowing from within him. And then they were one. Him and the subject. He was the subject. The subject was not himself—not anymore. The subject was dead, but not. The subject's soul had died or been replaced or been hidden, or something else entirely. Whatever the case, the subject was no longer present in the body, but the body remained alive, governed by Dionysus. He *controlled the limbs, the bones, the speech. He had inhabited the body.*

At first he was fearful that he had inadvertently become human again. That by some trick of the gods, he had devolved back into the pitiful existence of his predecessors. His fear was short-lived, however, as he had quickly realized that all of his powers, knowledge, and strength were still intact, they were merely housed in a new body. A younger body. One with more years separating it from a death caused by old age.

That's when he knew he had discovered the figurative fountain of youth. He could live forever. In fact, all angels could.

Dionysus smiled at the fond memory of his discovery. It had changed everything. He had switched bodies once more to retest his theory, carefully selecting a stunningly handsome Italian man for the job. The same man he now looked at every day in the mirror. He was the Italian man, or the Italian man was him, the semantics didn't really matter. Of course, he no longer looked Italian, because for some strange reason his hair had changed from a deep black to white blond when he had taken over the body, a trick of the transition.

Only a handful of other angels within his innermost circle knew the key to immortality, but none had chosen to follow the path yet. But they would. When their bodies began failing them, they would choose life. When the time was right, when the demons had been eradicated, he would tell the rest of the angel population his secret, and they would choose life too, helping him to enslave all of mankind.

Unfortunately, the last week had been a major step backwards for The Plan. When that damn girl, Taylor, transformed into an angel, she destroyed most of the Archangel Council—only Johanna, Sarah, and Percy remained. She had also eliminated his ability to use her aura to destroy the demons. When she was a human he could harness her aura to wield a weapon so powerful that the demons wouldn't stand a chance. However, as an angel, her inner light had changed—for some reason angels couldn't access each other's auras—rendering her useless.

The whole mess was an unexpected development, and had sent Dionysus into a fit of rage, the likes of which hadn't been seen in many years. His tantrum didn't last long, however, and now he had a new idea—one that was given to him by Taylor. Not intentionally, of course, but even an inadvertent gift was valuable.

If she could evolve, why couldn't he? Sure, he had evolved once before, from demon to angel, and his ancestors had once evolved from human to demon, but Taylor had been the first to evolve from human directly to angel. Perhaps he had been underestimating the evolutionary forces at play. Perhaps he had underestimated himself. Perhaps he could learn from the girl. *It couldn't hurt to try*, he thought. But how?

Out of the corner of his eye he spotted movement, subtle and small. Despite the tiny web-crawler's positioning in the far upper corner of the room, Dionysus could see the spider clearly. It had already designed and built an intricately detailed trap, beautiful in its simplicity—a web. Under normal circumstances, the spider would be motionless, waiting for his invisible net to capture dinner. In this case, however, the silky contraption had already done the deed—a fly was stuck in the corner, frantically buzzing and twitching in a fruitless effort to escape. The spider moved closer. Not only did Dionysus marvel at the beautiful appearance of nature in his fortress, but he also wondered at how a spider could have penetrated his innermost sanctuary. And even more incredible was the appearance of the fly. He would have to fire his housekeeper. But first, the spider and its web of perfection had given him an idea, one that excited him.

Assuming the success of his idea—and being an optimist he always assumed success—he would have all the firepower he needed to destroy Taylor, murder Gabriel, and eradicate the demons and their allies, like flies pitifully trapped in a web, waiting to be eaten alive.

But first he needed to rebuild the Archangel Council, and he knew the perfect recruits.

The spider crawled onto the fly.

Three

Taylor Kingston waited for him to arrive. She needed to talk to him. He was already an hour late.

She was wearing ripped jeans, flip-flops, a t-shirt, and her usual nine rings. Her straight, brown hair was unkempt—she hadn't bothered to comb it. As usual, she wore no makeup, although since her *transformation* her skin had become flawless—just another benefit of angelhood.

As she sat on the lawn waiting, she was subconsciously aware of the demons protecting her. One was on the roof of a nearby building, another high in the uppermost branches of a tree, and two more in a parked car. There were likely countless others in the vicinity as well, but as of yet she hadn't spotted them. She almost felt like yelling *C'mon out, guys, we can all sit and wait together!* but she held her tongue.

She gazed at the inside of her wrist—her new tattoo still looked fresh, having been inked only a week earlier. A pair of basic angel wings decorated her arm. They were a reminder of what she had become, and also what she had come from. Despite the increased strength of her skin, the tattoo-artist eventually got the job done, but only after breaking two needles and severely damaging the third. She had paid him extra for his efforts. Taylor's dad had shrugged when he learned about the new tattoo—after the second one he had come to expect it.

Taylor's new tattoo was the first to not feature the black snake. The deadly obsidian serpent that had plagued Taylor's nightmares her entire life was not important to her anymore—a mere shadow of the great tormentor from her past. Her first tattoo—on the back of her shoulder—was the largest and displayed only the snake; it had been etched while she was still in high school, as a symbol of her waning fear of the nightmarish creature. The second tattoo—on her ankle—showed the snake strung up on a sword, dead and gone. She had had it inked during her first semester at college after Gabriel had entered her dreams and slain the snake in its most fearsome form yet: a monstrous serpent bigger than any demon python or anaconda from some cheesy horror movie.

Taylor smiled as she ran her fingers over the freshly stained wings. She was an angel! A week earlier, she was a human girl, and now she had crazy-impossible-beautiful wings growing inside her back. Granted, she had been dating an angel and fighting alongside the demons to protect the earth, but she was still only a human, before. But somehow she had evolved like others had before her. She was still waiting on the test results, which would hopefully shed some light on the remarkable transformation she had undergone.

Naturally, her hand slid down to the second tattoo, on her ankle. Her thoughts reverted to her most recent dream. Awakening from the dream, she hadn't been scared or upset; rather, she had been surprised. It had been months since she had dreamed of the black serpent. The last time was when Gabriel had entered her dream and plunged his sword into its evil black heart. She wanted to know why the slithering Evil had made such a sudden reappearance. That's why she needed to talk to Gabriel, among other reasons.

Still bored, Taylor began playing with a lock of her hair, twisting and twirling it on her finger, braiding it and pulling it apart, flipping it in the air. It was the lock she always played with when she was bored. The white one. Taylor wasn't blonde all over; rather, she had acquired a single lock of white-blond hair when she had been changed. At first it had annoyed her, but now it was growing on her.

Taylor had only been back at college for a week, but was already growing tired of the daily routine: get up, go to class, eat lunch, more class, dinner, study, bed. After all she had seen and been a part of in the last few months, she wasn't ready for routine just yet.

She considered phoning Gabriel, but something stopped her. Most of her life she had relied on her instincts—her "good gut" as her mother used to call it before she was killed by a drunk driver. One of the few times Taylor had ignored her gut was when she had trusted Gabriel implicitly, and had almost died because of it. She wouldn't make that mistake again.

Now, her gut was telling her that something was wrong. She knew without a doubt in her mind that something terrible had happened.

Four

An hour earlier.

Despite all that had happened—from the kidnapping of his parents and their subsequent rescue, to Taylor's evolution to an angel and her destruction of most of the Archangel Council—the daily grind of the Great War went on. Most of the soldiers had heard rumors of the events that had taken place on the Warrior's Plateau, but few of them knew the details.

The daily battles continued as scheduled; angels and demons fought—and died—while the real fight was being fought behind closed doors, in the minds of their leaders.

Gabriel Knight yearned to fight again. Now was the time to strike, while the Archangel Council was in ruins, while Dionysus doubted himself, while they had a chance. For once, Clifford, the head of the Eldership of the demons, agreed with him. He said they were developing a plan, but that Gabriel needed to be patient.

He ran a hand through his wavy, sandy blond hair in frustration. Gabriel's request to fight in the day's battle had been rejected. Clifford had said he would have a much larger role to play in the War, and risking his life in a skirmish was out of the question. He could only watch from afar as his best friend, Sampson—an angel—and his demon girlfriend, Kiren, marched into battle.

He checked his watch. There were only thirty minutes until he had to meet Taylor. Because the flight to the University of Trinton, or UT, would take more than seven hours even at angel speed, one of Taylor's demon guards agreed to teleport back to the Lair—the demon's cave network that housed the demon army—and then teleport Gabriel to UT's campus.

High atop a cliff outside the Lair, Gabriel waited impatiently for the battle to begin. The opposing armies were completely out on the battlefield now and awaiting the signal for the clash to begin. With his ultra-powerful angel vision he could see Sampson hovering in the air, flanked by at least two dozen other angel fighters. Sampson's bright, white shock of hair was hidden beneath a sturdy helmet, but Gabriel could still easily recognize him. Like a sore thumb, Sampson's shorter, bowling-ball body stuck out amongst his taller, leaner comrades. Compared to his bull-like frame, everyone else almost looked fragile.

It was the first battle where a significant number of angels would fight on the side of the demons. They would be considered traitors by the angel warriors, and especially by Dionysus. The angel leader would likely be seething in the Command Center. Gabriel wouldn't have been surprised if Dionysus—known for his bad temper—charged from the mountain in a fit of rage, attempting to kill the angel traitors himself.

Below Sampson, his demon girlfriend, Kiren, popped in and out of view rapidly, like a magician performing a series of awe-inspiring disappearing acts. Compared to Sampson, Kiren looked thinner than a bean pole, although in reality her muscles were well-toned. Her short, punk-styled hair was orange today, although it changed color regularly.

Gabriel couldn't help but to chuckle to himself as he remembered the last time Sampson and Kiren went into battle together. When Sampson was injured early in the contest, Kiren was forced to rescue him, thus adding a bruised ego to his damaged body. His body had healed much faster than his ego, and behind closed doors Sampson had told Gabriel that he was going to make up for his poor performance in the battle today. Gabriel couldn't wait to see him try.

Sweat pooled in the center of Gabriel's back, but it was not from the hot, sunny day. Rather, it was in anticipation of the action. Action that he desperately wished he could be a part of.

From somewhere at the demons' end of the valley a horn sounded, clear and loud and ceremonious, and was quickly answered by a similar blast from the angels' side. The battle had begun.

With a flash of light, the first angel light-orb was fired, a massive pulse of energy that arced towards the demon army, until it was stopped in midflight by a well-aimed ball of fire set loose by a demon defender. The resulting impact was deafening, and filled the blue sky with an exquisite array of colors, whose beauty was marred only by the circumstances under which they were created.

Despite the forecast for clear skies and sun, a freak thunderstorm moved in as if by magic. For once, it wasn't the forecast that was wrong; rather, the demons had used their ability to control the weather to darken the skies, giving them a distinct advantage as angels relied on the power of light for most of their attacks. Giant spotlights flicked on throughout the battlefield—it was the angels' tactical response to the lightless skies.

Despite the smog-black skies, roaring thunderclaps, and icicles of lightning that filled the atmosphere, not a single drop of rain wetted the ground. While the demons preferred to fight in darkness, they also preferred to fight dry.

The scene rapidly became a spectacular lights, lasers, and fireworks display, although each magnificent color was filled with death. Fireballs charged through the legions of angels, while light-orbs pierced demon armor. Demon fire-swords clashed with angel light-swords, with each blow sounding like the beating of a bass drum. The battle was typical, neither side giving an inch or applying any unusual tactics.

Then everything changed.

The angels' horn sounded mid-fight, which Gabriel had never heard before. *Something was wrong.*

It was a signal.

Despite having heard the same horn hundreds of times before, the blast sounded ominous, dangerous, yet mellifluous at the same time. Gabriel squinted, his already incredible eyesight becoming further magnified—he was trying to see how the angel forces would react to the horn.

Like a flock of birds, the entire angel army lifted off the ground, at first leaping high into the air, and then using their powerful wings to propel them further skywards. In formation, they began to retreat. *What the hell?* Gabriel thought. Dionysus was a lot of things, but he wasn't the type to run from a battle, unless the dangers outweighed the potential rewards.

Something was wrong.

Deadly wrong.

But what? As he watched the angel army soar back towards their hideaway, Gabriel puzzled over the question.

The demon army seemed confused, unsure of whether to chase their fleeing enemy, stand their ground, or retreat. Before the demon generals had an opportunity to make a decision, the entire angel army changed course again, stopping abruptly in the air and turning back towards the eastern fringe of the battlefield.

It was the area currently occupied by Sampson and his demon-friendly angels, who had been given the nickname Hell's Angels. In Dionysus's warped mind, these angels would only ever be known as The Traitors. And he was targeting them.

Gabriel held his breath and could only watch as the mass of winged enemies crashed into Hell's Angels with rabid fury, slashing through them with ease. Despite the rapidity of the demon response—they realized the situation and took action, teleporting into the air to defend their exposed brethren—it was too late. Sampson and his squad fell from the sky, having been torn, slashed, blasted, and trashed.

In the chaos that ensued, bodies crashed into bodies as the demons attempted to catch the fallen angels, but mostly just got in each other's ways. Some of Hell's Angels crashed into the earth, some were caught by demons, and others landed on fallen demons.

Having successfully completed their task, the angel army took advantage of the confusion and carnage to perform a real retreat and escape back into the safety of their mountain refuge.

The entire event took about eight seconds.

Gabriel leapt from the cliff, his wings bursting instinctively with a slight *pop*, and then flew to where he had seen Sampson go down. He landed with a solid *thud* and pushed his way through the hordes of demons that had gathered amongst the injured. At least he hoped they were merely injured. He didn't let himself consider the alternative.

As he forced his way through the last circle of gawkers, he saw that Kiren was kneeling beside her boyfriend, her head tilted to allow her ear to rest on his lips. She was listening for breathing. She looked up, her eyes wild with panic, and said, "It's there, but very faint. He needs immediate help."

"Take me with you," Gabriel said.

Nodding, Kiren clutched Gabriel's hand and placed her other hand on Sampson's chest. The world twisted upside down and sort of sideways, as Gabriel felt himself being transported through space. He had teleported a few times before, but still wasn't used to it; flying was always his preference if he had a choice.

When the whirlwind stopped, they reappeared in a small room, next to a bed. Typical medical equipment beeped and droned along the edges of the space. Gabriel recognized it as a room in the medical wing within the Lair. He could hear shouts, screams, and cries outside the open door—the sounds of death resounded throughout the facility.

Kiren reached down and scooped up Sampson's bulky frame as if he weighed no more than a feather, and set him down on the bed. "Medic!" she yelled to whoever might be listening.

A shadowy woman in a black lab coat appeared across the bed. She hadn't used the door—there was no time for formalities. "Patient's condition?" she said simply.

The words rushed out of Kiren, no dams or rocks to slow them: "Multiple slash wounds, at least a couple of which penetrated his chest plate…Scorch marks on his body indicate he was hit by several light orbs…Breathing, but barely…Heartbeat is erratic…He's my freakin' boyfriend so please save him!"

"And my best friend," Gabriel added.

"No pressure there," the black-haired doctor said wryly. And then, "We'll do what we can."

Two more doctors appeared on either side of her and began setting up equipment, removing Sampson's armor and clothing, and securing various suction-like probes to his chest. One of them turned to Gabriel and said, "You have to go. You both do."

Gabriel took one last look at his friend. Despite his solid frame, he looked weak, exposed, like he was already dead. His face was even paler white than normal and his skin was glistening with bright, white blood. Because Sampson's eyes were closed, Gabriel tried to make himself believe that he was only sleeping, and not in critical condition, on the verge of death.

Kiren appeared to be in shock, her face bland and emotionless. She allowed Gabriel to take her hand and lead her from the room. In the hall, Gabriel pulled Kiren over to a row of chairs and helped her sit down. He slumped down next to her. Lifting her head, a single tear stained Kiren's face; it dangled precariously on her chin after having meandered down her cheek. "How did this happen?" she asked.

"We underestimated Dionysus's desire for retribution," Gabriel said.

"We should have known…"

"Yes."

The tear drop released itself from her chin.

They sat in silence for what felt like a few minutes, watching the nurses and doctors rushing around the hospital trying to save the dying angels. Gabriel's eyes wandered to his watch. "Damn," he said when he realized that over an hour had passed since the attack.

Five

The boy sat in silence, meditating. From afar, he could've been mistaken for his brother, Gabriel, only younger, with wavy, sandy blond hair, a wide, firm, kingly chin, and a physique that was fast developing into that of a soldier, strong and tight. The meditation was part of his training, but he didn't mind. Since his family had been abducted on the Warrior's Plateau and his filthy traitor brother had escaped unscathed, he had been spending more and more time wrapped up in his own head trying to make sense of the senseless.

Why had Gabriel betrayed his own kind? Why did his parents seem to agree with it? Why had the human girl killed the Archangels? There was only one answer that made sense—the same answer he had gotten from Dionysus: They were Traitors, Demon-Lovers, modern day Judas's.

The more he thought about it all, the angrier he became. Rage filled him, causing his fingers to tremble until he pulled them into tight fists. Sometimes he kept his hands balled for hours until they ached from the pressure. It hurt, but helped to douse the fires raging within him. It also helped to clear his mind. He had learned this technique from his master, Lucas, who had instructed him: "David, pain can be either a positive or a negative event, depending on how you use it." David Knight had always thought that pain was negative, to be avoided. And it was, for most angels. Most angels focused on the pain, rather than letting the pain focus them. Now, he used pain to his advantage, just like Lucas had taught him. His mind was clear.

He had tried to help his brother, to talk to him, to make him see the truth, but he was too far gone. Now David had only one choice to make things right, to fulfill his destiny. He had to kill Gabriel. And he would.

Six

Grudgingly, Taylor walked back to her dormitory. As a first year student, she was required to live in the freshman dorms—hers was called Shyloh Hall. As she approached the nondescript building, she had her student ID card in her hand. Reaching the security door, she robotically swiped her ID through the card reader. Her mind was elsewhere.

Something bad had happened—that much she knew. Selfishly, she hoped nothing had happened to Gabriel. He could be dead; or worse, captured by Dionysus. The knot in her stomach tightened at the thought. Gritting her teeth, she pushed through the door and took the stairs to the seventh floor—the elevator was broken as usual.

The trek up seven flights of stairs didn't bother her. Not anymore. Earlier in the semester she would have been winded, huffing and puffing and on the verge of collapse. Now she felt energetic at the top, ready to climb another seven floors. For a moment the exhilaration of the physical activity swept aside her fears about Gabriel. She opened her dorm room door, number 715—it wasn't locked.

"Hey, Tay," she was greeted as she walked in.

At first she couldn't see her roommate, although her voice seemed to come from the shadowy figure lying on the bed. "Hi, Taylor," a deeper voice said. *The demon is here,* Taylor thought.

Without speaking, Taylor outstretched her arm and performed a basic angel skill, the only one she had really mastered: flashlight. A strong beam of light shone from her hand, piercing the shroud of darkness around Samantha's bed.

As usual, Christopher Lyon was smiling from ear to ear. His tanned, muscular body was naked from the waist up. He wore a short, dark, well-trimmed beard that accentuated his black eyes, giving him a ruggedly handsome look that most girls would go crazy for.

Behind him, she could barely see a shock of blond hair: Samantha.

Chris kicked his legs off the bed and sat up, allowing Taylor's best friend to do the same. Typically, Samantha Collins looked beautiful. Whether she was dressed to the nine's or garbed in her "bumming clothes"—shorts and a tank top—as she was now, Sam was a classic beauty. Her long, toned legs seemed to extend a mile to the floor, and Taylor could almost believe that the term *hourglass* had been named after her friend. Even though she had clearly been lying on the bed, likely making out with Chris, her long, silky hair still seemed to fall perfectly across her shoulders. Her casual but dazzling smile revealed two rows of straight, white teeth. Looking at the couple, Taylor's breath caught for a second, in awe of their perfection. Her awe didn't last long though.

"Why don't you two get a room?" Taylor said sarcastically.

Chris laughed. "Nice to see you, too. And perhaps you should knock."

"It's my room, lover boy." Taylor liked Chris and was very happy Sam was dating him. He was funny, nice, *and* easy on the eyes. Finally her friend had found a boyfriend that lasted more than two weeks. Dating back to pre-high school, Sam had gone out with dozens of guys, most of them jerks. She usually didn't have the best taste in men. But Chris was great.

"Good point," Chris said. "Where's Gabriel?"

Abruptly, Taylor remembered why she had returned to the room. "I was going to ask you the same thing. Have you heard from him?"

Chris said, "No. Wasn't he supposed to meet you?"

"He didn't show. So you haven't received any calls?"

"Well, uh...I kind of turned my phone off...We were busy with something."

"Busy my ass. Turn your phone back on. I have a bad feeling."

Obediently, Chris fished his phone out of his pocket. Sam said, "Are you sure you got the meeting time right?" Taylor glared at her. "Okay, okay, I was just asking."

"Damn," Chris said.

"What?" Taylor asked.

"Twenty-six missed calls...Mission leader, squad captain, central command...Nothing from Gabriel. No messages either."

Taylor's face was emotionless. Just because he hadn't called or shown up didn't mean that something had happened to *him*. Just that something *had* happened. The twenty-six missed calls confirmed that fact.

Chris pressed a button on his phone and then raised it to his ear. Before the call could be connected, two bodies crashed onto Taylor's bed. Sam shrieked. As quickly as he had come, the darker of the two bodies disappeared, leaving only the blond-haired beauty.

"I hate *porting*," Gabriel said.

Despite the casualness of his comment, Taylor instantly knew something was wrong. Typically her boyfriend was cool, calm, and collected. At the present, however, she wouldn't use any of those C-words to describe him. Instead she might choose pale, tired, or even haggard. Regardless of what evil news he might be about to impart, Taylor couldn't help but to feel a sense of relief upon seeing Gabriel alive and relatively well.

Chris had removed the phone from his ear and was waiting expectantly. Even Sam was quiet for the moment, which was unusual for the girl who had been blessed with the gift of gab. Taylor went to Gabriel's side and said, "What happened?"

Gabriel's eyes were clear but had a look of defeat in them; they were half-closed, like he didn't have the energy to keep them fully exposed. His head slumped and he looked at the floor. "Hell's Angels were targeted in the battle today."

"Who?" Sam asked, not being privy to the code names used by the demon army.

"Sampson's squad," Taylor said. "What do you mean *targeted?*"

"Dionysus had one goal for the battle today: kill the angel traitors. He used a sneaky tactic that confused the demon defenses. There were casualties."

Taylor was afraid to ask the question *Is Sampson okay?* so instead she said, "Where's Kiren?"

Gabriel looked up, his blue eyes nearly fully black as his pupils dilated to soak up the light in the room. "She's in the hospital, with him. He's alive...but barely. The next twenty-four hours are critical." Like Taylor, Gabriel seemed to be afraid to say his friend's name, as if speaking it would curse him.

Sam said, "That's good, right? I mean, he's alive. He'll make it, I know it."

Chris put his arm around her. "Yeah, he'll make it. What about the others?"

Gabriel sighed. "Eleven dead. Ten in critical condition. A handful are already back on their feet."

"I hate him," Taylor said. "We can't let him get away with this."

Knowing exactly who she was referring to, Gabriel said, "Dionysus is pure evil and must be stopped, but first we have to plan. Given what you've become, we need to use your abilities to our advantage."

"What am I, Gabriel?" Taylor asked.

Seven

He laughed. "That was fun," he said.

Dionysus was celebrating the victory with his inner circle, comprised of Lucas, Cassandra, David, and the remaining Archangels—Johanna, Sarah, and Percy. They were in a large room with a long, rectangular table, named the War Room. Every surface in the room glowed from within, as if they housed miniature suns. The source of the power was hidden beneath the glow.

His laughter decreased until it settled into an arrogant smirk, and he took the time to read each of the faces in the room. He had been deceived once before, by someone he had trusted, and it had cost him dearly. Not wanting to make the same mistake twice, he considered each of his chosen ones in turn.

He started with the three remaining Archangels and glossed over them quickly. While he had had disagreements with all of them in the past, particularly Johanna, he knew that their vision of the future mirrored his own.

He moved on to his new Special Mission's Leader, Lucas, who had replaced Gabriel when he defected. Dionysus almost patted himself on the back regarding the selection of Lucas. He was a perfect example of the type of angel that could be trusted. Despite the fact that Lucas was smiling, his mouth still managed to look angry, as if his lips had been engineered into a perpetual snarl. There was a gleam in his eyes that couldn't be faked. The gleam showed his excitement at the destruction of the angel traitors. "Too bad Gabriel wasn't there, too," Lucas sneered. *Yeah, he was pure evil,* Dionysus thought, *perfect for mission he had planned for him.*

Next, Dionysus shifted his gaze to Cassandra. He knew little about her, but had trusted Lucas's judgment in selecting her. Looking into her eyes now, he knew it was a good choice. If there was a female version of Lucas, it was her. Despite her skin-deep beauty—she looked like a model in every sense of the word; tall, thin, symmetrical facial structure, perfect smile—Dionysus could sense the evil that lurked beneath her sparkling exterior. As he gazed at her, he could almost feel the malevolency simmering just beneath the surface of her skin. He looked forward to unleashing her on his enemies.

Lastly, Dionysus's eyes fell upon David, the boy. Of the group, he was clearly the biggest risk. He was young—barely fifteen-years-old—and had the most to lose if the angels defeated the demons; his entire family would be executed. But like Cassandra and Lucas and Dionysus himself, David was full of anger towards the demons. And the boy had demonstrated his dedication to the cause when he had stabbed Gabriel with a demon blade on the Warrior's Plateau. Anyone who would stab his own brother was okay in his book.

Satisfied with his selections, Dionysus said, "Do you know why you are all here?"

"To celebrate," Lucas offered.

Johanna snapped, "No, you imbecile! We are here to plan the next move. We angel leaders never rest on our laurels. We are always looking to the future."

Lucas scowled, but didn't respond.

Dionysus smiled. "You are somewhat correct, Johanna. And you can save your anger for the demons; it will be much needed if we are to succeed."

To Dionysus's surprise, David said, "We are here to rebuild the Council."

He stared at the boy who had looked so young not that long ago. In just a few weeks, he seemed to have aged, matured, *changed*. He was wiser, somehow. Ready to take his place. Ready to take action and to do whatever was asked of him.

"The boy is right," Dionysus admitted.

Johanna was in one of her moods. She said, "Then you're wasting our time. You need to have the prospective new Archangel Council members in attendance so we can consider them and vote."

Dionysus stroked his chin. "Actually, they *are* here."

"You can't be serious. These are children," Johanna growled.

"And yet I trust them more than our fallen brothers and sisters."

"That's blasphemy!" Johanna roared.

Dionysus managed to remain calm, choosing his words carefully: "Johanna, I realize that my methods will appear somewhat... unorthodox. However, the actions that I am about to propose must be carried out immediately if we are to ensure success. There is simply insufficient time to select additional Council members from the general population, train them, initiate them, and determine their trustworthiness. We have no choice but to go with those who have already proven themselves worthy."

Johanna started to respond, but then hesitated and held her tongue. She made eye contact with Sarah, who said, "You'll still need the support of one existing Archangel, otherwise you're outnumbered."

"Are you saying you disagree as well?"

"I haven't heard a proposal yet," Sarah said.

"Ahh. You are correct. Despite the urgency of the situation, we must adhere to the formalities required by our office. I'll give you a proposal: I propose that effective immediately, Lucas, Cassandra, and David be sworn in as members of the Archangel Council."

Out of the corner of his eye, Dionysus watched for reactions from his nominees. Almost identical smiles of victory exploded onto Lucas's and Cassandra's faces. Only the boy remained stone-faced, without reaction, as if he had already anticipated Dionysus's proposal. *Interesting*, Dionysus thought.

On the other side of the table, Johanna rolled her eyes, while Sarah scoffed. Only Percy seemed unaffected by Dionysus's declaration. Because he already knew about the proposal. Because he had already agreed to it. Because he was Dionysus's secret weapon against the two female members of the Council.

Johanna said, "Surely you're joking. Two of your nominees are barely old enough to drive and the third may not even be potty-trained."

Sarah said, "Can we check to see if he's wearing a diaper?"

"SHUT YOUR INSOLENT MOUTHS!" David roared. Shocked, all faces in the room turned towards the boy, who was fuming. He was on his feet, arms dangling awkwardly in front of him, his fingers curling into fists and then uncurling rapidly, again and again. Face beet-red, his eyes were night-black and yet were shining with rage.

For once, Johanna and Sarah appeared to be speechless, their mouths hanging open, gawking at the boy.

In a much softer but just as sharp tone, David said, "Percy, what is your vote?"

Not expecting the question, Percy had trouble speaking at first—his mouth opened and moved but no words came out. Finally, he found his voice: "Well, I...uh, I vote to approve the proposal."

Dionysus wanted to smile, but he couldn't seem to control the muscles in his face. Hiding emotions was usually one of his many talents, but his interest in the boy's outburst was written all over his expression: eyes wide, eyebrows raised, mouth formed into an O, head cocked slightly down.

David made eye contact with him, a direct stare that seemed to pierce him to the heart. The boy said, "Then it is done, my lord."

Still struggling to gain control of himself, Dionysus said, "Yes, it is. Sorry, Johanna, Sarah—we have a tie and as Head of the Council, my vote breaks the tie. David, Lucas, Cassandra: You will now be sworn in as members of the Archangel Council."

An awkward silence followed and more than a few glances were directed at the boy. He was sitting again, his face no longer red, his hands clasped loosely in front of him, his eyes no longer fiery. It was as if his outburst had never happened.

Needing to think, Dionysus handed over to Percy to take care of the formalities. Dionysus barely heard a word as each new Council member repeated the oaths and was officially declared a member of the Archangel Council. Instead of listening to the proceedings, he thought about David. Something had changed in the boy. Or something was changing. But what? And how? As the ceremony proceeded, Dionysus couldn't stop thinking about David's rage. *Anger, rage, power, the boy, the boy, boy, boy, boy...*

Eight

Gabriel was unwilling to answer her question until they had both visited Sampson. Taylor's seemingly simple inquiry of *What am I?* was evidently more complex than she had thought. She wondered whether Gabriel was withholding the information because it was bad news. Like perhaps during the act of evolving into an angel, a mutant gene had formed in her brain that would eventually cause her to turn purple and grow a third eye. Or maybe a long-dead angel spirit had inhabited her body and would slowly take over control until she was merely a trapped voice, unable to participate in her own life. While those possibilities might seem a bit farfetched, like something out of a bad sci-fi movie, given all the crazy crap that Taylor had seen over the last six months of her life—winged angels, fiery demons, and ugly gargoyles, to name just a few—she wasn't about to discount any ideas at this point.

Unfortunately, Sampson was not permitted to have visitors when they arrived, so instead, they waited with Kiren outside his room. Her eyes were closed when they sat down next to her.

"Kiren?" Taylor murmured, gently touching her shoulder. Kiren's eyelids rose slowly.

"Taylor...can you save him?" Kiren asked.

Taylor was taken aback by the question. *Save him?* She was no doctor. Hell, she could barely take care of herself when she skinned a knee. "Wha...What do you mean?"

"Please save him...like you did Gabriel on the plateau."

Taylor was stunned by Kiren's request. Of course, she *had* healed Gabriel, but now that she thought about it, she didn't know how she did it. It was as if a spirit had inhabited her body and taken control of her, performing incredible feats that Taylor wasn't capable of. Sure, she could already perform simple angel skills, like creating light and increasing the glow of her body, but she hadn't even flown yet. "I don't know how," she said.

"Don't think...just try," Kiren said.

Taylor looked at Gabriel. He shrugged. "It's worth a shot."

Taylor said, "What if I hurt him more?"

"You won't," Gabriel said.

"Okay."

"I'll get the doctor," Gabriel said.

"Thank you," said Kiren.

"Save it until afterwards."

At first the doctor—a dark-haired beauty that could have passed for twenty-two or forty-two—was skeptical about what they were proposing, but after Gabriel described what Taylor had done for him on the plateau, and her remarkable transformation, she became more and more interested in the idea.

When Gabriel finished, she paused for just a moment, and then said, "Okay, you can try. But my team needs to be there to monitor him the entire time and if we say to stop, then you must stop."

"Of course," Taylor said. Her mind was whirling, trying to remember what she had done to Gabriel, what technique she had used, what she had been thinking. Her mind was blank, as if that particular segment of her memory had been cut out and tucked away into a drawer full of lost memories. All she could remember was Gabriel looking dead on the ground and then he was suddenly awake. She followed the doctor into the room.

The room was well-lit, a far cry from the dark, torch-lit tunnels and caverns she typically associated with the Lair. Sampson was laying on his back on the bed, with his arms at his side, coffin-style. The comparison to death caused memories of movies about the undead to flick through Taylor's head. Vampires, zombies, demons of the night: they all tended to sleep the way Sampson did now. Trying to convince herself, Taylor muttered, "He's not dead yet…"

"What?" Gabriel asked.

Taylor's head jolted to the side and then she realized she had spoken. "Nothing," she said.

She moved to the side of the bed and touched Sampson's motionless hand. It was warm. For some reason, she expected it to be as cold as ice, ready to send chills up her spine and through the marrow in her bones. "He's not dead yet," she reminded herself again.

Sampson's face looked peaceful and serene and he might have passed for merely sleeping if not for the bandages on his head and the breathing tubes in his nose. He was in a coma, one he might never wake up from. Once again, Taylor tried to conjure up images of how she had healed Gabriel, as she put her hands on Sampson's head, like a priest about to give a blessing. Her mind remained blank. *Stupid, stupid, stupid*, she thought. *I'm no magical healer, I'm barely an angel.*

Unsure of what to do next, she closed her eyes and tried to think healing thoughts. Thoughts of scabs, Band-Aids, and ice cream floated randomly through her mind. Not helping. Despite her efforts to control her thoughts, they pursued their own agenda, bringing up memories of Gabriel: the first time she saw him when he found a four-leaf clover for her, the first time she saw him in angel form, their first kiss, their first night together.

Abruptly, she felt a warm sensation in her outer extremities. She opened her eyes to see her hands glowing, hot-white with energy. The light crept up her arms, over her shoulders to her neck, and then down her torso and through her legs until she was a full-fledged glow worm, the envy of the entire glow worm community. She realized that her mouth was moving, but no words came from her lips. Her body-and-mind-control theory was looking better and better.

And then Sampson was sitting up, gasping, choking, pulling the tubes out of his nose, yelling something. It sounded like "Crap!" No wait, that wasn't right, it was "Trap!"

When Sampson had reanimated, Taylor had been pushed away from him, and the doctor and her assistants had surrounded their patient, trying to calm him, to get him to lie back down, although he seemed unaware of them or his surroundings.

His yelling continued for thirty seconds—although an eternity couldn't have passed any slower—and then his mouth and eyes closed, his body went slack, and he collapsed to the bed once more.

"What was that?" the doctor hissed.

Taylor was thinking the same thing, except she would have phrased her question more like *What the flying, crazy, bloody, crikey, flaming hell was that?* And she had hoped the doctor would have been able to answer her pointed question, but instead she found the shadowy surgeon asking the very same thing. Not knowing whether to respond and hoping the question might have been rhetorical, Taylor remained silent.

Taylor was relieved when one of the assistants answered: "Not sure, but his vitals are stronger—heart rate is back to normal, BP is about right, fever is gone. He seems to be recovering."

"Really?" Taylor asked.

The doctor said, "Early indications are that whatever you did seems to have made a difference. But we'll have to wait a few hours to confirm."

"You did it, babe," Gabriel said, putting his arm around her waist.

"*I* didn't do anything. My new body did. Which reminds me: Can we talk about the test results now? I want to know who's inhabiting my body and how many eyes I'm going to have."

Gabriel frowned. "What?"

"Never mind," Taylor said. "Can we go talk?"

"Of course."

Gabriel told Kiren the good news before they left and she promised to take Taylor out for dinner once Sampson had fully recovered. "Where do you want to go?" Gabriel asked.

"Not here," Taylor said. "Anywhere but here."

"How about the Bird's Nest?" Gabriel suggested.

Exhilaration filled her. *The Bird's Nest!* Given all that had happened over the Christmas holidays, Taylor had almost forgotten about the place where it had all started. Just a few months earlier, Gabriel had first revealed himself in full angel form to Taylor. On that same night, he had used his powerful wings to fly them to a quiet and tucked away alcove high above UT's football stadium. Eventually the spot had become *their spot* and Taylor had nicknamed it the Bird's Nest. She longed to return there, for Gabriel to hold her, to laugh, to live, to love.

Since her magical transformation into an angel (or something angel-like), Taylor and Gabriel had spent very little time together. They were simply too busy. Taylor had been forced to return home, pack her bags, and return to college. And Gabriel had his war stuff to fill his waking hours. The power of her sudden desire to waste away a day with just Gabriel overwhelmed her for a moment. *Not cool*, she thought. Taylor hated feeling like she couldn't control her emotions or that she needed someone else to be happy. She wanted to always be independent, like her mom had been.

To cut off the unwanted feelings before they got out of control, Taylor slapped herself…literally. Smack! It wasn't a friendly love pat on her cheek, but a forceful blow intended to sting. And it did. Taylor winced. But with the pain came clarity of thought.

"What was that for?" Gabriel asked, a smirk crossing his face.

"Nothing. Bird's Nest would be perfect, but no hanky-panky. We have a lot to talk about."

Gabriel laughed. "What did you think, that I was going to try to seduce you or something?"

"Well, no, but I'm just saying….we don't have time for being in love right now."

"There's always time for love."

"Whatever, can we just go?" Taylor snapped.

Gabriel was still chuckling. "Sure, I just have to find a demon to port us back to UT."

"We'll use one of my guards," Taylor said. "They are always within sight, although they try to blend in like they're spies or something." She glanced up and down the hall. "Ah, there's one."

"Where?" Gabriel said.

"Dude in the ratty Yankees hat with the magazine."

"You sure? He might just be visiting someone in the hospital."

"Watch and learn, my friend." Taylor approached a demon who appeared to be concentrating hard on reading an article. She dipped her head around the top edge of his reading material so she could see it. "Interesting…'Sexy or Elegant: This Year's Choice in Eveningwear.' Good article?"

Startled, the guy looked up at Taylor. "Well, uh, yeah. Very well-written. You can never be too informed."

"Right," Taylor said. "Can you take us back to UT?"

"Sure." He flushed, embarrassed that he had been made so easily. He didn't turn red exactly, because it just wasn't possible; rather, he turned a slighter darker shade of dark.

Moments later and thousands of miles away, they were back on UT's campus, where night was fast approaching. They had instructed the demon to get them as close to the stadium as possible and he obliged by teleporting them onto the empty field. Now that the season was over, there was little risk of running into anyone except maintenance crews. They thanked the demon and Gabriel promised him that he would protect Taylor for the rest of the night.

"I don't need protection," Taylor said when the demon left.

"I know, I only said it to get rid of him."

"I can protect myself."

"I know that."

"Fly me," Taylor said.

"Why don't you give it a try?"

"No, thanks. I still don't know what the hell I'm doing."

Without another word, Gabriel snatched Taylor in his muscular arms and leapt into the air—his jump was impossibly high, the equivalent of a high-jumper clearing the bar without using a pole. Then, with a slight *pop!* his wings escaped from his sinewy back. With powerful strokes, Gabriel's wings propelled them higher and higher until they were looking down from above the stadium. The sky looked beautiful: clusters of stars winked off and on; wispy clouds caught final red rays of the already-set sun; a giant, low-set full moon illuminated a broad pathway across the landscape.

"Unnecessary and show-offy flying: a clear attempt at seduction," Taylor said.

"You're crazy," Gabriel said. "I'm just enjoying the evening."

"Right."

Unexpectedly, Gabriel dropped sharply, allowing them to momentarily free fall until they had cleared the upper ramparts of the stadium. "Woohoo!" Taylor yelled, enjoying the butterflies in her stomach and the thrill from the extreme maneuver.

Turning sharply to the left, Gabriel headed directly for a corner of the stadium. Just when it looked—and felt—like they would surely crash into the steel rafters, he weaved between two flagpoles and landed on his feet on a hidden platform set against the stadium wall. "Honey, we're home!" Gabriel joked.

"Very funny. Thanks for the ride; I didn't realize how much I'd missed that."

"Giving in to my charms already, I see," Gabriel said, setting Taylor back on her feet, only to clamp his hands around her waist and pull her tightly against his body.

Unlocking his hands from her hips, Taylor said, "Nice try, angel-boy, but I want to get straight to business."

"Okay," Gabriel said as he sat down with his back to the wall, "what do you want to know?"

"You said my test results were ready."

"Right. The actual report is a couple hundred pages long, but the summary is all up here," he said, pointing to his head.

"Am I turning into a three-eyed hobgoblin?"

"Yes, in fact, you are," he joked. "But I promise to love you all the same and will even attempt to gaze romantically into all three of your eyes at the same time."

"Thanks. What's the real story?"

Gabriel smiled. "The real story is much better. Simply put, you're an anomaly."

"So a freak, right?"

"Yes, but a very powerful freak. You are the first of your kind. Previously, only one angel had evolved—Dionysus—and all other angels were his offspring. In other words, I am technically related to him, although we don't really see it that way, just as you probably don't think of Adam from the Bible as your relative. And even Dionysus evolved from the demon race; there have been no instances of humans evolving directly to angels. Well, until you, of course."

"Okay, I get that, but how did it happen?"

"We're not sure exactly, but what the researchers do know, is that your inner light is stronger than the average angel. Actually, much stronger. It's similar to how your aura was much stronger than all other humans, except now you are stronger than all other angels, too."

"I'm stronger than *all* angels?" Taylor asked incredulously.

"Yes."

"So I'm stronger than Sampson, the walking, talking tank?"

"Yes."

"And stronger than Dionysus and his remaining Archangels?"

"Yep."

"Then that must mean....I'm stronger than you, too!"

Gabriel sighed. "I wouldn't get carried away, but yes. Their theory is that the size of your aura as a human and the constant *use* of your aura by me caused some kind of a metamorphosis. Your blood was probably the first to change—from red to white—and provided the source of nourishment to allow your body to change."

"And my wings to grow."

Nodding, Gabriel said, "Exactly. And for some reason you are more powerful than all other angels, almost like a real *archangel*."

Taylor frowned. "But I thought Dionysus and his Council *were* archangels?"

"That's just a name Dionysus made up. While they tend to be the most powerful—and evil—angels, there is nothing truly special about them. You, on the other hand, are genuinely special, one of a kind, unique..."

Gabriel continued on with his synonym list, but Taylor stopped listening. She was remembering that first night with Gabriel, when he had told her he thought she was special. She had made a joke out of it. Now he was saying it again, but for a different reason. It felt like déjà vu.

Gabriel was saying, "...singular, distinct, exceptional—"

"Enough!" Taylor snapped. "I get it, I'm different. I've always been different though, so it's cool with me."

Gabriel laughed. "You are definitely different."

Taylor said, "Is that it? That I'm unique and powerful."

Gabriel shrugged. "Pretty much."

"So what happens next?"

"The demon Elders wanted me to ask you something." Taylor waited expectantly. "They wanted to ask if you would be willing to use your newfound abilities to help kill Dionysus."

Taylor stared at Gabriel. *Dionysus.* Just thinking his name sent snakes of anger wriggling through her. Her heart rate leapt, her hands sweated, her eyes narrowed. Her mom had taught her the strength of the word *hate*, and had counseled her never to use it or to feel it. But in this case she would make an exception. She hated the Evil that was Dionysus. And she would do anything in her power to destroy him.

"Damn straight I'll help."

"I thought you might say that," Gabriel said. "Training begins tomorrow if you're ready."

Nine

While the fiercest portion of his anger had subsided, a smaller, more controllable fury remained below the surface, simmering, like a witch's brew filled with eye of newt, unicorn blood, vampire fangs, and clippings from anything else that goes *bump* in the night. It was the heat from his rage that seemed to sustain him, to give him power. He was changed by it. There was no reason to question whether the changes were for the better. The joy that he felt confirmed it.

After he had received his appointment to the Archangel Council, David had made his way back to his small room to get his stuff. He would be moving to one of the dead Archangel's rooms—Thomas's maybe?—and was excited to escape the rat hole he had been living in. No longer an apprentice to anyone, David would be an equal to all but Dionysus. Sarah and Johanna might not understand how a fifteen-year-old boy could rise to such a position, but they would soon see the light.

He didn't even feel like a child anymore, although he knew that in age and in body he still was. In mind, he was a god, all-knowing and judging. It was like a thousand years had passed in the blink of an eye, wizening him. He didn't know how it had happened, but it did, and for that he was thankful. It would give him the ability to kill Gabriel the next time he had the chance, regardless of his lesser stature and experience.

As he zipped up his duffel bag full of clothes, there was a knock at the door and Lucas pushed through. "Ready?" he said.

Without responding, David slung the bag over his shoulder and followed Lucas out. As they walked, Lucas talked incessantly. About how cool it was that they were on the Council, how he couldn't wait to get his revenge on Gabriel, and even how awesome it was that David shut down Johanna in the meeting.

David wished he would shut his mouth.

Ten

"Are you okay?" Gabriel asked.

Taylor raised her eyebrows. They were camped out in Gabriel's dorm room eating barbecue chips and drinking Pepsi, talking about anything but angels and demons, when he had suddenly asked the question. Before answering, she tried to think of all the reasons that she might not be okay. Her evolution into a one-of-a-kind angel? No, she was ecstatic about that. The fact that she was involved in a century-old war between the two most powerful armies the world had ever seen? That used to be a problem, but now that she was as strong—or stronger—than the other angels, she felt like she could contribute.

Having to lie to her father? It was for his own safety, so no, not a problem. She couldn't work out what he meant.

"Why wouldn't I be?" she asked.

"The dream."

Ahh, yes, the dream. Taylor had completely forgotten about the nightmare she had had the previous night. Gabriel's purported death, her lust for revenge, the snake wrenching her warm, white heart from her chest, Dionysus's face, Gabriel's reanimation and subsequent catching of her bloody, still-beating heart as it plummeted towards her face: Each memory flashed by with such intensity that she felt a physical burning in her head more painful than a migraine or a brain freeze effected by the overzealous consumption of rocky road ice cream.

Taylor screwed up her face and groaned, in an effort to lessen the pain.

Gabriel grabbed her, while saying, "Taylor? What's the matter, Tay?"

She held her head for moment, gently massaging her temples. When the bulk of the pain had passed, she said, "It's nothing, I'm fine. Just a weird flash-headache."

"Flash-headache?"

Taylor explained: "Yeah, you know. Like a flash-flood, except a headache. A quick and unexpected pain in your head with unknown origins."

"I've never heard about that before. You get them often?"

"Never. But I read about them somewhere."

"It seems to me like the origin was me mentioning the dream," Gabriel said.

"Maybe," Taylor admitted. "How do you know about the dream anyway?"

"I tried to stop it, Tay. Desperately tried, but Dionysus was too strong. I have been monitoring your dreams for a long time now, trying to prevent our enemies from messing around with them."

Taylor had never really gotten used to the angels' and demons' ability to participate in, and even modify, the dreams of anyone they chose. But she was an angel now, wasn't she protected? "So Dionysus can enter angels' and demons' dreams, too? I thought it only worked with humans?"

"Technically it works with anyone, except for gargoyles, although we're not sure why they're protected."

"Then why doesn't Dionysus mess with your dreams? And other demons' dreams? And why don't you mess with his?"

"Because from a very young age, angels and demons are taught how to protect themselves. I will be teaching you as part of your training."

"Show me now," Taylor demanded.

Gabriel shrugged. "I guess it could only help at this point." He moved to the floor, a narrow space of shag carpet between his bed and desk. Pulling Taylor after him, he instructed: "Sit cross-legged, arms out to the side, hands open and relaxed meditation-style."

Once in position, Taylor instinctively closed her eyes before being told. "Now what?"

"Clear your mind."

Damn, that might be a problem. Taylor had never been good at this meditation crap. Anything that required intense concentration and thought control was difficult for her. She had given up on meditation, prayer, and even yoga a long time ago. Now, even as she tried to focus, all she could think about were rabbits: brown ones with floppy ears; white ones with black spots and twitching noses; big ones, small ones, cute ones, ugly ones; some were hopping, others eating carrots and chewing on grass. She even spotted a giant Easter bunny, complete with a basket full of painted eggs. As she watched the lumbering animal hop towards her, it opened its mouth to reveal several sets of razor sharp teeth. Two or three mauled rabbits hung from its lips, dripping blood and contorted grotesquely. Taylor shuddered at the thought and opened her eyes.

Gabriel was staring at her oddly as if he had seen into her thoughts. "Not able to clear your mind, huh?"

"You don't wanna know," Taylor said.

"It gets easier the more you practice. Try this. Close your eyes again..." Obediently, Taylor snapped her eyes shut and waited for the furry freaks to reappear, but for the moment they had disappeared. Gabriel continued: "If you can't clear your mind, you can think of things that have a similar effect. For example, try imagining yourself in a well-lit room. I'm the only other person there."

To her surprise, Taylor was able to conjure up the image. It was the hotel-like room that Taylor stayed in whenever she visited the Lair. She pictured herself sitting on the couch next to Gabriel. "Now, imagine there's a bed in the room," Gabriel said.

"It's already there. Hey…wait a minute…you're not trying to seduce me in my thoughts are you?" Taylor asked, her eyes snapping open.

Gabriel sighed. "No, Taylor. Can we continue?"

Taylor stared at him for a few more seconds, trying to detect a lie. Finally, she closed her eyes and reimagined the picture that Gabriel had painted.

Gabriel said, "Now watch as I turn off the lights. It is completely dark now." Taylor saw the Gabriel-thought in her head stand up and walk to the wall. He flipped the light switch and all went black.

"Okay," Taylor confirmed.

"Good. Now, think about feeling your way over to the bed in the dark. What do you feel?"

Concentrating hard, Taylor thought about how she would stand up, reach with her arms, and take the three steps required to get to the bed. On step two, she felt a pain in her knees and then she was falling, falling, crashing, tumbling, hitting her head, and coming to a stop against the foot of the bed. "Ouch!" Taylor yelped.

"What happened?" Gabriel asked, a high-pitched twinge of alarm creeping into his voice.

"Just my uncontrollable brain working overtime again. I tripped on something." Gabriel laughed and Taylor said, "Shut the hell up."

"Yes, ma'am." With sarcasm added, Gabriel said, "Okay, now pick yourself up and dust yourself off from your imagined fall, and then get into bed."

Taylor daydreamed how it would feel to clamber onto the bed and snake-crawl her way to the pillow. It felt awkward, but the bed was soft and warm and cozy. Weariness overcame her, as if she hadn't slept for days. She could feel the overwhelming pull of gravity on every bone and muscle in her body.

Gabriel said, "Now imagine falling asleep and dreaming about only good things that have happened in your past. Like birthdays, family holidays, first kisses, love, friends, that kind of thing."

Into Taylor's head screamed an unwanted vision: She was in a car, in the backseat; someone else was driving. A woman—her mother, Nancy Kingston. Her mom was humming along to some old tune playing on the car radio. Taylor didn't recognize the song. It was dark out, but her mother seemed wide awake, snapping her fingers and driving with one hand. The car approached a familiar T-intersection; the light was green. As they peeled through the crossroads and gradually turned left onto the adjacent road, something caught Taylor's attention out the left window. A dark and sinister monster bore down upon the four-door sedan, staring at them with pale, gleaming eyes. Tires screeched; someone screamed; metal shrieked and crunched and ripped and tore. All was silent, silent, silent. And then knocking. On the passenger-side front window. Taylor turned her head. A teenage kid was pounding on the window. His bike lay tossed aside on the cement sidewalk. A witness to the accident. He was shouting, but Taylor couldn't make out the words. Remembering her mom, Taylor climbed over the front consol. Her mother was slumped in the driver's seat, her body pinned to the leather upholstery by a tangled mass of metal from her door. Flakes of shattered glass coated her like sprinkles on a cupcake. A deflated airbag served as a blanket, pierced in three or four places by plumes of metal. Then she saw the blood and her breath caught in her throat. There was so much blood. She realized her mom's eyes were open and that she was staring. But when Taylor followed her gaze, she saw that she was looking at nothing; her eyes were blank, lifeless, unrepresentative of the previously full of life orbs that had once laughed, cried, reprimanded, and empowered. Her mother was dead. Again.

Taylor was suddenly aware of arms holding her, warming her. She opened her eyes but her vision was blurred by fountains of tears welling from tiny ducts, spreading their salt along warm riverbeds.

"It's okay, Taylor," Gabriel said. "It's going to be okay. We are done practicing for today."

Taylor pulled her boyfriend close and for once allowed herself the luxury of being vulnerable, of being held, of being protected, of being cared for. Eventually the tears stopped and she used the shoulder of her shirt to wipe away the residual wetness. She looked at Gabriel. "Thanks," she said. "I saw…"

"I know," Gabriel said, cutting her off. "Next time, you might want to try using something more pleasant, although your technique of thinking about the saddest memory will technically also work to keep Dionysus from penetrating your dreams. You have to practice this every night if you want to be successful."

"Will I dream about the things that I was just thinking about?" Taylor asked numbly.

"Not necessarily, but it will allow your mind to block any unwanted intrusions."

"Okay."

"You should rest."

"Yeah."

"Want me to stay with you?"

"Yeah."

"Okay."

Gabriel helped Taylor to her feet and then scooped her up and set her on her back at the far side of the bed, against the wall. He slipped in after her and pulled the covers over both of them.

Taylor smirked. "What?" Gabriel asked.

"Just because you ended up in bed with me doesn't mean you successfully seduced me."

Gabriel laughed. "I know that. But the result is the same."

Taylor nodded. She kissed him deeply while clawing at his shirt.

Eleven

Samantha cleared her throat. She said, "Cliff, there must be some way that we can move the planning phase along a bit quicker. People are getting hurt out there."

Clifford smiled at her; it was a fatherly smile. He liked Sam and she knew it. And she milked it for all it was worth. No one else could get away with calling the head of the Eldership of the demons by a shortened version of his first name. But Sam could. In Clifford's eyes, she could do no wrong.

After Sam and Chris had learned of the unfortunate attack on Hell's Angels, they had talked for a long time. Taylor and Gabriel had left to visit Sampson and to do who knows what else and it gave the couple a chance to think about things. Despite her generally peaceful nature, Sam was of the opinion that the only choice was to take the fight to the angels immediately, and not stop until Dionysus was either captured or dead. Chris didn't think it was that simple, but he agreed that a plan needed to be finalized—and fast.

Once they were in agreement, Chris had teleported them to the Lair and they had requested a special audience with Clifford, which had been granted almost immediately. Given his rapid rise through the ranks of demon leadership, Chris was entitled to certain privileges. They were in Clifford's office, sitting side by side—the top demon was on the other side of a wide, thick, wooden desk. Clifford sat in a tall, plush chair that was adorned with gold plating and jewels; it was reminiscent of the seat you would expect someone of the same stature as King Arthur of Camelot to rest his buttocks upon.

Despite the fact that he had aged well, Clifford appeared ancient next to Chris, with deep lines in his forehead and around his eyes. A dark mop of hair sat upon his head like a toupee—and Sam wondered if a strong enough gust of wind would knock it straight off. His black eyebrows were as bushy as raccoon tails, as if they had been growing unchecked for decades. A well-trimmed beard coated his cheeks, chin, and just under his nose. Every time Sam saw him she thought of Sean

Connery, although Clifford was a much darker, more mysterious version of the aging actor.

Clifford said, "We have to be patient." Sam had heard him say this single phrase so many times she was beginning to think it was his personal mantra. "The incident today was unfortunate, but we lose dozens of demons every month—sadly, casualties are a major part of war. But we can't overreact each time it happens."

"I understand that, Cliff, but this is not a normal time for the War, don't you agree?" Sam said.

"I do, and that's why we are close to finalizing our strategy for what we hope will be the final act of this grand play."

"Let's be honest, Cliff, you've been saying that for a week. How close are you really?"

"It's classified," Clifford said.

To this point Chris had been silent, despite Sam's agreement to let him do most of the talking. Finally, she turned to him, giving him a beseeching look.

He said, "C'mon, sir. You're going to tell me eventually and then I will tell Sam, you know that."

"I do, which is why I have kept you out of the loop thus far."

"Why does it matter if Sam knows?" Chris asked.

Sam frowned. She was missing something. Something important. The pieces to the puzzle were on the table, but either she couldn't figure out how they fit together, or she was missing one. Chris was always privy to the latest war news, especially the crap involving strategy. And, of course, he always told her what he knew. But now he was being blocked out because of his relationship with her. But why?

It clicked.

Her eyebrows rose and her eyes widened. "Taylor is involved! Seriously involved! Let me guess: You're sending her on a highly risky mission, one that she may never come back from—alive that is."

Clifford sighed. He stroked his dark beard and looked at the ceiling. Without saying a word, he had as much as admitted the truth of Sam's guess.

Sam's elation at having solved the mystery gave way to nagging frustration. "I'm not some child that needs to be told her dad's on a business trip when he's actually abandoned his family, that he's never coming home, that birthdays and Christmases and track meets will be a broken-family affair. She's my friend—no, my best friend—yeah, but it's not like I would try to stop her from going or something. Not if that's what she wanted to do. But I deserve to know what she's doing, especially when her life is in danger, before she is brought home in a body bag—or worse, not brought home at all." Having not taken a breath during her rant, Sam paused to suck in a swell of air. It gave Clifford a chance to respond.

"Sam, please. I know you're not a child, but I was only trying to protect you. I was going to tell you, or have Taylor tell you, but I wanted it to be nearer to the start of the mission. That way, you would be able to enjoy your friend's company without worrying about her."

The sincerity in his eyes, in his voice—the fatherly concern—caused Sam's narrowed eyes to widen and her mouth to form into an O. "Oh," she said. "Oh, Cliff, I'm sorry. I didn't mean to—"

"I know, my dear. I know. You were right, I should have just told you. And you, Chris."

Chris said, "It's okay, sir, we all make mistakes. So….what is this mission exactly?"

Sam immediately imagined the worse. Maybe Taylor would be sent alone, directly into the belly of the beast, on a suicide mission with the best case scenario being that she would kill Dionysus just before being killed herself. Or perhaps she would be traded for Gabriel's brother, David, and left to be beaten, brainwashed, or slaughtered, vulnerable to the whims of a madman. Sam held her breath.

Clifford said, "She will be part of a special task force with one ultimate goal: to kill Dionysus and the remaining Archangels—Johanna, Sarah, and Percy. We hope that if we cut off the head, we might be able to subdue the rest of the beast."

Sam let out a stream of breath, her lips puckered like she was giving someone a kiss. *A task force.* That sounded like a team—in other words, not alone. Team was better than alone. Sam said, "Who else will be on the task force?"

Clifford paused. "Chris, for one." He paused again, as if to give Sam a chance to soak up the information.

Sam nodded and bit her lip. "That's good. I trust Chris to protect Taylor." Chris put his arm around her and squeezed.

"But they will have plenty of help. Kiren has been selected, as well as each of our Special Mission Leaders. We had hoped to include a select number from Hell's Angels, too, but given today's attack, I'm not sure that will be possible."

"And Gabriel?" Chris asked hopefully.

"No, we have other plans for him. The second head of the two-headed attack." Chris seemed ready to ask another question, possibly to request more information about Gabriel's mission, but then stopped himself, his mouth snapping shut. Sam noticed.

Sam didn't want to linger any further on the topic of the task force team members. She couldn't. If she thought about how many of her friends' lives would be at stake, she might break down. She forced herself to move on. "How will they do it?"

"That's the bit that we haven't completely finalized, but we are thinking of using bait to draw Dionysus out of his fortress. Kind of like he has been doing to us."

Sam's heart sank. The bait had to be Taylor. Chris asked for her. "What bait?"

"Not Taylor," Clifford said quickly, as if he could read Sam's thoughts. "We are hoping to capture one of his favorites, someone he will be loath to let die. He has shown a special attachment to Lucas and Cassandra."

"And David," Chris added.

"True. And David. But we are hoping to use one of the others. For Gabriel's sake."

Chris nodded. Sam said, "Okay, but what does Taylor do until you've procured your bait?"

Clifford smiled and said, "Something you can both participate in: training."

PART II

"Admire me, admire my home
Admire my son, he's my clone
Yeah, yeah, yeah, yeah
This land is mine, this land is free
I'll do what I want but irresponsibly
It's evolution, baby

I'm a thief, I'm a liar
There's my church, I sing in the choir:
(hallelujah, hallelujah)
I am ahead, I am advanced
I am the first mammal to make plans, yeah
I crawled the earth, but now I'm higher
2010, watch it go to fire
It's evolution, baby
Do the evolution
Come on, come on, come on"

Pearl Jam- "Do the Evolution"
From the album *Yield (1998)*

Twelve

The room had been prepared. The team had been working on it for forty-eight hours straight. Two-dozen of his best electrical and weapons engineers had been hand selected to perform the task. They worked ceaselessly, in twelve-angel teams, for twelve-hour shifts until the job was done.

And despite Dionysus's perfectionist nature—which usually resulted in the need to berate, criticize, and punish his employees—he had to admit that what they had created was perfect. A work of art, poetry in motion, the Eighth Wonder of the World: the room was beautiful in its simplicity.

None of the workers knew the purpose of their creation, nor would they ever. It was classified. Each of the engineers had been fitted with a security device while they were sleeping. The device transmitted anything they said, as well as their location, to security personnel who were monitoring everything they did and said. None of the engineers so much as stirred in their sleep while the device was implanted in the backs of their necks—the heavy sedative in their food had guaranteed that. The security personnel had been charged with an important mission: Monitor the engineers for any signs that they were gossiping, blabbing, or even thinking about the room they had built—for they had been expressly forbidden from doing so. If an offender was discovered, they would squash him like a bug. In the less than six hours since the room had been completed, three engineers had already died in unfortunate accidents. Surely there would be more. *It was a shame to lose such good engineers at such a critical time*, Dionysus thought. He didn't dwell on it.

Like it was a priceless piece of art—Van Gogh's *Starry Night* or da Vinci's *Last Supper*, perhaps—Dionysus could not take his eyes off of the room. In his travels around the world, he had come across many great and beautiful things, but none had given his eyes cause to linger like the room did. The Eiffel Tower, the Grand Canyon, the Great Wall of China, Niagara Falls, and even the Egyptian Pyramids were mere eyesores compared to what stood before him now.

The only comparison he could make was his own naked body, at which he regularly stared for hours at a time, in awe of his sculpted physique, perfect symmetry, and statue-of-*David*-like features. Each time he did, he was thankful for the wrap-around mirrors he had had installed, allowing him to see his perfection in its full three-hundred-and-sixty-degree splendor.

While perhaps a degree short of the beauty that was his body, the room got close. Damn close. Built at the highest peak of the mountain, the room was two-hundred feet in diameter and featured a large sunroof built using triangles of magnifying glass fitted tightly between energy-conducting copper frames that spiraled outwards much like a spider's web, which, of course, had helped inspire the design. At the direct center of the skylight was a circle cut of glass—the eye of the web. Upon receiving direct sunlight, the fragments of exquisite glass would sparkle like diamonds, throwing off beams and charges of light in many colors. The domed, translucent ceiling formed a three-dimensional semicircle atop the room, like half of an orange. However, the remainder of the room was not rectangular as one might expect. Instead, the metaphorical orange continued down the walls and curved to create a floor that sloped in all directions, outward from the center. The bottom half of the room was also made of a glassy material, but dissimilar to the roof, the see-through panels were square and allowed man-made light to penetrate their sheening surface, rather than the pure light of the sun.

Each panel protected and magnified the energy provided by a powerful light source. Currently, the flooring was dark as the room was not in use. The roof also lay in shadow, as a thin vinyl cover blocked the sunlight from directly penetrating the glass.

While the roof cover and extinguished lighting prevented Dionysus from viewing the room in its complete glory, they were necessary precautions until he was ready to use the room. He wouldn't really know what the room was capable of until he had tried it. For all he knew it might be dangerous. Deadly even. Which was why he wouldn't try it on himself—at least not yet. What he needed was a guinea pig, a lab rat, a flunky, a poor unsuspecting soul who was devoted enough to do what he was told and stupid enough to not consider whether he should. But he couldn't pick just anyone, because if the room worked, if it really, truly worked the way he somehow knew it would, the guinea pig might be in a position of power, for a time; at least until Dionysus could use the room on himself to equalize the matter.

And so he had chosen wisely. In most instances, using a child would be the easiest and safest. But he couldn't use David. Not anymore. Perhaps a few weeks ago he would have considered it, but given the changes in the boy, he didn't want to do anything to him that he couldn't control, that he couldn't predict the outcome of.

As had happened so often over the past few hours, his thoughts paused on David. When he had first taken the boy, he had been an eager, young, comic-book-reading, head-in-the-clouds, moldable child that he had hoped to use for a few specific purposes and then throw out with the trash. Now the boy was an enigma. A question mark. An unsolvable Rubix Cube. Dionysus liked that the boy was ruthless, like he was, but he was also unpredictable. The margin for error in the War had grown so slim that Dionysus couldn't afford to have loose cannons on his side of the battlefield. But he also didn't want to destroy David either, because his instincts told him that there was something truly special about him, something that if harnessed and honed could give the angels the edge, and help them finally defeat the demons once and for all. The way he had shut up Johanna was a prime example of what he was capable of. He wished he had David around for the past few years. Johanna and Sarah's girl-power duet had been a thorn in his side on numerous occasions, making it difficult for him to get plans finalized, strategies ratified. If he had had David, he could have simply tapped the kid on the shoulder, signaling him to spout threats until they gave in.

No, the boy was not a good guinea pig. He had, however, considered using the newest member of his inner circle, the one who with a whip of her blond locks and a seductive smile could steal the hearts of most mortal men—Cassandra. He was most inclined to use her *because* she was a woman. From experience—particularly from his dealings with Johanna and Sarah—women were a liability.

A chauvinist by nature, Dionysus believed women were most valuable for sex and child-rearing. Rarely did they have leadership potential. That being said, he thought Cassandra might be an exception. By her actions thus far, she had demonstrated her unquestionable loyalty. As for the leadership potential, before Dionysus had selected her, she was already a rising star in the angel army. He would hate to waste such talent if his little experiment went awry.

Clearly he wouldn't choose one of the current Archangels, although Johanna and Sarah provided some temptation, nor were any of them stupid enough to agree to it. That left Lucas. *Ahhh, Lucas*, he thought. His do-it-all guy, his yes-angel, his new Gabriel. The truth was, while Lucas would score a 10 for tenacity, dedication, and demon hatred, he was likely near the back of the line when they were handing out brains. Unfortunately, he wasn't half as smart as Gabriel, but at least he wasn't a traitor. Lucas was someone Dionysus could trust, and he would readily agree to the experiment, regardless of the dangers. If the experiment was a monumental disaster, it would be a small loss as Lucas was highly replaceable, and if it was a success, Dionysus could count on Lucas to wait patiently for the rest of them to undergo the same procedure before he did anything stupid.

Just as Dionysus was thinking that his guests should arrive any minute, the large portal at the south end of the room opened without so much as a creak. The double-trio entered ceremoniously in order of seniority. Percy followed Sarah, who followed Johanna to round out the Archangels from the old regime, and his newest Archangels came in height order—Lucas, Cassandra, David—which was, coincidentally, in order of age and army experience as well.

Each of the Archangels had one thing in common at the moment: They were swiveling their heads around and around, taking in the unequivocal beauty of the room in admiration and awe. That is, except for David, whose eyes never left Dionysus's. The smallest angel in the room was smiling. Not a wow-this-is-so-fun-being-an-Archangel smile, nor a childish I-smile-at-everything smile; instead, it was a knowing smile. Like he was inside Dionysus's head and knew exactly what the room had been built for and who it would be tested on. The smile, while located on the face of a school boy, was a far cry from a school boy smile. It was intense, rather than happy-go-lucky; heavy and dense, rather than pure; evil, rather than good. Dionysus had a sudden urge to physically wipe the smile off the boy's face with a backhand slap to his face. His fingers trembled with desire, but instead, he fisted his hands and tucked them under his armpits until the impulse passed.

"This place is truly amazing, my lord," Lucas said.

Dionysus smiled, not at the compliment, but because Lucas's constant butt-kissing affirmed his decision to use him as the test rat. "Thank you. It is a spectacular feat of modern engineering, regardless of whether it fulfills its purpose."

"And what, may I ask, is its purpose?" Johanna said.

David said, "Isn't it obvious? Evolution." The boy's voice was condescending and harsh. Cold. Knowing. Powerful. It almost sounded like nails on a chalkboard. With some effort, Dionysus was able to keep his facial muscles unchanged when all they wanted to do was cringe. David's voice softened as he said, "I'm right, aren't I?"

"Very astute thinking, David. Yes, you are correct." Johanna glared at David, but he just smiled at her. Dionysus watched the exchange with interest. He had seen strong angels buckle under Johanna's piercing green eyes. David didn't flinch, twitch, or even blink. He just curled the edges of his lips and stared back.

Eventually, Johanna broke the eye contact first, and said, "Okay, so the room is for evolution. Evolution of what?"

"Ahh, now that's a good question," Dionysus said, warning David off with his eyes. The boy looked as if he was ready to answer her question again. He knew that the answer would be correct—it was as if the boy knew everything he was thinking. David's lips parted, but then closed. Dionysus said, "That's exactly why you're all here. I'm looking for a volunteer."

"But we're already evolved," Johanna argued.

"Are we?" Dionysus asked. Silence. "You were all there on the Warrior's Plateau. Can you do what that filthy bitch of a girl did to us? I think not. Evolution is a journey, not a destination. Evolution continues in perpetuity, it is not a single event. Back when I was a demon I could have considered myself fully evolved, but I saw an opportunity for improvement, and I grabbed it, forcing the powers of the universe to let me see the light. And they did. Nature serves those who serve themselves. Survival of the fittest. Only the strong survive. Dog eat dog. No matter how you describe it, it all comes down to one principle: adapt or die. And right now we are on the precipice of extinction. And why? Because one lousy human girl could dream a bigger dream than us. I for one am not going to sit idly by and watch while all of our meticulously formed plans are destroyed and us along with them. So do I have a volunteer to take the next step in the evolution of angels?"

To Dionysus's pleasure, Lucas said, "I will do it, my lord."

"I thought you might, my son," Dionysus said. He made it sound sincere, like a compliment, when it was really an insult to Lucas's level of predictability. "Now," Dionysus said, taking on the stern and well-practiced tone of a university lecturer, "this room contains approximately ten thousand panels of magnifying glass, each angled precisely to harness light, magnify it, and redirect it throughout the room. Some of the panels direct the light towards the absolute center of the sphere, while others redirect the light to other panels, which reflect it toward other panels still, each time building up the energy contained in the light beams. The room is the perfect combination of natural energy as provided by the sun via the roof and upper walls, and synthetic energy as provided by our high-power lights via the floors and lower walls. The goal, of course, is to provide the angel—in this case, Lucas—with an overload of light energy, thus forcing his body to evolve in order to process and use it all. Any questions?"

Dionysus expected even the dimwitted Lucas to ask something about the safety of the procedure, whether it would hurt, whether it had been tested on animals, something. But all he said was, "I'm ready, my lord."

Dionysus smiled. "Good." He saw that Johanna was smiling mischievously—clearly, she understood what was happening.

Dionysus directed Lucas to the center of the room, where a glass-free rubber circle was cut into the floor. "This will rise up when the device is turned on, shifting you to the evolutionary position." Lucas nodded, his face stoic, filled with pride. Dionysus laughed inside. Sometimes puppets were funnier than clowns at the circus. "Good luck, my son."

"Thank you, my lord."

Dionysus ushered the remaining Archangels from the room and into the control module, which provided a one-way view of the activity in the room. A single engineer manned the controls. He would be disposed of later.

"Raise him," Dionysus ordered. Obediently, the engineer flicked a safety switch and then gradually raised a lever. The circle beneath Lucas quivered and then inched upwards. Lucas was jarred by the movement and temporarily lost his balance, but managed to remain upright by extending his arms and bending his knees. The pole that raised the circular platform telescoped upwards. Ten feet, thirty feet, fifty feet, one hundred…

Upon reaching approximately one-hundred-and-fifty feet, the spindle ended its altitude gain and eased to a halt. If not for the angels' extraordinary vision, Lucas would have been a speck, unidentifiable from such a distance. However, they could see him clearly, his white blond hair silhouetted against the covered glass dome. He still wore the arrogant expression that Dionysus had left him with, and he had extended his arms like he was some kind of a savior, come to save his people. Dionysus smirked. *What a tool*, he thought.

Dionysus said, "Ramp up the lower lights—thirty…no, fifty percent. Keep the sunlight covered until I give the order."

"Yessir," the pawn said. Another couple of switches and then a few keystrokes entered into the computer and the lights exploded on in the room. The effect of the magnifying glasses was magnificent, creating a blinding glare even through the heavily-tinted control room window. They heard a sound—a scream of pain, of agony?—and as Dionysus tilted his super-hearing ears towards the noise, he realized what he was listening to. It was laughter. Joyful, uninhibited, childlike laughter. He glanced around the room and noted they were all as shocked as he was—not one mouth was open wide enough to emit so much as a giggle. Judging by the distance and frequency of the silence-shattering tittering, it could only be coming from Lucas. Evidently, he was actually enjoying the effect of the bolts, beams, and lasers of light that pierced his frame.

Dionysus squinted and through the brightness could just barely make out a figure in the distance, brighter than the surrounding room by a factor of ten. And the figure was convulsing in a way that could only be in pain or....in laughter, apparently.

Dionysus said, "Increase the power of the lower lights to one hundred percent."

Two keystrokes and the intensity of the light in the room doubled, but not enough to obscure the glowing image of Lucas, who continued to laugh, harder and harder and louder and louder. "He seems to be okay," Dionysus said to himself.

"Of course he is," David said.

Turning sharply, Dionysus made eye contact with the boy. His eyes contained a rich blackness that could only be described as the absence of color. "Turn up the heat," David said. "He'll be fine."

The matter-of-fact way in which the boy spoke, as if he knew the outcome without a doubt because he had the ability to see into the future, unnerved Dionysus. But he knew his words were true. "Remove the outer cover," Dionysus barked.

The engineer hesitated for the first time since they had entered his domain. "The entire thing, sir?" he asked.

Dionysus hated being questioned, hated insolence. With the speed of a damn mongoose attacking a pesky cobra, Dionysus closed the gap to the engineer and shoved him forcefully. The engineer flew backwards like he was made of straw, and crashed into the side wall of the vestibule, leaving an indentation the shape of his body in the stone barrier. Rocks crumbled and cracked and generally rolled over his slumped body, but Dionysus wasn't looking at the aftermath of his actions. Instead, he had punched the required commands into the keyboard.

He turned his attention back to the room. He waited, gazing at the covered roof. A pinpoint of light appeared in the absolute center of the ceiling and then birthed four slits of light, which extended in opposite directions, like a cross. As the four quarters of the cover slid away, each branch of the cross grew wider and wider and exponentially increased the brightness of the room. By the time the final corners of the cover had slid away, the room was white. Dionysus couldn't see Lucas, couldn't see the walls, the roof, the floor. He suspected that Lucas could be immediately next to the viewing window and he still wouldn't be able to see him.

The noise from within the chamber had continued throughout the procedure, but it had changed in quality. Something was different and Dionysus tried to discern what had changed. And then someone was grabbing him from behind, yelling something in his ear. He ignored the voice as he focused on the sound from within the room. *Screaming*. Unlike a get-your-attention kind of scream, this was a scream of pain. More like agony. The tortured cry was shrilling, piercing, mind-shattering, something heard only in horror movies and nightmares. It was a sound that generally preceded death. The sound made Dionysus smile.

Thirteen

They made love as the afternoon sun waned in the west. That night, Sam didn't come home so they made love again. Sleep took them soon after.

Taylor awoke when the first full beam of light spilled over the horizon and through her east-facing window. Squinting, she said, "Gabriel."

His body was flush against hers—a necessity, given that students were only entitled to single beds, which created a logistical nightmare when opposite-sex sleepovers occurred. But they managed it well, even enjoyed it. Early on in their relationship, they had each learned that sleep came easier and was more restful when they did it together. It was just another sign that they were meant to be together. Or that they missed being in the womb. It was definitely one or the other.

Taylor felt Gabriel's body shift against hers. "Yeah?" he murmured, his eyes still closed.

His face looked peaceful, as if he were still in a dream full of grassy meadows and bubbling brooks. He also looked beautiful. Such a shame that she had to do it.

"Hiyah!" Taylor exclaimed, using the best impression of a karate master that she could muster. She brought the pillow down on his face as hard as she could.

"Oww! What the—" Gabriel groaned.

Taylor said, "Ding! Welcome to Hotel Taylor. This has been your sunrise wake-up call. We hope you enjoy the rest of your stay."

Slowly opening one eye, Gabriel said, "I don't remember scheduling a wake-up call and even if I did, I would have expected something a little more delicate. I might have to complain to management."

"I am management and your concern has been noted and denied." Knowing retribution was forthcoming, Taylor leapt from the bed. In the time it takes to blink, she had repositioned herself on Sam's bed, lying down; her head rested casually on her hand. Gabriel had tried to grab her as she made her escape, but was left grasping at air.

Taylor smirked. "Looking for someone?" she said.

"Damn. All of this talk about you being a faster, stronger form of angel has already gone to your head. It was bad enough when you were faster, but it is even worse now that you know you're faster."

"You ain't seen nothing yet."

"Great," Gabriel said. "Hey, how was your sleep last night?"

Taylor frowned. "Fine, why do you ask?"

"I just wanted to see what impact our little meditation session had on you."

"Oh." Taylor remembered how she had learned to block angels and demons from corrupting her dreams. "Well, it worked, I think. No Dionysus messing with my head last night."

"What about the other thing? Any bad stuff there?"

"Thankfully, no. If I had any nightmares about my mom's death, I don't remember them."

"Good," Gabriel said. Even as he enunciated the "dah" on the *d*, with lightning-quickness he launched Taylor's pillow across the room at her head. Unflinching, she grabbed it with one hand and tossed it aside. Gabriel smiled, shaking his head. "You really are amazing."

"I don't think being able to out-duel you in a pillow fight qualifies as amazing, but thanks."

"I guess we'll find out today. Are you ready to start training?"

Taylor's eyes lit up. "Hell yeah! I can't wait to see what I can do."

"Me, too," Gabriel said. "And I've managed to locate the perfect arena for it."

"Where?"

"It's a surprise."

"Great, you know how I love surprises," Taylor said sarcastically.

"Yes, I do," Gabriel said, playing along.

They agreed to meet in an hour so that Gabriel could confirm that his "training arena" would be available, and so he could make a few calls to ensure the necessary equipment could be requisitioned. Taylor, not one to primp, was ready in five minutes and found herself calling Sam on her iPhone. Although it wasn't unusual for Sam not to come home—sometimes she stayed at Chris's dorm room or at the Lair—Taylor still wanted to make sure she was okay.

Her friend answered on the third ring with a tired, "Taylor?"

"You can call me Archangel Taylor for now on."

"What?" Sam asked, confused.

"Haven't you heard? Gabriel told me the test results showed that I am the most powerful angel around, almost like an archangel."

"No, I didn't hear that. But I did hear about your mission."

"Yep, training for it starts today."

"I heard that too. I'm going to come to help out."

"Great!" Taylor said, even more excited now. "We're starting in an hour. Gabriel will tell Chris where it is. See you there." She hung up and realized the call had only killed about 45 seconds. She groaned—still about fifty minutes to waste. Deciding that watching TV or reading a magazine would be impossible given how jumpy she was, Taylor waved at a dark figure that was pretending to repair a bike on the lawn outside her window. Seconds later, the dude was in her room.

"What can I do for you?" the demon guard said.

"I wanted to see how the injured members of Hell's Angels are doing, particularly Sampson. Have you heard anything?"

The demon shook his head. "Not lately. Want me to radio in to find out?"

"I'd prefer to go there in person. That is, if you don't mind?"

"Fine by me. Let me just clear it with my mission leader."

A minute later, Taylor was following the demon out of the dark teleport room in the Lair. Although it would have been quicker to teleport directly to the demon medical wing, it required special approval that would take too long to obtain. All teleporting within the Lair was monitored and approved to prevent the chaos that would ensue if there were demons constantly popping in and out of view. For the most part, teleporting could only be conducted using a designated room.

From the teleport room, the duo made their way down a torch-lit tunnel. Unfinished, the tunnel walls and ceiling were comprised of rough, bare rock, giving it an

Indiana Jones feel. The tunnel led to a security door, which opened upon the demon's command. They were expected. From there, they took one of the many transporters—futuristic-looking trains that zipped personnel and guests throughout the Lair at sometimes rollercoasteresque speeds—to the hospital.

Taylor led the way to Sampson's room, remembering where in the maze of halls, corridors, and exam rooms he was located. Without knocking, she pushed open the door. The room was empty, the bed sheets having been laundered and replaced. Taylor frowned. "They must have moved him," she said.

At the nurse's station, they inquired as to Sampson's new room. "He's gone," the nurse said solemnly.

Shock, sadness, frustration, fear: such were the feelings that were included in the muddled mix of emotions that hit Taylor at that moment, leaving her nauseous and light-headed. Just yesterday he had been on the mend, how could this have happened? The nurse must've read Taylor's pain on her face, because she said, "No, no, I mean…I shouldn't have said it that way. Sampson's fine. He's been discharged, that's all. He made such a speedy recovery that he didn't need to stay here any longer."

Relief washed over Taylor, leaving her feeling fresh and clean again. The pit left her stomach and she felt a slight fluttering of butterflies. She had trouble finding her voice, however, and only managed to mumble, "Thanks," before walking off.

Despite her reassurances, the demon insisted that he follow Taylor around the Lair as she searched for Sampson. He wasn't worried about her safety; rather, he wanted to know when she was heading back to UT's campus, so he could resume his security detail with the rest of her guard. "Fine. But you can damn well stay at least twenty feet away. I'll be damned if I have a freaking entourage walking around this place." The guard, taken aback by the directness of her demand, backed off immediately much to Taylor's satisfaction.

It didn't take Taylor long to find her friend. Sampson was in the demon café, scarfing down platefuls of food as if he hadn't eaten since his birth more than eighteen years earlier. He was sitting with a group of his fellow Hell's Angels, but stood and strode to meet Taylor upon spotting her.

As he approached, Taylor outstretched her hand to fist-bump him and then blow-it-up as was their typical greeting, but instead he moved past her arm and hugged her firmly. It was the first time they had hugged, and although Taylor thought it would be awkward—as they just didn't have that type of touchy, feely relationship—it wasn't. The hug felt natural, sincere, brotherly.

When he released her, his face was serious. "Taylor, I don't know how to thank you."

"C'mon, don't get all mushy on me. You can thank me by not making a big deal out of it. I want the jokester, doesn't-take-himself-or-life-too-seriously Sampson back."

Sampson screwed up his face, fully closing one eye and bugging the other eye out. Touching his tongue to his nose, he mumbled, "Isth thut besser?"

Taylor laughed. "Much better. Thanks. Hey, I've got training today, do you want to come?"

With a gleam in his eye, Sampson said, "I would love to, but I have an important briefing to attend. I've been booked on a mission. You may have heard about it. It's called Operation Kill-the-Bastard-Head-of-the-Archangel-Council."

"What!? You're on my mission? But don't you need to rest and recover?"

"Thanks to you, I'm already at one hundred percent. Clifford asked me if I would do it and I said yes, of course."

Taylor couldn't hide her excitement as a smile filled her face. "I'm so glad, Sampson. It will mean a lot to me having you there."

"Me, too," Sampson said. "Now, where's that chump of a boyfriend of yours?"

"Preparing to train me back at UT. That's where all the action is. Sure you can't come?"

Sampson said, "I'll try to stop by later. I heard it's being held in the football stadium, right?"

"What? How's that possible? Gabriel said it was a surprise but that's outrageous!"

"A surprise? Oops, I guess the cat's out of the bag. Listen, can you pretend you didn't find out from me? Or even better, that you didn't find out at all? Just act surprised."

"I'll do my best."

"Thanks."

Taylor checked her watch—only five minutes until Gabriel would come by her dorm. She swiveled on one foot, panning her surroundings and quickly locating the demon. While she knew it seemed cold, she refused to learn the names of her demon guards and preferred to refer to them as Demon A, Demon B, etc. They preferred it, too. Less personal was better in war. If something happened to any of them while protecting her, she wouldn't even know their names.

Sensing that she was ready to leave, the demon met her at the tunnel that would lead them to the transporter that would deliver them back to the teleport room. Taylor set the pace, a light jog down the passageway. They needed to hurry; Gabriel was generally very punctual.

In four minutes and thirty seconds they appeared in Taylor's room. With no reason to linger, the demon said a muffled and succinct "Goodbye," and disappeared. Less than ten seconds later there was a knock at the door.

Out of habit, Taylor checked the peephole and saw Gabriel's distorted head through the portal. Opening the door, she said, "You would look really funny if your head was twice as big but on the same body."

Gabriel smirked. "And you would look like some bizarre big-headed chicken from Mars."

"What are you saying, that I have chicken legs?"

Using his best chicken voice, Gabriel said, "Bawk, bawk, bagaw!" and then tried to grab her bare legs, left exposed by the old denim shorts she was wearing.

Taylor felt as if he were moving in slow motion, as she easily sidestepped and kicked him in the butt as he lunged through her room. Almost crashing into the microwave sitting on top of the mini-fridge, Gabriel barely managed to avoid losing his balance. "Damn, you're fast," he said.

"You've already said that."

"I'm still getting used to it."

"You will," Taylor said. "So…where's this secret place you are taking me for training?"

"You'll see," Gabriel said.

Leaving Shyloh Hall, the pair took the long way to the stadium, which basically meant walking rather than flying. As they strolled along, hand in hand, Taylor thought about her life before Gabriel. Dull, boring, uninspired. It wasn't that she hadn't been enjoying her life, or that she didn't have a lot of fun. That wasn't it at all. God knows her and Sam had fun—and laughed a lot, although mostly at each other. But there had also been something missing. Something that maybe she wasn't aware of until she met Gabriel. Something that might have left her life when her mom died. Something she needed and would never again be able to live without. Excitement, adventure, inspiration. A reason to wake up in the morning and to get a good sleep at night. It wasn't only the thrill of battles and wars and angels and demons and auras; rather, it was the feeling of being part of something important. She would cling to that feeling desperately, firmly, as long as she could and hopefully forever.

Taylor was still lost in her thoughts when they reached the stadium, but was jarred back to reality when Gabriel said, "We're here."

Taylor thought, *No kidding we're here*, but then remembered she was supposed to pretend to be surprised. Her reply was a tick late. She said, "What do you mean we're here? This is the stadium."

"I knew it! Someone told you, didn't they?"

She was caught in her lie and lamely tried to recover: "What? Uh, no. I thought it would be somewhere less public."

Gabriel was not to be fooled. "You weren't paying attention. I practically let you lead the way here and you never wavered or questioned the direction we were taking. You knew exactly where we were going. Who told you?"

Busted, Taylor thought. "Sampson," she said.

"Yeah, like I'm going to believe that!"

Taylor was glad to know something that Gabriel didn't know for once. He probably assumed Sampson was still bedridden, barely able to eat or talk. But she knew better.

"I'm not lying. I went to visit him this morning while I was waiting for you. He's fully recovered and walking around as if he was never critically injured. He'll stop by later to watch the training."

Gabriel looked dazed. "Incredible," he whispered.

"What? That I wasn't surprised by the venue or that I cured Sampson so fast?"

"The latter. You may be even stronger than any of us think."

"You keep underestimating me. I'm one tough chick," Taylor joked.

"Evidently," Gabriel said, still looking dumbfounded.

Taylor turned her attention to the stadium. Her eyes scanned the exterior. The massive structure was constructed on a base of concrete blocks, which gave way to exposed steel girders and cross-beams. Typically the uppermost rising seats could be seen through gaps in the top portion of the crater-shaped stadium, but were now hidden beneath the retractable domed roof, which could be closed in the event of rain during a sporting event. The dome was closed, but the skies were blue, the sun was shining. The place looked like a fortress, impenetrable to all but the most heinous enemy weapons.

"How'd you get us private access to this place? And get the dome closed? What about the maintenance staff, isn't there a chance they will show up?" Taylor rattled the questions off while counting on her fingers.

"I'm awesome, I'm awesome, and no," Gabriel said, laughing. Taylor rolled her eyes. "Just kidding, Tay. I actually had nothing to do with it. There is a woman in the demon army whose husband is one of the top dogs on the stadium operating council. He made this all possible. We won't be disturbed. The only rule is that we have to clean up any mess that we make."

Taylor was impressed. And excited. Training in the massive enclosure that was the football stadium would be incredible! She couldn't have asked for a cooler location. "Awesome," she said. "Let's do it."

Gabriel grinned. "Follow me."

He led Taylor through a player's only entrance which he happened to have a key for. Three hallways later and they were in the locker rooms. Taylor always expected that a football team locker room would stink of dried sweat and body odor, perhaps with the slight metallic hint of blood from past gridiron battles. In this case, however, all she could smell was lilac and cotton candy. *Weird*, she thought. Evidently, even tough-guy football players appreciated a well-perfumed preparation area. She spotted five or six automatic, continuous air fresheners plugged into simple wall outlets—the source of the lilac and the cotton candy.

From the locker room they followed a wide, high-ceilinged corridor that grew lighter in the distance. It led directly to the field. As Taylor walked out of the tunnel, she realized why football players always appeared so energetic and emotional when they ran out onto the field before a game. The stadium looked mesmerizing: rising seats pyramided upwards in what might have been a stairway to heaven; bright lights gave the field the appearance of being a giant stage on Broadway; the perfectly trimmed grass seemed to stretch on for miles, rather than merely a little over one-hundred yards. Even without the band, or the cheerleaders, or the fans, or the cameras, the sight was still thrilling. Taylor tried to imagine what it would be like with the stadium filled to the rafters, fans cheering and clapping, and dozens of players streaming all over the field. She had been to many games, which all proved to be fun and exciting, but she now had a whole new appreciation for the experience.

On the field, Taylor noticed a handful of dark figures—demons—as well as several angels who were hovering in the air by gently fanning their wings. Gabriel explained: "They're here to help. A few demons volunteered to assist with your sword work, and a few guys and girls from Hell's Angels came along to demonstrate flying and light powers."

"Hell yeah," Taylor said. "I can't wait to try flying for real this time."

Fourteen

Lucas was screaming. Dionysus was grinning. Cassandra was the angel who had grabbed Dionysus's shoulder from behind. She was yelling, "Stop! Stop the machine! It's killing him!" Dionysus ignored her, soaking up the beauty of the tortured cries from within the room.

It was nothing personal against Lucas. He certainly didn't want him to die and truly believed that he wouldn't. His theory was simple: no pain, no gain. In fact, Dionysus had only heard such a cry of anguish once before. More than five decades earlier, he himself had once issued a similar noise. Because it hurt—really, really hurt—when he evolved from a demon to an angel. The pain had been worth it then and it would be worth it now for Lucas.

Which is why Dionysus was smiling.

Because it was working. Or so he believed.

What he really wished was that the blonde would stop yelling in his ear. Without turning around, he angled a fist backwards over his shoulder and fired off a powerful orb of light. At such a close range the impact was deafening. BOOM! He heard the girl crash to the floor; she would be unconscious for at least an hour.

He heard laughing from behind—probably Johanna finding his response to Cassandra's yelling amusing. She was always amused by the pain of others. *At least she was consistent*, he thought. Whether angel, demon, human, or gargoyle: sadistic Johanna loved watching the destruction of others.

Dionysus was aware that the screaming had stopped, which meant one of two things: Lucas had died from the strain on his body, or Lucas had evolved. There was a third possibility—that he was still alive and no evolution had occurred—but Dionysus the optimist discounted it immediately.

He shut down the system and waited. Slowly, bit by bit, the cover slid over the dome, blocking out the sunlight, as the lower lights were extinguished, restoring the room to a dull gray; the only light was provided by the filtered rays of sun finding their way through the covering. The process took about ten minutes.

When the shutdown process was halfway complete, they got their first glimpse of the raised platform, which had partially descended and was continuing to creep towards the floor. On the platform, Lucas remained standing—or had regained his feet. He stood up straight, his spine in line with his legs, his head tilted back, his eyes looking up as if towards heaven.

Lucas shone.

As the room continued to darken, the contrast of his gleaming body against the dim background became more severe, until he looked like a beacon of hope—a lighthouse?—in a sea of rough, stormy waters.

Lucas remained like a statue when Dionysus entered the room, with the other Archangels—minus Cassandra the nag—following closely behind him.

He approached Lucas. Lucas the Shining; Lucas the Beacon; Lucas the Archangel perhaps? Even as Dionysus moved within Lucas's line of peripheral vision, he remained still as stone, head craned skywards. "My son," Dionysus said, "how do you feel?"

No response.

David said, "He's changed, my lord. For the better."

Dionysus knew the boy was right, if only because Lucas *wasn't* responding. Typically, he spoke a mile a minute all the time. His silence was a clear indication that he was improved, in some way.

Lucas's face appeared to have undergone a subtle change. All of his features were the same, and yet different, more distinct, improved. His athletic frame looked even more toned, as if he had just finished lifting weights.

Moving closer, Dionysus extended his hand, placing it on Lucas's shoulder from the front. Lucas's head snapped down and he made eye contact. He seemed startled by Dionysus's sudden presence, but he wasn't scared. "My lord," he said.

"Speak, my son," Dionysus said encouragingly.

"The pain...." He trailed off.

"I know, Lucas. Evolution is painful. But how do you feel now?"

"Perfect," he said. He could have said good, or great, or fantastic, but Dionysus sensed that his word choice was important. *Perfect.* Time to put that perfection to the test.

Without warning, Dionysus whipped his fist at Lucas's head with as much speed and power as he could muster. Lucas was quicker, raising one arm sharply to catch Dionysus's fist in his hand, stopping the attack cold. *Impressive.* Before the procedure, Lucas couldn't have thwarted the attack and would now be lying unconscious on the ground.

"Release me," Dionysus said.

Obediently, Lucas dropped his fist.

Dionysus turned to face the others. Johanna, Sarah, and Percy looked impressed, while David's eyes were as unreadable as ever. Raising a fist in the air, Dionysus said, "For sixty years, ever since I evolved from a demon, I have been focused on one thing: cleansing the face of the earth from the demon scum—the filth—that plagues it. All that time I was perpetually mired in a belief—which I now know to be a false belief—that I was at the top of the food chain, fully evolved, perfect in every way. Much time has been wasted as I sought the girl who I thought would provide a weapon destined to end the War. I was not wrong about the importance of the girl; rather, I was wrong about how she would come into play. Her weapon was powerful, yes, but she was never going to help us. Instead, her purpose was one of education, of opening my eyes to my mistake. For behold, Lucas is the proof that our kind have never been perfected, that we have been strong—oh, how strong—but not perfect. Now I give you perfection! And with this knowledge and this procedure, we, the Archangel Council, will become the true archangels we were always meant to be, to govern the angel race, finally destroy our darker ancestors, and take our place as rulers of the world!"

Dionysus paused to catch his breath. In the zealousness and anger of his words, spittle had escaped his lips and bubbled on his chin. He wiped it off with the back of his sleeve. He said, "I will take my place next and then I expect each of you to follow. Will you do it?"

"Yes, master," David said fiercely. His eyes were gleaming in the dim light.

"And you, Percy?" Dionysus asked. Percy nodded. Letting his eyes slide to Sarah, he waited.

"I will do it," Sarah said.

Before he could question Johanna, she said, "Hell yeah, I will."

"Let it be done," Dionysus said.

Fifteen

Taylor's training began with instruction on harnessing the power of light, from which all other angel abilities originated. She wanted to fly first, but understood the logic that flight was also powered by light and therefore she needed to walk before she could run, so to speak.

Gabriel started by showing how he could capture the lights in the stadium just by wanting them. He explained that his eyes needed to be open, as they were the conduit for the energy to enter his body. Unblinking, he stood still and let the light wash over and into him. His body began to glow. At his sides, his hands were filled with orbs of light that appeared as tangible as basketballs, clearly defined and formed.

Something didn't make sense. In the past, Taylor had seen Gabriel harness light countless times. Usually he used his hands more. Taylor said, "I thought you needed to aim your hands at the lights to obtain their power?"

Like a university lecturer, Gabriel said, "Very astute observation. You've probably seen me do it before, right?" Taylor nodded. "That's exactly how you'll need to start out. While the only requirement is to desire the light, that can be quite difficult in practice. Because your hands and arms are instruments of your mind's will, it sometimes helps to direct them at what you desire to help focus your mind. Understand?"

"Focus. Right," Taylor said.

"Good. Now you try."

Wanting to prove him wrong and show him that she could focus without using her hands as training wheels like some twelve-year-old angel learning the basics, Taylor remained still, like Gabriel had, directing her thoughts at the beaming stadium lights. *Monkeys! Cute, little chimpanzees running amok through a supermarket, throwing cans and boxes and fruit and rolling cantaloupes down the aisles like bowling balls. And ice cream! No, no—an ice cream maker! A giant, shining metal machine filled with churning, oozing, viscous ice cream. Chocolate, her favorite! And then it was overflowing, dumping gallons of the cold treat onto the floor, creating a tsunami of flavor! Dammit, get out of my head, damned monkeys and ice cream!* Taylor silently screamed.

Gabriel interrupted her thoughts when he said, "Taylor, just try it using your hands to help the first time, nothing is happening."

"No, shut up," Taylor said through clenched teeth. "I can do this."

Refocusing herself, Taylor tried to imagine that she was reaching her hands out to grab the lights, to steal away their precious energy. *Now the monkeys had left the supermarket and were at the ice cream factory. Happily, the marsupials swam in the ice cream lake, swallowing mouthfuls of the chocolaty delight and spitting it back out. Others had started an ice cream ball fight, rolling piles of snowball-like projectiles and launching them across the room. Splat! One monkey was hit in the face, but instead of hissing or growling, it squealed with delight as it licked the sugary slime off its face. No, no, no, no, no, splat! Another monkey hit. No, no, no! Get the hell out of my thoughts, monkeys!* Taylor cursed in her head. But it was to no avail, the monkeys continued to swing and swim and splat across her mind.

Grudgingly, she admitted defeat. "Can't concentrate," she said.

Gabriel said, "What did you see?"

Taylor sighed. "Monkeys."

"Monkeys?" Gabriel said, smirking.

"And ice cream."

Gabriel's smirk turned into a chortle and then a guffaw, and soon he was laughing so hard he was crying.

His case of the laughing-flu soon became airborne and the various demons and angels who had been watching Taylor began chuckling, too. If there was one thing that Taylor's mom had taught her to be, it was a good sport. "Taylor, if you can't laugh at yourself every once in a while, you will become so uptight, even dogs won't like you," she used to tell her—and so Taylor was soon laughing with the rest of them.

When she stopped, she said to Gabriel, "Did you enjoy that? I hope you peed your pants," which started a whole new round of laughter.

After wiping the happy tears from his eyes, Gabriel said, "Are you ready to try to do this my way?"

Ignoring him, Taylor outstretched her arm and aimed it at one of the massive stadium spotlights in the corner. Seeing her hand reaching out for the light, Taylor was easily able to visualize her fingers pulling at the beams of light, like cords of rope, extracting them from the fixture. And there were no monkeys this time.

She felt her body begin to warm as the light was soaked up by her eyes and start to flow through her veins. In seconds her arm was glowing, and then her entire body. "I think I'm getting the hang of this," Taylor announced. "How do I make an orb?"

"Just visualize it. Again, it might help if you use your hands to help. Pretend you are rolling the orb out of the incoming beams of light."

Licking her lips in concentration, Taylor imagined that the beams of light were coming so fast that she could barely keep up with them. She made a motion with her hands like she was squeezing something together to make a snowball. She felt like she was a mime on the streets of New York, performing for a group of tourists while dressed as if she had recently swam in a bag of flour. Or maybe she was playing charades, trying to act out making Christmas cookies so her team could guess it.

Something began to form in her hands. An amoeba of light, ill-defined and wobbly, bounced and waggled through her fingertips. *More power*, she thought, *I need more power*. She reasserted her claim on the light's energy and imagined her eyes were huge vacuums, sucking generous watts of electricity from the bulbs. The amoeba was not an amoeba any longer, having formed into a glowing ball, an orb. As Taylor strained to get every last drop of energy, the ball suddenly grew bigger and bigger and brighter and brighter and then was gone, having imploded into nothingness. There was a crackle and a pop and a shower of sparks from above, as one by one, the dozen or so bulbs exploded and burnt out, leaving a quarter of the field in shadowy darkness.

"Nice one, Tay," Gabriel said.

"What the hell....but I did everything right!" Taylor said.

"Almost everything," Gabriel said. "I wanted you to make your own mistake on this one to ensure you learned the lesson. In this case you tried to soak up more power than you needed to form the orb you desired, and thus, it had the opposite effect. Not knowing what to do with the extra energy, the orb reversed itself and was unmade."

"Unmade? What is this, the freaking science-fiction channel? Speak English, you mean *destroyed*?"

"You could put it that way, but it's not like a piece of paper going through a shredder—there are no scraps—rather, it's like a drop of water evaporating into steam. The orb is still there, it's just changed—back into light."

Taylor frowned. "But why couldn't I just store the energy I didn't need?" she asked.

"Actually, you could have. You just didn't know how."

Growing impatient, Taylor snapped, "Why didn't you just tell me how before I started?" She glared at him.

Gabriel stared right back, emotionless. He said, "Taylor, I am attempting to teach you ten years of technique in only a few months. You are just going to have to trust me. Sometimes you will need to make mistakes and figure things out on your own in order to learn. Can you handle that?"

She wasn't sure why she had gotten so angry. She knew he was only trying to help her. The speed that the anger had boiled up took her by surprise. She felt chastened. Raising her eyebrows, she said, "I'm sorry, you're right."

With a wink, Gabriel said, "I never thought I would hear those words."

"Don't push your luck, buddy," Taylor said lightly.

"Okay, now try again."

Taylor outstretched her arm.

Sixteen

While the War Room remained nearly half-empty—with five of the twelve chairs unused—somehow it felt fuller than before. The New Archangels, as Dionysus was calling the current members of the Council, were seated and discussing the future, which was feeling brighter by the minute. It had taken more than two hours to use the room to evolve the remaining angels. Even Cassandra was able to participate after being revived with smelling salts and a bucket of water on her head. Although there was anger in her eyes, it dissipated after seeing that Lucas was not dead and was, in fact, improved, perfected. Given Cassandra's bold reaction when she thought Lucas was dying,

Dionysus suspected there was romance in the future for the two of them. He would have to monitor *that* situation carefully to ensure it didn't impact their judgment, although he suspected it wouldn't, given they were cut from the same mold manufactured by Evil Corporation, of which he was the President.

While each member of the Council had been attractive to begin with, the act of evolution had taken that beauty to a whole new level. To his frustration, Dionysus could barely take his eyes off of Cassandra. Her skin was like porcelain, her features perfection. The use of makeup would be silly, like trying to improve upon a work by Michaelangelo. And she was aware of the attention he was giving her, batting her eyes and pouting her lips like some damn showgirl. He would come up with a solution later— maybe a bag over her head or clown's makeup or something.

The others were changed too: Lucas seemed calmer, more reserved, more intelligent even; Johanna and Sarah looked like Amazon women, as fierce as they were beautiful; Percy looked like a Swedish-god, with strong features and captivating blue eyes; Dionysus was also improved, but the differences were more subtle.

However, the most impressive changes had surely been wrought on David. While he had looked a year or two older than his age at the start of the day, the boy now appeared to be a half-decade older. His boyish features had dissolved, and in their place was a vision of a man. If he looked like Gabriel before, he appeared as his twin brother now. In fact, if the brothers were standing next to each other, it would be difficult to discern who the eldest was. The similarities in appearance between the brothers were so great that it was disconcerting for Dionysus to rest his gaze upon the boy's face for too long. It was as if his greatest enemy from the past had found a way to inhabit his brother's body and thus learn all of Dionysus's darkest secrets. But the comparison ended when the boy spoke, his words harsh and uncaring, eerily mature and wise, definitive. Dionysus realized he was speaking now.

"My lord, we now have the firepower we have been seeking. I recommend we march out in the next battle and decimate the demon army. In our evolved state we cannot be stopped."

The strength of David's words resonated with others around the table. Percy and Sarah were nodding, and Lucas seemed to be hanging on his every word. Only Cassandra and Johanna appeared unmoved: Cassandra was more interested in gawking at herself in the portable mirror she had brought to the Council meeting, and Johanna was probably still angry with the boy for the way he had spoken to her in earlier meetings.

Dionysus said, "What about the girl?"

"She is only one, we are many. We will crush HER!" David slammed his fist on the table when he said *her*, emphasizing his point. Cassandra flinched and almost dropped her mirror.

"Your point is well-taken, but I would propose a slightly different course of action. Look, we are in no danger at the moment. The demons, as usual, are probably waiting for us to make the next move. And we will. But not yet. At this point, we do not fully comprehend what the girl is able to do, or what our new bodies are capable of. We need to know what we're dealing with."

David said, "What do you propose?" The man-child's voice sounded so different that Dionysus found himself shuddering each time he spoke. He would need to do something about that too, maybe force him to speak in a voice changing device that made him sound like a little kid again.

"I propose we train. We learn about our new powers and ensure we understand how to use them most effectively before we fly into battle like a bunch of testosterone-crazed teenagers that just hit puberty. At the same time, we'll enlist one of our demon spies to keep tabs on the girl, and gather intel about her powers. Once we are informed, we'll plan our next move."

"Interesting," David said. "I am willing to live with that." Dionysus smiled. He had been somewhat concerned that there might be dissension in the New Archangels, especially because the boy was so unpredictable. Now he knew that David was on his side, just another pawn to be used. "Thank you, David. Your agreement is appreciated. I propose a vote!"

As expected, the voting was unanimous.

Seventeen

A single bead of sweat twisted and turned and meandered down Taylor's face. It paused mid-cheek and quivered for a moment, as if it were fighting gravity and losing, before continuing to her chin. The droplet reached the edge and fell to the ground, making a tiny splash that went unnoticed by anyone in the stadium.

"I can do this," Taylor said under her breath. Despite her stronger, more capable body, her muscles ached and her lungs burned. She had been training for two hours straight—no breaks, no water, no rest—and had barely learned anything. All she had been able to do was to create a small orb about the size of a basketball, which had taken more than an hour to accomplish. During that time, she had basically been standing still, so she was surprised at the toll it had taken on her. Gabriel explained that every angel act—whether mental or physical—had a physical component to it. Therefore, the thirty or forty attempts to harness the power of light to create a ball of energy had been the equivalent of running about twenty miles, based on Gabriel's estimations. Taylor felt like she had run a hundred miles—or more. But her new and improved body managed to sustain her in a way that never before would have been possible.

For the last thirty minutes she had been trying to fly. "You can do this," she repeated as she took her first step. They had started with hovering, but Taylor was unable to encourage her wings to break from the skin and muscles in her back. You can't hover if you don't have wings. Changing tactics, Gabriel had instructed her to try a running start, almost like an airplane speeding down a runway. The hope was that the forward momentum, along with a high jump at the end, would allow her instincts to take over, thus forcing her wings out.

The first three times she had crash landed before ever really taking off. But she had stayed true to her promise to Gabriel that she would not get frustrated, and had kept trying.

She sped up, turning her light jog into a run, faster than any human being could move. She hissed over and over again: "You can do it, you can do it, do it, do it, do it…" Taking her already blazing speed up another notch, she began sprinting down the field. Unlike even the fastest football players, who might be able to go end zone to end zone in thirteen or fourteen seconds, Taylor got there in three. Waiting until the last possible second—just before she reached the end of the grassy field—Taylor leapt skywards with all her might, higher than she had ever jumped, willing her body to take over, releasing her mind to her angel instincts. *The monkey tittered at her while licking an ice cream cone. Chocolate, of course.* Gravity took over and slammed her down forcefully. Except this time she didn't have soft grass to land on. She careened into the metal bleachers, crunching them under her steely angel frame. "Ahhh!" she yelled.

In seconds Gabriel was by her side, still smiling. He had been smiling the whole day. Either he was trying to be positive for her sake, or he was amused by her struggles. Either way, it annoyed her, but she dared not complain. "You're bleeding," he said.

"You think?" Taylor said sarcastically, giving herself a minor reprieve from her pent up anger.

Lifting a mangled piece of metal bleacher that had wrapped around her arm, Gabriel said, "It's not deep. Watch it heal."

As soon as the offending metal was removed from the wound, Taylor watched as the steady stream of white blood that poured from her skin became a trickle and then stopped completely, of its own accord. The three-inch gash became two-inches, and then one, her skin knitting itself together as if she was watching the speeded up process of an injury healing through the use of stitches over the course of a few months. "Awesome," Taylor breathed.

"Okay, break over," Gabriel said, clapping his hands together. "We need maintenance over here!"

Grudgingly, Taylor picked herself up. Gabriel didn't offer a helping hand. *That was a break? Taking two minutes to watch my arm stop bleeding?*

Taylor watched as two demons jumped effortlessly from the field to the raised seating area. They carried a fresh segment of metal bleachers. Working quickly with metal saws, they cut away the section she had destroyed, and replaced it with the fresh piece. All day the maintenance team had been chasing her around, cleaning up after her mistakes. Like replacing light bulbs she had fried, replacing divots of grass she had torn up, and now, repairing stadium hardware, like the bleachers.

Trying to control her simmering frustration, Taylor hopped down from the seats and strode back onto the field where Gabriel waited for her. He said, "Flying's not so easy, even with wings."

"I don't have wings. At least, not anymore. It's like they've disappeared."

"Trust me, they're there. The scans showed them healthy and strong and ready for flight. The first time's always the hardest."

"But it's not the first time," Taylor said, remembering how she had hovered magnificently in the air before wreaking havoc on the Archangels. At the time, the experience had seemed so real, vivid, but now it felt like just a memory of a hazy dream.

"The other one doesn't count. You weren't trying then. It's harder when you're trying."

"Whatever you say, boss," Taylor said, hoping he was right.

"Try again, but this time, don't think about flying. Assume you are just going to leap in the air and then come falling back to the ground, like you would before—when you were human."

Taylor nodded, and without responding, took off down the field. Two seconds and fifty yards later, she planted both feet firmly on the ground and propelled herself up. Expecting to come back down, she kept her knees bent and her stance wide, as she controlled her body in anticipation of recontacting the field. She closed her eyes

There was a *pop!* and she felt the wash of wind through her hair. It felt good, as she was still warm and sweaty from the exertion of the day. The breeze was inconstant, however, hitting her from behind and then not. From behind and then not. Like a turning fan, it provided cooling relief one out of every few seconds. She enjoyed the breeze for a few minutes, preparing herself mentally for her next attempt at flying.

She heard, "Way to go, Tay!" It was Gabriel's voice, but sounded distant—he was still at the other end of the field, most likely. He had been sarcastic with her all day, with comments like *Nice one*, or *Impressive!* after each of her failures. It was really starting to piss her off. Taylor opened her eyes, ready to yell something like, "Who saved your life when you got the poo beaten out of you by Lucas?" Instead, she yelled, "Holy Shnikes!"

Her feet were dangling beneath her and the field was getting smaller and smaller. At both edges of her peripheral vision, there were white creatures flashing about. *Angels!* she thought. Dionysus had found her and captured her and was carrying her away. She glanced to the left, ready to kick and claw at her attacker. Her breath caught in her throat when she saw what was there. A brilliantly white, feathery wing gracefully arced high above her shoulders, and then powered down with a *whoosh!* With each successive cycle, the wing pushed air across her face, simulating a gust of wind. She was flying!

But how? She wasn't thinking about it and yet the wings performed, propelling her higher and higher, as if they had minds of their own. Finally, she thought to look up, and when she did, she saw that she was nearly to the top of the domed roof. "How do I stop these things!?" she yelled to Gabriel, who now looked like an ant scurrying across a small rectangle of grass.

Faintly, she heard Gabriel say, "You control them, not the other way around! They are just like legs or arms, your brain just isn't fully aware of them yet!"

Taylor glanced up again; she was getting dangerously close to the roof, and she didn't want to find out what would happen if she collided with it. A vision flashed in her mind: her wings clipped the dome, cracking in four places and failing her, like the propeller on a helicopter stopping in midflight, allowing gravity to carry her to the earth hundreds of times faster than she had left it.

"I'm the boss," she growled through clenched teeth. *Flying is just like walking, once you get the hang of it*, Gabriel had explained. Concentrating on these words, she tried to garner control.

A burst of air hit her as she suddenly shot forwards, cruising along the edge of the dome. Despite having flown with Gabriel many times before, Taylor was unprepared for the rush of excitement she felt. Like every carnival or amusement park ride twisted into one—all the rollercoasters with their demon drops and loops and corkscrews, the plunges from incredible heights protected only by a thin safety strap, the spin-factories and Ferris wheels—flying solo was a thrill seeker's wildest dream.

And then she was in control.

Somehow she intuitively understood the nature of her new appendages, and she dove rapidly for the field, loving the drop in her stomach that resulted and wishing she could fall forever. She leveled out and soared towards

Gabriel, who was still earthbound and watching her. Seconds before crashing into her boyfriend she turned and whipped around him, leaving him in the wash of moving air that she had created, as if she was a truck powering down the highway.

Heading upwards again, she looked back over her left shoulder for Gabriel's reaction. He was gone. Something brushed by her right side and past her. She heard Gabriel say, "Tag, you're it."

Turning to face forwards again, she saw him flying out in front of her, putting more and more distance between them. "It's on!" Taylor yelled, as she mentally spurred her wings to speed up. They completed a lap around the dome. And then another. Despite her best efforts, however, he seemed to continue to gain on her. *There has to be something else I can do,* Taylor thought.

She stopped flying to think about it for a moment, hovering delicately in the air. A thought was on the tip of her tongue, but she couldn't quite pluck it off. Something to do with angel abilities. Powers. How to magnify her powers! That's it! She remembered Gabriel telling her at the beginning of the training that harnessing the power of light was the most important thing she could learn, because it would need to be combined with all her other powers to magnify them. To catch Gabriel, she would need to use more light power.

She waved her hand in front of her face to gauge her current energy level. Her hand was glowing, but only dimly, barely even noticeable under the bright stadium lights. Reaching her hand towards the nearest pocket of overhead lights, Taylor tried to extract their inherent power. Immediately her hand glowed brighter and brighter until it wasn't glowing anymore—it was shining! Not nearly as bright as the sun, and just short of a light bulb, her hand's light appeared more distant, like that of a star. Realizing she might blow out the bulbs like she had earlier that morning, she picked the next set of lights and stole as much of their energy as she could. Growing in confidence, she started flying again, but continued to soak up light-energy wherever she saw it.

She picked up speed.

Ahead of her, Gabriel had stopped to watch what she was doing. When she resumed her pursuit, he turned and raced off, moving faster than Taylor thought possible. But Taylor was faster, narrowing the gap by half, and then by half again, until she was less than five body lengths from catching him. Sensing her, Gabriel looked back and smiled. "Good luck!" he yelled gleefully.

With reckless abandon, he twisted his body so that he was flying blind and upside down and then dove for the ground, arcing his trajectory so that when he pulled out of the dive he would be heading in the opposite direction. Taylor dove after him and realized too late that he was attempting to go under her, and because of the way he had positioned his body he would be able to seamlessly complete the maneuver, whereas she would have to come to a stop or slow down to turn. Taylor only had one option: speed up. Mustering all the energy she had absorbed, while continuing to soak up more power, Taylor increased her speed. When Gabriel was directly beneath her and just coming out of his arc, she burst towards him, grabbing his waist as she collided on top of him. "Oommf!" he groaned, absorbing the impact.

"Gotcha!" Taylor declared victoriously as they plummeted towards the ground. Thrown off balance by their midair meeting, Taylor was spiraling out of control. She tried everything in her power to stop the spin, to stop their fall, but her body just wouldn't respond. Evidently her reserves of energy had been expended. She felt a jerk in her back and heard a zipping noise and she knew her wings had retracted.

Holding on to Gabriel's back for dear life, she used him as a landing pad as they smashed into the field. They sank deep into the soft grass, leaving a two-foot crater that would require more than just a few panels of pre-grown grass to repair.

Climbing out of the hole unscathed, Taylor looked back and said, "You okay?"

"Uhhhh," Gabriel said, still face down in the dirt.

"I guess I got a little carried away," Taylor said.

Rolling over, Gabriel said, "Ya think??" His face was covered in splotches of dirt, and bits of grass clung to his nose, chin and ears. Taylor clamped a hand over her mouth to stifle a laugh.

Muffled by her hand, she said, "You look….good, Gabriel."

Before he could respond, Taylor heard a girl's voice say, "Hey, Tay."

Turning her attention away from her battered boyfriend, Taylor saw her best friend jogging up to meet her. Chris was next to her. "What are you doing here, Sam?"

Smiling, Sam said, "Clifford told us about your training and recommended that we come and see if you needed any help."

Chris winked. He said, "It seems like you're doing just fine though. That was an incredible maneuver, especially for your first time flying."

"Second time," Taylor corrected. "You saw that?"

"We saw the whole thing, Tay, but didn't want to interrupt. You were amazing," Sam said.

"Tell that to the Training Master of the Universe over here," Taylor said, motioning to Gabriel, who had sat up, poking his head out of the hole like a gopher on the prairie.

Frowning, Gabriel said, "It was a really, really impressive display of flying, Taylor."

"But?" Taylor said.

With a wry smile, Gabriel said, "But….it was also extremely reckless. In a real battle you could have been badly injured. Not to mention that you completely exhausted your stores of energy, which would have allowed your enemies to destroy or capture you as soon as you hit the ground. This isn't a game, Taylor."

"Hmmm, let me remember....I think your exact words were: 'Tag, you're it.' Is that right?"

Gabriel froze. "I, uh, well, I was just trying to make it fun for you."

"You've been tough on me all day long and suddenly you wanted to make it *fun*?" Taylor said incredulously. "You egged me on and I responded. And...I...beat...you."

A voice said, "That's why he's so mad."

Taylor turned to see who the newcomer was. A white tank rolled their way. It was Sampson. And next to him was Kiren, whose neon pink hair looked even brighter next to her bulky boyfriend.

"Hey, guys," Taylor said.

Continuing his previous line of thought, Sampson said, "In angel training, Gabriel was always the top of the class—First Angel. His best subject was flying, and during our breaks we used to play a game called Flying Tag. In all the years I've known him, Gabriel has never lost. Until now, that is. And let me tell you, us kids were far more reckless than Taylor was today. We tried everything: teaming up, daredevil moves that we hadn't even learned in school yet, free falls; but nothing worked. Despite our desperate desire to dethrone the king, we never could. That's why he's so pissed, not because you were reckless."

Taylor turned to look at her boyfriend, whose face was already turning red. "Is that true?" she asked, a smile widening across her face.

"Maybe," Gabriel said.

"Definitely," Sampson said.

"I dethroned the King of Flying Tag?" Taylor asked to confirm.

"Fine, yes, whatever," Gabriel said.

"And bruised his ego," Sampson added helpfully.

In a blur of movement, Gabriel was on top of Sampson, pinning him to the ground. "Slow as ever, buddy," Gabriel said.

"Hey, you're messing with someone who is still recovering, that's cold, man," Sampson said.

"I saw what Taylor did, you're in perfect shape."

"What did Taylor do?" Sam asked.

"Saved him," Kiren said.

Shaking her head, Taylor said, "Look, guys, I'm no hero and I didn't save him. My new body did. It can do things…things I can't even seem to control. I just let my body help him, that's all."

"Semantics," Gabriel said, "but all that matters is that he's okay now. I'm glad you're okay, man."

"Glad enough to get off of me?" Sampson asked.

"Never," Gabriel said, laughing. He pushed him hard into the ground before releasing him.

When Gabriel regained his feet, Taylor punched him hard in the shoulder. "Oww!" he said, wincing. "What was that for?"

"For being an egotistical jerk sometimes," she said.

"Can we kiss and make up?" Gabriel said, reaching for her.

But Taylor was already gone, her wings spreading and lifting her off of the ground. She was flying…and loving it.

Eighteen

Two months later.

Dionysus smiled. They were ready. After two months of hard training, the New Archangels had mastered their new abilities to the greatest extent possible. They could fly faster, attack more powerfully, wield swords more precisely, recover from injuries more quickly—basically do everything they could before but at a much higher level. While they had all progressed significantly, the greatest change was wrought in David. He had been a mere child before evolving; he was First Angel in all of his courses, yes, but only at a fifteen-year-old level. Now he was fighting with a strength and skill near—if not equal to—Dionysus's own.

His smile was prompted by the sparring match he was watching. Even to a sword-master like him, the display was impressive. Even better was the suspense as to who would win. Johanna versus David—it was the grudge match he had been waiting for days to see. Johanna had been reluctant to fight the boy at first—using all sorts of excuses, like she didn't want to hurt him, and he was only a boy, and blah, blah, blah—but Dionysus had eventually convinced her. Like him, her ego was her weakness. A few well-placed lies about how the boy had said he would easily defeat her and that she was too scared to fight him did the trick, and soon she was begging Dionysus to schedule a duel between them. All in the name of training.

Now the two were locked in an eighty-minute struggle that showed no signs of ending. Dionysus watched as Johanna slashed and David parried and counter-slashed. Johanna easily blocked the attack. Using her non-sword hand, she fired a light orb at David's feet, but he hopped over it casually, like he was jumping rope. While still in midair, David swung his sword at her head, and at the same time kicked at her stomach. Johanna blocked his sword with her own blade, but was thrown off-balance by his foot, which connected solidly below her ribs.

Falling backwards, she led with her arms, which she threw back over her head, using them to catapult herself into a back-handspring. But her escape move was too slow, as David sprang forward, poking at her legs when she landed on her feet. His sword pierced her skin in three or four places, and white geysers of blood erupted.

In desperation, she went back on the offensive, erratically whipping her blade at David. He casually ducked under the first two swipes and then caught the sharp metal in his hand during the third wave. Milky blood dripped from his fingers, but still he held on. While Johanna was still hobbling from her injuries—and with her sword temporarily restricted—he kicked her damaged legs out from under her. As she fell, David wrenched the sword from her grip, although he paid a price, his fingers slicing off one by one as the pressure from the blade edge tore through his hand.

Before she could move to stand up or roll away, David had his foot on her chest and the point of his sword on her throat. His face was full of rage—maybe from the pain of his lost fingers, or from the excitement of the battle, or perhaps from something else entirely—and for a moment Dionysus thought he might finish the job, run her through, kill her. Rather than making a move to stop him, Dionysus just watched with interest. A trickle of blood dribbled down her neck as the razor-sharp blade cut into her skin. *Would he do it?* As the seconds ticked away, his suspense grew. Dionysus almost found himself wishing that he *would* do it, even though that would leave him another Archangel down, and a powerful one at that.

His face still contorted in rage, David finally lifted his white-hot sword from her throat; in seconds, the blood had dried up and the minor wound had healed. Stepping off her, he said, "Good fight," and stooped down to collect his dismembered fingers. Then he walked to the training room door and exited, leaving a trail of blood from his damaged hand.

Dionysus was speechless. The boy was so strange, so unlike anyone that he had encountered before, that he didn't know what to make of him. Clearly, he had his uses. The anger, the hate, the rage: If he could manage to harness the boy's fury and direct it at his enemies, it might be the edge that he needed to win the War. As long as the boy didn't destroy the New Archangels first, Dionysus was happy.

Johanna was still lying on the ground, breathing heavily, her chest rising and falling. Dionysus watched her. *Wait for it, wait for it*, he thought.

One second she was on the ground and the next she was in his face, having used a karate-style kick to regain her feet in one swift motion. "What the *hell* was that!?" she roared, inadvertently—or maybe purposely—spitting in his face as she spoke.

Using a sleeve of his robe to casually wipe the spittle from his cheeks, Dionysus said, "No harm done."

"No harm done! The boy nearly killed me, was going to kill me, I could see it in his eyes. He's freaking crazy, one of these days he will kill one of us and it could be YOU!"

Remaining calm, Dionysus said, "I am aware of the risks, Johanna, but at this time his benefits are greater. Now, if you don't get out of my face and calm down RIGHT NOW, I may order the boy to KILL YOU!"

Before she could react or respond, Dionysus pushed past her and exited the room. His smile had returned; in his mind, a little dissension in the ranks was a positive thing. Fingers could be regrown. Yes, they were definitely ready. All that remained was for them to find out where the girl went each day. Two months earlier, Dionysus had contacted his last demon spy with a special mission: to follow the girl everywhere she went.

On day one of the mission, the demon reported that he had followed Taylor to class and then back to her dorm. For the next eight hours he waited, but she never came out. The next day, the same thing happened. And the next. He knew something strange was going on, but despite the demon's attempts to get the latest gossip from within the army, no one seemed to be able to give him any straight answers about the human girl who had turned into an angel. Evidently, anything related to her was highly classified, only known by the demon Elders and their innermost advisors.

Dionysus had to know what she was up to, so he instructed his spy to take whatever measures were necessary to find out the truth. The spy continued to tail her daily and stake out her dormitory whenever she was there, but her curtains were always drawn, preventing him from gaining any insights. Eventually he realized he was going to have to do something drastic. And to his credit, he did.

Earlier that day, Dionysus had received an excited call from the spy. The mystery had been solved. While Taylor was at class, the demon had broken into her dorm and hidden under her bed, behind some boxes. When she arrived home, he heard voices discussing whether it was time to go. He recognized one of the voices as being that of Christopher Lyon, a high-ranking officer in the demon army. Another voice was clearly that of Gabriel Knight. While even the thought of the traitor had made Dionysus want to punch something, between gritted teeth he asked the demon spy to continue.

Based on the conversation he heard, the spy knew they were about to leave the room, but not via the door. They were going to teleport, which explained why the girl was never seen coming out of her dorm after getting home from class. The demon explained to Dionysus how there was a risky form of teleporting that could be performed in dire situations. Demon children were not taught this technique, but those in the army received remedial training in what was called *drop-porting*, and were advised to only use it if there was no other way to accomplish what was needed. In this case it was the only option. The technique involved teleporting to the exact spot where another demon had teleported just before, thus dropping in on the other demon's teleport. The window of opportunity to perform the maneuver was extremely short, and the risks to the dropping demon were many and deadly. In some cases, the dropping demon had been known to disappear, never to be heard from again. There were other tales of the demons being transported to faraway places, like deep under the ocean, or into outer space, although no one knew how anyone would know about the stories if they were true. In any case, the demon spy took a chance, peeking out from behind the boxes to watch for the perfect opportunity. When Chris, Taylor, and Gabriel had teleported from the room, the spy had dropped in, and was sucked into the same teleportation tunnel as them.

The catch was that the dropping demon generally ends up near the teleporting demons, but not in the exact same spot. In this case, the demon was fifty yards from his enemies who luckily had their backs to him. Acting quickly, he teleported again behind the closest cover he could find, which happened to be several large padded structures used for football tackling drills. From that vantage point, he was able to take in his surroundings.

The girl had been taken to the football stadium...for training! All the while that Dionysus and the New Archangels had been training, the girl had been doing the same. The demon described her feats as being "extraordinary," and "unlike anything I have ever seen." While Dionysus believed she was powerful—as he had already seen what she was capable of when she destroyed half the Council—he knew the New Archangels were powerful too, and there were more of them.

Abruptly, the time had come for action. They would go immediately. Kill the girl. Kill Gabriel. Get revenge. Kill, kill, kill.

Nineteen

Straightening her body, she threw her arms forward like the point of an arrow, and tucked her wings tightly behind her, allowing her to pass through the narrow circle without touching the sides. With a sharp cut to the left, she deftly slipped through another ring, and then dove ten feet to clear the third hoop in the series. It was the first time she had successfully navigated the most difficult sequence in the course.

Coming out of the dive, she prepared herself for the attack. It came swiftly and from all directions, as demons popped in and out of view around her, aiming kicks, punches, and fireballs at all parts of her body. While the demons couldn't fly, they could teleport into the air to attack and then teleport back to the ground. And they did. Again and again while she tried to block their attacks. She used all parts of her body in unison to defend herself. Sometimes her foot was blocking a kick, while one of her wings deflected a punch to the head; meanwhile, her arms conjured up light orbs that she used to obliterate the fiery projectiles before they did any damage.

Eventually, the attacks ceased, and she moved on to the next task, still unscathed. Fourteen angels descended upon her, falling in behind her flight path. Using the most complex evasive maneuvers she could think of, Taylor tried to shake her pursuers. First she arced to the roof of the dome, glossing a hand along the metal surface as she flew against it. She reached the first line of girders and beams, and then the fun began. Like a skier slipping through slaloms on a snowy ski slope, Taylor weaved in and out of the metal supports, using them to help hide her next move. Slowing slightly, she allowed her first two pursuers to catch up. Sensing they were close, she grabbed a cylindrical flagpole as she passed it, using it to swing backwards in the direction of the chasers. As she came out of the spin, she spread her legs and tilted her shoes up, so that her heels were exposed. The two angels tried to swerve, but it was too late. Each caught a heel in the chin. Their heads snapped backwards and Taylor knew they were knocked unconscious. She had to trust that they would be caught by someone below. *Twelve left*, she thought.

There was no time to celebrate her small victory, as the next two pairs of angels were upon her, flying in a diamond formation. She knew they were already too close for her to be able to outrun them, so she hovered in midair, waiting to defend herself. After eight weeks of training, her instincts governed almost every move. Her body was trim and toned and agile, her mind sharp and fast. The flying diamond came in slow, wary of their prey. Instantly, Taylor's mind computed that, given their reluctance to come in fast, there was a three in four chance that they would launch an attack from a distance. Given they were angels, it would likely be some sort of a coordinated light attack.

Motionless—except for her magnificent wings, which swept the air again and again, maintaining her height—Taylor powered up her body, unsure of what line of defense she would use. As expected, when the angels were within fifty feet, they fired off dozens of twisting, turning orbs of light, each designed to paralyze Taylor. Her chances of eliminating so many rockets with shots of her own were slim, and therefore, her mind told her that her best chance was to fly, and try to avoid as many as possible. But her instincts were saying something else entirely.

She mentally urged her wings to carry her away, to *fly, fly, fly, dammit!* As usual, her fifth and sixth appendages ignored her, choosing to obey a growing instinct that was about to act. Her field of vision was completely yellow now, like she was staring into the sun, each of the orbs having locked on to their target—her. Closing her eyes, she held her breath and waited to be stunned, shocked, paralyzed, shot from the sky, like she had been so many times over the course of her training.

Typically he revived her with smelling salts, but sometimes Gabriel chose to dump a bucket of cold water on her head, or enter her dreams, scaring her back into consciousness. She wondered which method he would use today.

The shock came, but felt different than ever before. It didn't hurt, or even cause discomfort. Instead, she felt as if her muscles had bulged, her skin hardened, and a suit of armor had been fitted over her clothes. Invincible—that's how she felt. Opening her eyes, her vision was buttery and hazy, like she was looking through a fogbank wearing yellow sunglasses. Past the sunflower mist were the orbs. They looked the same as before, except they seemed to be moving away from her now, heading directly for their masters. With no time to escape, the foursome was hit by an explosion of light. Their bodies went rigid, their wings stopped beating, and they dropped from the sky. *Eight left*, Taylor thought, although she didn't know how she had done it.

Two more angels, who were trailing closely behind the four, became victims of shrapnel from the blast; each attacker was stung by thin, concentrated beams of light in at least thirty places. Like dead leaves, they fluttered towards the bleachers below. *Make that six*, Taylor thought.

Her heart raced wildly as she realized she had never made it this far through the training course. She'd defeated the demon onslaught a few times, and even taken out six angels once, but never eight. The last phase of the challenge was meant to be conducted on the ground. Eagerly, Taylor dove to the distant field below, swooping over the heads of the dark spectators.

She recognized Clifford. He wore a bright red tunic and a big grandfatherly smile. When she passed over him, he waved. The other spectators were the demon Elders, in attendance today to evaluate her progress and readiness to embark on her mission. Landing at midfield, Taylor allowed herself to be surrounded by the six remaining angels, one of whom she called friend and another lover.

The small audience cheered. The final showdown had begun.

Taylor drew the sword hanging from her belt. From her touch, the blade received power, turning yellow and then bright white, glistening with light energy.

Mirroring her, the six angels brandished their brilliant weapons. One held his sword high over his head like a torch; another spun her blade like a baton; the third held a spear straight out, as if he were pointing it at Taylor's heart; the final three, including her boyfriend and friend, held their swords casually, as if they were no more dangerous or deadly than a bouquet of roses.

Dozens of Gabriel's favorite training tips poured through Taylor's mind as she tried to concentrate. *Offense is the best defense…Use your enemy's strength against them…Trust your instincts…Use overwhelming force to surprise your enemy.* Although Taylor understood the words, she was unable to discern their meaning, or how any of them applied to her current situation. Her mind was a blank slate, wiped clean from the stress of the situation; her comprehensive knowledge and experience were of no use to her now. Her only choice was to act swiftly and hope for the best. *Trust yourself,* she thought, this time remembering a piece of advice provided by her mother, rather than Gabriel.

Whirling around, Taylor tried to judge her enemies, looking for the weakest link. None of them looked weak to her, although one had edged slightly closer than the others. He was thick, but at least half a head taller than Sampson, making him the biggest of the bunch. Without thinking too much about it, Taylor threw her sword like a spear at the angel, who hadn't expected an attack to come so quickly. At the same time, she chased the sword with a powerful blast of light from her palm. Despite his surprise, the angel recovered and slapped Taylor's flying sword with his own, only to be hit flush in the chest by the orb.

Even as she fired the orb, Taylor had sprinted after it, timing her approach in line with the glowing shell. While her enemy was groaning—and falling—Taylor snatched the two swords from the air. The remaining five angels made no move to help their fallen comrade, each realizing that it was too late for him, and that an emotional reaction could lead to a similar fate for them.

Taylor held the two swords like ski poles, one at each side, points in the grass. Although her heart hammered rapidly, Taylor said, "Who's next?" with a smile. Although it felt moronic saying such a cheesy line, Gabriel had counseled her to *Never show fear even when you are about to pee yourself.* And this was definitely a time when she feared losing control of her bladder.

As she planned her next move, the attack came from the back. And from the side. Each collision felt like being hit by a freight train, and squeezed every last bubble of air out of her lungs. In the several seconds it took for her to fly through the air, land on her back, and skid across the field, Taylor had many thoughts, her computer-like angel brain attempting to analyze the situation. The first of the plethora of questions she had was *Who da?* And her response was to laugh at the ridiculousness of the question. However, even as her brain was messing with her, it had deduced that there were two additional attackers—of whom she wasn't aware—who had joined the fray. And had they been angels, she would have seen them coming, so they must have been demons, teleporting close and then barreling into her. Another thought she had was *Breathe, breathe, breathe, freaking breathe, Taylor!* which was likely a result of the strange wheezing sound she was making as she struggled to take in gulps of air from a seemingly airless atmosphere.

While fighting to breathe, the rest of her body acted on its own, as if it was a separate and distinct entity, outside of the craziness that was her mind, brain, whatever. She managed to turn the skid into a roll, which allowed her to avoid two fiery swords that were swung at her wildly. At the same time, she used her hands and feet to direct four orbs at her shadowy assailants.

Like she had planned it the whole time, Taylor came out of the roll and up to her feet, although she was still gasping for oxygen. The familiar demons were down. "Chris, Kiren?" she said.

Groaning, Chris said, "Nice one, Tay."

"Yeah, well done," Kiren added, lifting her head slightly.

"Thanks," Taylor mumbled.

Kiren added, "Do me a favor, will ya? Kick my boyfriend's ass."

Taylor grinned. "Sure. And I'll kick my boyfriend's while I'm at it."

Stalking away from the downed demons, Taylor sized up the remaining angels. Besides Gabriel and Sampson, there were two tough-looking chicks and giant dude. *Ladies first*, Taylor thought, as she planned to engage the long-haired angels next.

But Gabriel didn't give her the chance, lunging at her with his sword. Metal clanged metal, and then scraped, as their swords met and slid apart. With unexpected ferocity, Gabriel slashed again, while swiping a leg along the grass. Taylor hopped over the attempted trip and swung her second sword at his waistline. Clang! The blow was deflected by Sampson's blade. Her friend had crept in from the side just in time to save his best friend.

White hot adrenaline pumping through her veins, Taylor parried both angels using her duel swords as if she had been borne ambidextrous, although as a human she could barely even answer the phone with her left hand. When one of her attackers slashed, she would block and then slash back with double the force, pushing them backwards towards their allies.

The other three angels were not interested in being bystanders, moving in behind Taylor, and forcing her to back off from Gabriel and Sampson to protect herself. When they fired orbs at her, she used her swords like tennis rackets to bat them away.

Again, instinct took her to another place, to another level. Not knowing what she was doing, Taylor jammed each sword into the grass and injected them with charges of light. Like a fuse being lit, snapping sparks and crackling electricity buzzed along the ground in two directions. They headed for the two glowing chicks. When the energy reached them, the angels jumped to avoid the danger. Instead of streaming harmlessly underneath them as even Taylor anticipated, the trails of light stopped and then burst from the ground, forming hands and arms, which grabbed the angels by the ankles, pulling them back to the ground, where they collapsed.

Ignoring Gabriel and Sampson who were still behind her, Taylor plucked her swords from the ground and charged the tall dude, who looked like he had just seen a ghost, his face pale and his eyes bugged out. His single sword was no match for Taylor's pair and she quickly disarmed him. Under the rules of her training, a sword to the throat and the pretend enemy was considered dead, which left Taylor to defeat only the final two knuckleheads.

Taylor spun around to face them.

"This should be fun," Sampson said, grinning.

"Yeah, for me," Taylor retorted.

Gabriel said, "I don't know, Sampson, are you sure we should hit a girl?"

Sampson said, "You're right. We're too gentlemanly for that. Let's just let her win."

"That would certainly save you the embarrassment," Taylor taunted.

"On second thought, I have no qualms about decking a chick," Sampson joked.

Tiring of the verbal-jousting, Taylor launched herself at her opponents, spinning through the air, twirling her swords like a propeller. Rather than blocking with their swords like she expected, the best friends jumped back, avoiding her completely. Taylor grinned. "Why fight when you can run," she said.

Gabriel strode forward, swinging his sword back and forth. Taylor deflected his blows and watched out of the corner of her eye as Sampson curled in behind her. Instincts flashing, Taylor knew that the two old army buddies had a strategy prepared, and it was likely one that had worked many times before. She had to finish them off before they could execute it.

For the third distinct time that day, Taylor gave herself over to her instincts, letting them dictate her actions, even if they seemed to push her to do something that didn't initially make sense. In this case, her instincts really weren't making sense, as she felt her hands unclasp the hilts on her swords. Her weapons thumped to the grass ominously, like they were tolling the bell on her life.

Seeing the surprise on Gabriel's face, Taylor tried to shrug off her strange behavior by saying, "I just want to make the fight fair."

She raised her hands in the air, not knowing why. Light energy poured through her body, up her arms and through her fingers. With a few chirps, two tweets, and at least one cheep, a flock of glowing golden birds flew from her fingertips, like something out of an annoyingly perky Disney movie. Taylor waited to hear herself burst out into some painfully cheerful melody against her will, while the birds chirped and tweeted and cheeped at all the right times, and simultaneously dressed her in some excruciatingly girly pink dress with satin bows.

Gabriel and Sampson were mesmerized by the sudden explosion of migrating fowls, watching them soar overhead. Lowering their swords, they followed the birds with their eyes.

Despite her fears, Taylor did not sing a single melody, tune, or even a note. And the birds turned out to be as un-Disney-like as they could possibly be. Initially one by one, and then in bunches, the flock began falling from the sky, dive-bombing the two unsuspecting male angels. Sampson and Gabriel, on opposite sides of Taylor, were hit by dozens of falling birds, each detonating with a powerful *BOOM!*

And then it was over. The Elders were standing and applauding. Angels and demons alike were rushing to Taylor, and then picking her up, carrying her around the field. It was like some stupid movie where the runt football player kicks the winning field goal and becomes the hero. But Taylor enjoyed every minute of it.

Twenty

"You were incredible," he said.

"Tell me something I don't know," Taylor replied jokingly. Although she had impressed even herself with her performance, she knew she couldn't have done it on her own.

They were sitting on Taylor's bed, in her dorm room. After she successfully navigated the obstacle course and defeated all enemies in her path, a celebration was held in the stadium. There was drink, there was food, there was laughter. Taylor had been forced to shake all one-hundred-and-fifty-one Elder hands. When the party looked like it might go on late into the night, Taylor whispered to Gabriel, "Can we get out of here?"

"I thought you'd never ask," he had said. They had left after promising Clifford that a final training session would be held the following night in the stadium. Next steps would be planned, hard decisions would be made, team members would be selected. But that was tomorrow. Tonight was a chance to be alone with her boyfriend. Of course, he wouldn't stop badgering her.

"Teach me," Gabriel said seriously.

"Ahh, grasshopper, the student becomes the master."

Ignoring her flippantness, Gabriel said, "How did you do it?"

"Do what?" Taylor said.

"The birds….the ground strike….the cube of light around your body? I didn't teach you any of that. Hell, I don't think I could've done any of those things, or have even thought of doing them."

"What cube?" Taylor asked.

"Stop messing around, Tay. Remember the gaggle of orbs headed for your head while you were flying?"

"I'm not messing around, Gabriel. And, yes, I remember the *gaggle*, but then I closed my eyes, so I'm a bit hazy on what happened after that."

"You closed your eyes?" Gabriel asked, the corners of his lips curling up ever so slightly.

"Look, it's like this. When I don't know what to do, I just stop trying to think and let my body do the work. It's like I'm a squirrel or something, and I just know that I have to gather and store acorns in my tree for the winter."

"You store acorns?" Gabriel joked, looking around the room as if he expected to see hordes of tree fruit piled up around them.

"Ha ha. It's called a simile."

"Okay, so you're saying you let your instincts take over."

"Duh."

"Alright, fine. So let me tell you what I saw you do then. You were high in the air, hovering in the corner of the stadium, a *gaggle* of orbs heading your way, ducking and diving and twisting. You were dead in the water, dead meat, dead girl walking, deader than dead—"

Taylor cut him off: "I get it. I was dead."

"Sorry, I guess I got carried away. Anyway, you were practically road kill...," Gabriel said.

Despite her efforts to look tough, a smile escaped Taylor's closed lips. Gabriel laughed, too. "As long as I can always make you laugh," he mused.

Taylor hugged him. "As long as I can always make you cry," she joked back. Releasing him, she said, "What happened next?"

"So the ducking-diving-twisting light-rockets were about to blast you out of the air, when a cube of light forms around you, as if you had been trapped inside a block of frozen lemonade."

"I was stuck in lemonade?" she asked, sniffing her arms as if she expected the fresh scent of lemon juice to waft from her skin.

"Touché," Gabriel said. "That was a simile, too."

"Oh," Taylor said, pretending to be confused.

Ignoring her act, Gabriel said, "Although you were surrounded by light, it didn't look like a spotlight or anything, it was much more tangible than that, like it had substance…Like it was hard, a barrier."

"Like a wall."

"Exactly. When the orbs hit the pillar of light, they bounced off like it was made of rubber. Did you see what they did after that?"

"Yeah, they hit the same angels who originally shot them at me."

"Right, plus a couple extra."

Taylor didn't get it. So what? Evidently it had been a nice trick, but why was Gabriel so focused on it? She had seen him do amazing things, too. They were angels after all—inherently amazing, if only for the fact that they existed. "What am I missing?" she said, almost to herself.

"What do you mean?" Gabriel asked.

"I mean, why are you making such a big deal out of what I did? A pillar of light, wow. I'm sure you've used that trick many times before while in a real battle."

Gabriel's eyes widened. "Taylor, did you think you were carried around the field just because you made it through an extremely difficult training course?"

Not wanting to sound stupid, but having only one answer to the question, Taylor said, "Uh, yeah."

"No, Taylor. No, no, no. They cheered because no one has ever seen anyone—angel, demon, human, gargoyle—do what you did. I might be able to pull off the pillar of light one time, but I would be so weakened from the effort that I would be killed soon after. And the swords-in-the-ground trick? No way I could pull that off, pushing the light energy through the ground the way you did, and then morphing it into hands. Don't get me started on the flock of birds. I've never—never—seen anyone handle light with such ease, with such grace. It was poetry, Tay. That's why they cheered you. In you they found hope."

Gabriel's monologue stunned Taylor into silence for a moment. The gravity of his words lay heavy in the air, pressing down on her shoulders, and although her usual response to such a moment was to make a sarcastic comment, the mere thought felt wrong, sacrilegious. They sat unspeaking for a time, until Gabriel said, "You okay, Taylor?"

Taylor looked at him for a long second before saying, "I'm fine. Do you think I am what they say I am? That I have the potential to change things?"

Looking deep into her eyes, Gabriel's face looked more certain, more full of truth than Taylor had ever seen before. He said simply, "Yes. I do."

Something her mother once told her popped into her mind: *Taylor, the only support you need is your own. If you believe in yourself, that is enough. But if you can turn that self-support into the support of another, and then another, until you have hundreds of hearts behind you, the effect will be magnified, and the sum total of that support will be unstoppable, immovable.*

Taylor said, "Thanks, I'll do my best."

Gabriel put a hand behind her head, her neck, and pulled her in close. He kissed her deeply, lingering on the edge of her lips. They kissed again.

Tonight they wanted love; the pain would come later.

Twenty-One

The demon spy had checked in. The girl would be training the next night again. Except this time they would be there. He could almost feel her neck between his hands, bones cracking, muscles withering, life ending.

David hated her. She was the great corrupter. If not for her, he would be standing side by side with his brother, fighting for the cause. Instead, he would have to kill Gabriel too. He deserved nothing less.

He wondered if Gabriel, his own brother, would recognize him now. He hoped he would. That he would see how strong he had become without him. That he was better off on his own. That Gabriel was no longer his idol.

Then he would tell him how badly he had hurt him. How he might not have become who he had become if not for his relentless anger towards Gabriel. He hoped Gabriel would see that he was partly to blame. After breaking his mind, he would kill him.

Given her seniority, Johanna would lead the mission, but David knew he had become the true second-in-command over the New Archangels, the one everyone feared. Even before he had defeated her in a test of strength and skill, Johanna had feared him. And while Lucas still tried to treat him like his apprentice—like a child—David knew that he feared him, too. That was good—to be feared. It was a form of respect, something that Dionysus had taught him. And now Dionysus feared him, too, but not as much as the others. No, he was too arrogant for that. Which is why David still respected him, and would serve him.

David cracked his knuckles and smiled. Tomorrow would be a good day. At long last, his growing lust for blood would be fulfilled.

Twenty-Two

They slept in the next morning. Samantha had stayed at Chris's so they were alone. Sleeping in didn't always involve sleeping, but did mean that they stayed in bed. Sometimes kissing, sometimes doing more, they spoke little.

Eventually, they arose and had a late breakfast—a brunch—at one of their favorite on-campus spots. The food was good, the atmosphere was light, and the excitement level was high. Taylor didn't know why she should feel excited. The end of training meant going on her mission. The mission might mean death, or worse. Yet she was excited.

Gabriel seemed to sense it, and spurred her forward, his words upbeat and positive. At this time more than ever, she was glad he was her boyfriend. He knew what it was like to embark on a first mission, although his had been of a somewhat different nature—to destroy the world, rather than save it—but the feelings were similar: a twinge of fear, a burst of excitement, a dash of optimism, a slice of pessimism.

"Back when I was your age…," Gabriel joked.

"You are my age," Taylor commented.

"Good point. I have no advice for you."

"Come on, there must be something you can say."

"Not really. Just to…..trust your instincts. As you proved yesterday, they are your greatest weapon."

"And you'll be there to watch my back, right?" Taylor asked.

"No."

"No?" Taylor repeated, still assuming he was joking.

"I'm sorry, Taylor. I have a different mission."

"But I thought—" Taylor started.

"It was never the plan," Gabriel said.

"But Clifford implied you would be going when he said I would have a team of the best angels and demons," Taylor pointed out.

"He never said *I* would be going, but you'll probably get Chris, Sampson, and Kiren. There's a second mission. One that I will lead. Clifford thinks it's my destiny, although I'm not sure I believe all that legend stuff."

Taylor said, "He thinks you will lead a great angel rebellion against the Archangel Council. He thinks you're the chosen one."

"Clifford thinks a lot of things. All I know is that he wants me to travel the world, trying to convert angels to our cause. I don't know about legends and myths and stories, but I do know that it is a good plan. We can use all the help we can get and if I can turn Dionysus's own people against him, he won't stand a chance."

"It is a good plan. I understand. Be careful, I'm not gonna be around to save your butt next time you get stabbed."

"I might not last a day without you," Gabriel joked.

"Probably not," Taylor said.

From the diner, they spent time walking around campus, eating ice cream cones, talking about anything but wars and missions and rebellions. It was nice for a change. To act normal. To do human things. Taylor was surprised at how much she missed it. She had a sudden urge to see her dad, and even her brother, in a weird, from-across-the-room sort of way. Just to know they were alive and well. She considered calling them just to say hello, to hear their voices, but decided against it—she worried that by speaking to her family she might lose her nerve.

And then the day was gone, having melted away like butter in a frying pan. They returned to Taylor's room, where Chris would meet them to secretly transport them to the stadium via teleportation, or porting as Taylor like to call it.

When they walked in, Samantha and Chris were already waiting. "Hey, Tay!" Sam said. "Ready for tonight?" Her friend's enthusiasm was almost oozing from her.

"I was born ready," Taylor said. Backtracking, she said, "No, not really. I had a good day full of normal human stuff."

Sam laughed. "Yeah, we're a boring species, but our simple lives can be quite enjoyable sometimes."

Her best friend fit in so well with the demons that Taylor sometimes forgot she was still human. "I'm sorry, Sam, I didn't mean to say—"

Sam cut her off: "I was just kidding, Taylor. I am as happy as ever to be a lowly human—there's less pressure. I get to focus on being a college kid while you're out saving the world. The only hard thing is that I am left worrying about you guys when you run off with your swords and guns and such."

"We'll be fine, Sam. At least I am capable of defending myself now that I am trained."

Chris said, "I can vouch for that. I'm still sore from the orbs you knocked Kiren and me senseless with."

Taylor grinned. "You asked for it when you snuck up on me."

"True," Chris said. "Should we get going? We need to be on time tonight."

"Let's do it," Taylor said.

They formed a chain by holding hands and then Chris flipped-spun-ported them to the stadium. A handful of angels and demons were already there, including Sampson and Kiren, who ran up to greet them.

Sampson said, "Time to get back on the horse. I haven't seen any real action for a long time."

"You needed some rest after the last time you saw action," Gabriel noted.

"Well, I am certainly well rested now. I can't wait to work with your super-angel girlfriend on the next mission," Sampson said, motioning towards Taylor. "You have got to teach me how to do that bird thing."

"Already tried that," Gabriel said. "She claims it was all instincts, but I think she might just be holding out on us."

Taylor was aware that her friends were laughing, but she was too focused on something else. She was about to start a mission and would have Chris, Sampson, and Kiren with her, which should be comforting, but it wasn't. Instead, all she could think about was that Gabriel would have none of them. It didn't feel right. They should both be amongst friends, especially when they were in dangerous situations. It was at those times that you needed people who loved you, people you could trust.

"What's eating you, Tay?" Sam said.

Taylor realized it was the second time her friend had asked the question. "Oh, umm, nothing. Just thinking about the mission."

"Don't worry, Tay. I know it will be fine. You've come through so many times before, you'll do it again."

"Thanks, Sam."

"Sure."

Gabriel said, "Let's get started."

The two demons, human, and angel went to sit on the bleachers to watch, while Gabriel and Taylor headed for the twenty yard line, where she would start her drills. She had told Gabriel that she wanted it to be like any other day of training, nothing special.

And for the most part, it was. Gabriel started by stretching her out. From there, she practiced some complex aerial maneuvers and then it was on to sword work. She battled Gabriel, who managed to disarm her the first two times, before Taylor won five in a row. Two hours had passed in a hurry, and at the end, Gabriel said, "There's nothing more I can teach you."

"Thank you, grasshopper," Taylor joked, "but I was really hoping to learn how to catch a fly with chopsticks."

Gabriel laughed and hugged her. "I'm not sure the world's ready for an angel like you," he said.

Waiting for Clifford to arrive, they sat in the bleachers with their friends, laughing and joking. Around eight-thirty, the head of the demon Elders arrived alone, appearing out of nothing in one of the end zones. Despite the fact that he could have teleported over to them, Clifford walked slowly to the bleachers; he looked older—and wiser—than usual.

Upon reaching them, he hopped over the small wall and railing with an ease that was elf-like, youthful, like he had just then cast off thirty years from his age. Smiling, he sat next to Sam, who had Chris on her other side. Taylor was next and then Gabriel, with Sampson and Kiren sitting in front of them, down a row.

"Hi, Cliff," Sam said.

"Ahh, my dear, how nice to see you again," Clifford replied.

"You, too. So which mission am I going to lead?" she joked.

Clifford laughed, a hearty *ho, ho, ho*, that reminded Taylor of gifts and colorful lights and North Poles.

Clifford said, "My dear, your mission is to keep me company. Whenever you're not in class, that is."

Putting an arm around Clifford, Sam said, "Well it just so happens that tomorrow is the start of spring break, so I've got the whole week to keep you company."

Clifford's eyes lit up at the information. "That is great news. I was worried about Taylor falling behind in her studies."

Taylor frowned. "Really? The world is on the verge of destruction and you're worried about my grades? You sound like my dad."

Clifford said, "When all this is over I want you to have a chance at a normal life, or at least semi-normal, if that's what you want, Taylor. College will help give you that chance."

Taylor laughed. "Semi-normal—that's a good way of putting it. And thanks, but don't worry about my studies, I can always catch up later."

Clifford nodded. "I have just finished meeting with the Eldership. We have finalized some of the details for the missions," Clifford started, emphasizing the *s* at the end of missions and watching Taylor's face carefully.

Taylor said, "I know about the second mission—Gabriel's mission. You don't have to worry, I understand how important it is and won't try to change your mind."

Clifford nodded again. "I wish it didn't have to be that way, but thank you for your support. The first mission will be Gabriel's and he will go with only a demon escort. This will allow him to get around fast and travel light. He needs to cover as much ground as possible in a short time."

Taylor's thoughts from earlier wormed their way through her mind, into her throat, and out her mouth: "I want Sampson to go with him."

Alarm on his face, Gabriel said, "No, Tay. You need all the firepower you can get. My mission is much less dangerous. I'm just going to talk to people."

"Yeah, talking to people about changing everything about the way they think. It is not going to be an easy message. Some will be angry. There could be violence."

"Then I'll handle it," Gabriel said firmly.

"I am not questioning how capable you are. But there are many benefits to bringing Sampson with you. For one, two witnesses to the evil that resides within the Archangel Council will be much more powerful than one. And secondly, if something does happen, you'll have someone to watch your back."

Still shaking his head, Gabriel looked to Clifford for help.

He didn't get it. Clifford stroked his short, dark beard thoughtfully. "The girl has made a good argument. Request granted. Sampson will accompany Gabriel on his mission."

"Thank you," Taylor said. She looked at Gabriel. "You'll thank me later."

Gabriel frowned, but didn't argue further.

Clifford continued with the informal briefing: "The goal of the first mission will be to gain support for the demon cause amongst the angels. We expect this to be a most difficult undertaking, one that will require powerful words from a powerful leader. We believe that leader is you, Gabriel."

Gabriel said, "I know, I know, legends and dreams. I'll do my best."

With a wry smile, Clifford said, "I know you will." He shifted his eyes to Taylor. "And you, young lady, will lead the second mission. Christopher and Kiren will accompany you, along with a dozen of the other top angels and demons. Your goal will be to kill Dionysus. The angel mountain is a fortress, and we believe getting into it while the angels are strong is nearly impossible. Therefore, you will need to draw Dionysus out from his stronghold, into the open. To do this, you will need bait."

Taylor interrupted: "So we capture one of his favorites, right? Like Lucas or Cassandra."

"Exactly right," Clifford said. "How you do that is up to you and your team."

Taylor glanced at Chris and Kiren, who both looked significantly more capable than she felt. She expected to lean heavily on them for advice during the mission.

"If there's nothing else—" Clifford started to say before being cut off by a loud cracking-tearing-grinding sound from above. Taylor looked up and saw a single star shining through a hole in the roof. Another crack, another tear, another grind: Like an orange being peeled back, the roof was slowly ripped from its moorings, revealing the clear night sky beyond. Glowing shapes were silhouetted against the blackness of the cloudless sky. Taylor counted six bright figures.

Taylor said, "Is this part of the training?"

Clifford was already on his feet. He said, "No, my dear. I think we're under attack."

Almost as a response to his statement, a massive boulder of light tumbled at them from above. "Incoming!" someone yelled, maybe Sampson.

Taylor watched as Chris teleported Sam from the area, and then she spread her wings and rocketed away from the danger zone. *BOOM!* She looked back to see the boulder explode in a frenzy of sparks, fire, and shrapnel. The bleachers were flattened by the impact—huge chunks of concrete and metal were launched through the air. Instinctively, Taylor fired half-a-dozen medium size orbs, destroying the deadly projectile rubble before it could do any serious damage.

She heard Gabriel yell, "All fighters to me!" His voice had come from behind her. Performing a tucked and twisting front flip, Taylor hung in midair and then accelerated forward in the opposite direction. She was able to easily locate Gabriel, who was hovering ten feet off the field in the north end zone, which was painted with the football team emblem, a ferocious-looking, sharp-toothed beaver with a mohawk. Sampson, Kiren, Chris, and Clifford were already beneath him—along with a group of other angels and demons who were there to help Taylor train—forming a shield around Sam, the only human in the group.

Taylor reached them in less than two seconds, and Gabriel lowered himself to the field. He barked orders, naturally assuming a leadership role. No one questioned his authority, not even Clifford. "Angels—you will fly with me and we will attempt to target one enemy at a time and force them to land. Demons—you hit the fallen angels hard and fast when they reach the field. Clifford—you'll get Sam the hell outta here."

Clifford was already reaching for Sam's hand as Gabriel was speaking. Once his fingertips touched hers, he started to teleport, his body becoming fuzzy. And then a glowing form was upon them, snatching Sam from his grasp and leaping from the ground.

Clifford disappeared without Sam.

Sam yelled, as she was flown towards the roof. Taylor saw her kicking and clawing at her assailant. She was about to fly after her, but Chris said, "I got this," and was gone. A dark form appeared on the angel kidnapper's back and the lot of them—demon, angel, and Sam—disappeared. Chris appeared a second later, hanging in the air for a moment, clutching at the nothingness that used to be Sam. He yelled, "Nooo!" as gravity took him back down.

Chris crashed to the field, spraying grass and dirt in his wake. Taylor and Gabriel rushed to his side. He was bloodied from the crash, but the scariest part was the look on his face. It was something Taylor had never seen from her best friend's boyfriend. Fear, agony, hopelessness, defeat. Under enormous pressure, Taylor had seen Christopher act calmly and confidently. Now his face was ghost-white, a far cry from the shadowy ruggedness that typically dressed the area between his scalp and chin.

Gabriel sensed the change in him as well. He said, "We'll get her back, Chris. I know we will. I need you to pull yourself together so we get through this."

The pep talk was all Chris needed to recover. The color in his face returned, and his stunned cheeks firmed into a stony determination. He was back.

They stood up and surveyed the sky. Five angels could be seen soaring within the stadium. "Attack!" Gabriel roared, as he threw himself off the ground.

Taylor followed her boyfriend, and was soon joined by a dozen other angels in flight. Gabriel looked back and growled, "Lucas is here. We target him first."

As she followed him into a sharp turn, Taylor saw an angel hovering in front of them, waiting. When they approached, he stretched his arms forward and fired six orbs, three from each hand. "Evasive maneuvers," Gabriel yelled, as he barrel-rolled to the side. Taylor went the opposite way, but as she came out of the spin she could see that the orbs had combined together to form into the shape of a giant six-fingered fist. Still in its path, Taylor gained as much altitude as she could, narrowly avoiding one of the blazing knuckles as it shot past her.

Glancing back, she saw that half of the other angels had not been fast enough and were crushed by the fist. Flailing, they fell to the field below, creating tiny craters in the earth. The single attack had knocked out half of the angels, and a quarter of their entire force. *Something wasn't right*, Taylor thought. Scanning from side to side, Taylor located Gabriel and flew to him where she was joined by the remaining angels.

"What the hell was that?" Taylor said.

"I don't know," Gabriel said. "It appears his power has increased significantly. Almost like yours, Tay."

Although she didn't have a clue what to do, Taylor found herself saying, "Get to the ground and rally the demons. Tell everyone to stay as far away from each other as possible. We need to ensure that one attack doesn't hit more than one of us if we're going to survive this. I'll take Lucas."

Leaving Gabriel speechless, she headed for Lucas, who was still hovering arrogantly, like he was untouchable. When she got within yelling distance, she stopped and shouted, "Finally found your mojo, Lucas?"

His smile was wicked, Grinch-like. "Didn't you hear? I'm one of the New Archangels. Stronger, faster, deadlier. I'm pretty much your worst nightmare."

"We'll see about that," Taylor hissed as she darted towards him. An explosion of light filled her field of vision as Lucas attacked. This time it was a shockwave of light, rolling towards her like a dust storm. She never even slowed, her body turning hot-white just before she met the onslaught of energy. Like a fantastical creature passing into a looking glass, Taylor went through the light storm, her passage marked only by slight ripples in the filament of power.

She came through the other side like a charging bull, her eyes locked on Lucas's. When she collided with him, she could see the surprise plastered on his face. While she had the upper hand, Taylor managed to land three quick punches to his head, which allowed her to climb on his back and grab his wings. Standing on him, Taylor wrenched the wings in opposite directions. The motion was unnatural and the wings resisted it. Slowly, however, Taylor was able to bring them together like an accordion, and then snap them past each other. With a cringe-worthy *crack!* the bones splintered, leaving the wings hanging awkwardly from his back. Lucas cried out in pain and fell from the air.

Taylor rode him to the ground like a surfer, forcing him to collide violently onto the field.

She stepped off him casually, and was about to request for a demon to teleport him away as a captive, when a demon appeared next to her. She had never seen him before.

"Hello," he said, and then touched a hand to Lucas's back. They disappeared.

Taylor knew immediately that the demon was a spy and had just rescued her prisoner. He was probably the one who had taken Sam too. "Dammit," she muttered.

She surveyed the rest of the battle, trying to decide what to do next. She was glad to see that the angels and demons had scattered and were doing their best to protect themselves from the powerful attacks from the remaining four enemies. She found Gabriel, who was locked in a swordfight with a familiar female angel. If not for the shining armor, blazing sword, and enraged face, the woman would have belonged on a Milanese catwalk. She was beyond beautiful, her long, blond hair swirling around her with each stroke of her blade. *Cassandra*, Taylor thought. *Time for revenge.* The last time she had seen the evil witch, Cassandra was attempting to kill Gabriel, and might have succeeded if not for Taylor.

Taylor approached her from behind, drawing her sword. She could see that although Gabriel was fighting brilliantly, he was overmatched. Slowly, she was pushing him backwards, her attacks gaining confidence with each stroke. "Hey, bitch," Taylor said. "Remember me?"

Cassandra jumped away from Gabriel and glanced back. Upon seeing Taylor, her eyes blazed with renewed anger. "You! I've been waiting a long time to meet you again." With an animal-snarl, Cassandra threw herself at Taylor, attempting to overwhelm her quickly with an explosion of force.

After weeks of training, Taylor was ready. She slid under Cassandra's initial swipe—which had been aimed at Taylor's head—and hacked at her leg; she aimed for a weak spot in the armor, where the upper leg plate met the lower. She was rewarded with a satisfying shriek of pain from her opponent.

Turning quickly, Taylor followed up the move by grabbing the witch from behind, locking both her arms behind her and ripping her sword from the clutches of her hand. "Gabriel!" she yelled, but he was already by her side, helping her to subdue the kicking, screaming Cassandra.

Gabriel yelled, "Christopher! We need you now!"

Evidently, Chris was close enough to hear his name and appeared next to them; black blood poured from his ear, which looked like it had become a chew toy for a Doberman. "I've got her," Chris said, placing a hand on her shoulder. Taylor and Gabriel released her and she was gone, Chris likely having teleported her to a prison cell somewhere in the Lair.

Taylor and Gabriel looked around them. Destruction was everywhere. Three of the attacking super-angels were shooting light-arrows from invisible bows, cutting down demon after demon. The dark bodies lay twitching on the field, the golden arrows sticking out of their arms, legs, chests. Even Taylor knew that an attack using the force of light should explode, or at least dissipate upon contact with its target. The arrows, however, defied all the rules by remaining intact in their victims, continuing to send shockwaves of pain through the unfortunate bodies.

Gabriel said, "We've got our prisoner. It's time to retreat." Taylor nodded and dashed off to help round up the rest of the squad, both the living and dead. Gabriel did the same, heading in the opposite direction.

Taylor found Kiren first, who, despite having an arrow through each leg, was still fighting valiantly; blasts of fire shot from her hands at the three hovering angels. Each blast was knocked aside easily by the enemies, but she kept trying. "Kiren!" Taylor said. "We gotta get out of here." Her mouth dry and lips cracked, Kiren only nodded. "Teleport the wounded back to the Lair. Get anyone else who can still walk to do the same."

Taylor scanned the field for anyone else still standing. There were a couple demons at midfield, but Kiren was already headed in that direction. She heard a yell from behind her: "Gabriel! No!"

She whirled around to see Sampson sprinting down the field. Her eyes travelled ahead of him to see what had caused his reaction. Gabriel was walking slowly down the field, arms out pleadingly. He had deserted his sword, which lay behind him on the grass. Taylor's eyes continued on, until she saw a glowing figure, hanging above the field. *Gabriel!* The figure appeared to be Gabriel again, except not. Her head bobbed back and forth between the two Gabriels, trying to understand.

While she was puzzling over the mystery of the twin Gabriels, she chased after Sampson, who was nearing the walking Gabriel. She watched as the muscly angel reached her boyfriend and thrust an arm around him, trying to pull him away from the second Gabriel. With a quick motion, Gabriel threw his elbow back, contacting Sampson's face just below the eyes. Sampson's head snapped back and he toppled over, white blood spurting from his nose.

As Taylor closed in, Gabriel approached Gabriel number two. That's when Taylor realized who it was: his face was Gabriel's but not; his body structure was similar but different; the second was not Gabriel, but was from the same gene pool. *It was David.* But he was changed—

not the boy he had been two months earlier when Taylor last saw him. At that time he had done the unthinkable: stabbed his own brother—Gabriel, his idol—in the leg with a demon blade.

Taylor stopped ten feet short of Gabriel, afraid that she might spook him if she rushed in the way Sampson had. Gabriel, unarmed, said, "David, let's talk."

The look on David's face was anything but brotherly. The sneer reminded her of Dionysus. The hate in his eyes, the rage on his face, the tension in his arms: It all pointed to one thing—he was about to attack. Recognizing the danger Gabriel was in, Taylor took off just as a golden snake sprung from David's arms, its fangs reaching for Gabriel's neck.

Twenty-Three

Samantha kicked at the angel's shins, she clawed at his face, but his grip was like iron and the ground fell away below her. Screaming, she felt something land on her back. *Help had arrived*, she thought. And then she was spiraling through a strange vortex, left trying to remember which way was up.

All went black.

It was the deepest blackness she had ever experienced, and for a moment she thought she had been struck blind.

She heard a scratching. "Who…Who's there?" she said.

No response. More scratching, getting closer.

When everything went black, she had found that she was sitting on a hard floor, somewhat cold, somewhat wet. The cold and wet came from the floor.

She stood up, ready to run from whatever was scratching. She would risk running blind if she had to, using her arms as a battering ram to prevent herself from running headfirst into a wall, or worse. The stone was cold on her bare feet. Where had her flip-flops gone? They probably fell off when she was ripped from the ground against her will.

Moving away from the scratching, Sam strafed her arms back and forth, but felt only dense air. Another few tentative steps and her knuckles scraped against something hard. A wall. Left or right? Left. Why not, she had no idea where she was and staying in one place wouldn't get her anywhere. Using the wall as a guide, she moved left until she reached a corner, intersecting with another wall.

She still heard the scratching but it seemed to be well behind her.

With no other options, she turned left, following the new wall. The wall ended after only five steps when her hands clasped something cold and hard. It was thin— perhaps a pole of sorts. No, a bar, she realized. Like on a cell. Like in a prison.

Her heart hammered in her chest. *Oh, God, no*, she thought. This couldn't happen to her, she wasn't Taylor. Not tough, not feisty, not capable. Taylor would know what to do, what to say to her captors, and would probably save the day in some way. But Sam wouldn't do any of those things. Under pressure, she would probably cry. She wouldn't last one day in prison, much less the potential years that lay ahead of her. Taylor wouldn't mind wearing the same clothes, being a bit dirty, having no makeup. *No makeup! How will I survive?*

Sam began breathing hard, unable to catch her breath. She was hyperventilating and she knew it. Stop thinking, stop thinking. Stop, stop, stop. Just breathe. Breathe. Breathe. Her inhalations slowed and her exhalations followed suit. Okay, everything is going to be okay. Why? Because her best friend was a powerful angel and her boyfriend was a ridiculously tough demon. And because she had spunk. Many people had told her that before, even Clifford, who didn't hand out compliments lightly. She might not have the toughness of Taylor, but she was an optimist by nature. She could rely on that optimism and spunk to get her through whatever trials were coming.

Something scurried over her bare feet, scratching her skin as it passed. She screamed, loud and long. *Yuck, yuck, yuck!* Definitely a rat. A nasty, diseased, filthy rat had infected her feet, which would likely contract a strange fungus, turn black, and eventually fall off.

Screw spunk. Screw optimism. She wanted to get out of the cell now!

Twenty-Four

Searing pain burst through her chest as the snake of light tore into her. Despite being formed from light energy, Taylor could feel the fangs burrowing into her skin, searching for her heart, trying to pierce her, to maim her, to kill her. There was so much blood. On her skin, on her face, in her eyes. Her vision blurred, until she blinked away the glowing liquid.

Gabriel loomed over her. At least she hoped it was Gabriel and not David. He was shouting something but she didn't know what. He clutched the snake by the tail and pulled. She felt her skin coming apart as its fangs were wrenched from her body. Upon leaving her, the snake disappeared.

Her vision went black for a moment and then returned. Gabriel was asking her something, but she still couldn't hear. Her hearing returned when a blast rocked the night. Gabriel was thrown away from her, and she was left seeing the night sky through the damaged dome roof. It was so beautiful, clear and full of lights. Twinkling stars, the glow of the moon. The pain had left Taylor. *That was good*, she thought.

Gabriel loomed over her again. *No, not Gabriel—it was David.* She was glad she could tell the difference, although it was hard. He pointed a single finger at her and laughed.

Taylor closed her eyes and prepared to die.

Nothing happened. She didn't feel anything. No pain, no movement, no impact. And then there was a terrific roar, as if a horde of angry lions all decided to voice their opinions simultaneously. What horde? What lions? They were in a football stadium on a university campus, not on some African safari or in a circus.

She opened her eyes. David was flailing in the air, held between two massive jaws full of shark-like teeth. The angry gargoyle bucked its head and David went flying through the air, away from Taylor. She smiled. "Thanks buddy," she whispered. All went dark.

Twenty-Five

Taylor opened her eyes. A dark room, torches flickering. Hurt to move.

Gabriel said, "Amazing."

Taylor turned her head to the left, saw her boyfriend. He was sitting next to her, holding her hand. "What's amazing?" she asked.

"That you're awake already."

Hours, days, weeks: Taylor had no idea how long she had been asleep. "How long?" she asked.

Gabriel checked his wristwatch. "Exactly thirty-five minutes. The doctors didn't even have to stitch you up; your body took care of the healing on its own. A wound like that…" Gabriel shook his head. "Not many angels would survive that. I don't know if I would have."

"The snake?"

Gabriel said, "Not real, and yet real, somehow. Gone. Disappeared. My brother has evolved somehow, like the others. Lucas, Cassandra, and the rest—all evolved. Stronger, like you."

"Where is he?"

"Who?"

"Your brother."

"Gone. Escaped. Managed to fly off even after being chomped on by Rocky. Was so fast no one could catch him."

"Rocky?" Taylor said. "But the gargoyle that saved me was huge. Rocky is just a little guy."

Gabriel laughed. "You haven't visited your friend in a while, have you?"

"I guess not," Taylor said. "But that big?"

"It's been two months, Tay. He's full size already. And he is well above average in height and weight."

Taylor's mind flashed back to the gargoyle that had saved her. He didn't resemble the Rocky that Taylor remembered. While staying in the Lair over the Christmas holidays, Taylor had befriended a newborn gargoyle. Rocky was unlike any other gargoyles—a free spirit. He allowed Taylor to feed him by hand and seemed to actually look forward to her visits. Even the gargoyle master, nicknamed Gargo, had told her it was a unique relationship. But she had been so busy with her training that she had forgotten all about him. And now he had saved her life.

"Where'd he come from?"

"After securing Cassandra, Chris brought Rocky back. He thought we might need reinforcements."

Taylor said, "He was right." Her muddled brain was trying to process everything that had happened. She was forgetting something. "Chris, Sampson, Kiren…" She ticked them off on her fingers. Gabriel looked at her strangely. Then she remembered. "Oh, no."

Gabriel squeezed her hand. He said, "They took her, Taylor. Sam has been captured."

Taylor took a deep breath. *It will be okay. We will get her out.* "Trade Cassandra for Sam," she said.

"That's the plan," Gabriel replied. "We expect that Dionysus will go for it considering how powerful she is now."

"A New Archangel," Taylor murmured.

"What do you mean?" Gabriel asked.

"That's what Lucas called himself. I think what happened to me—how I evolved from human to angel—inspired Dionysus to push the limits on the Archangel Council's evolution."

"Well it worked," Gabriel said. "They were tough as hell. I used to disarm Cassandra in about three seconds in a swordfight. Now…"

"We have to get Sam back. How's Chris?"

"Beside himself with worry, but focused on getting her out. I will be meeting with Clifford and Chris in a few minutes to modify our plans as necessary."

"I'm coming too."

"Taylor, you need to rest, recover."

"I'm fine," Taylor said, pulling the covers down to her waist. She was wearing a hospital gown. Unworried about modesty, she peeled off the gown and looked at her chest, expecting to see deep bruising and a bloody hole in her. Instead, there was nothing. Her skin was smooth and free of damage.

"My gosh, Taylor. If the New Archangels heal that quickly, they may be invincible."

"Don't say that. There's a way to beat them, I know it."

Gabriel stared intensely into her eyes, and then said, "Okay, let's go."

Taylor changed into a fresh set of clothes that someone had left beside her bed. The jeans were about a thousand years old, ripped in all the right places, as comfortable as being naked, except without the embarrassment. Her t-shirt was dark and contrasted sharply with the soft glow of her skin.

They took a transporter from the medical wing to Clifford's office. When they walked in, Chris was already there, speaking in hushed tones to the head of the demon Elders. His mouth opened when Taylor came through the door, but not because he was going to say something. In fact, he appeared to be speechless. Taylor put her hand under his chin and pushed up, closing his mouth.

"Me angel. Me heal fast," Taylor said, doing her best Tarzan impression.

Clifford smiled. "Indeed," he said. "I'm glad you're here."

Taylor said, "So the first priority will be to get Sam back?"

Chris said, "Yes, we will trade our prisoner."

"Yeah, Cassandra," Taylor said. "Any possibility I can slap her around a little before we let her go?"

"Only if I get to participate," Gabriel said.

Clifford said, "You won't have much time. Dionysus has already agreed to make the trade today. It seems he values her highly."

"Tell him what you think," Gabriel said, encouraging Taylor.

Taylor explained how Lucas had referred to himself as one of the New Archangels and how Taylor believed they had managed to evolve into a more powerful form of angel.

Chris said, "It's like I was telling you, sir. They're tougher, stronger, faster. We had them way outnumbered but could barely defend ourselves."

Clifford stroked his beard, his usual sign of deep thought. "Hmmm….," he mused. "If they have evolved, it's only a matter of time before Dionysus allows more and more of his army to do the same, to ensure they win every battle. I fear that when we lose our prisoner, who we were hoping to use to draw Dionysus out of his stronghold, that we will lose our only advantage."

Chris's face sharpened. "Are you saying we shouldn't trade Cassandra for Sam?" he said. His tone was accusing.

"Not at all, my dear boy. I am simply saying that we need to find another way."

"Like capture someone else?" Chris asked.

"No, like use a different kind of bait. Like me." Clifford's eyes were sparkling and he wore a wry grin.

"You would be the bait? I'm not following," Chris said.

Clifford leaned back in his chair, his hands behind his head. He sighed deeply. "Besides destroying the demons as a whole, Dionysus wants to see me destroyed. I was his father, and he hated me for it. When I found out that his view of the world was different than mine, I gave him a hard time about it. Told him he was crazy, that he was a fool. I didn't listen to him, or even try to understand. He never forgave me for that. I know him. He never forgets a grudge. I can draw him out. I can be the bait."

Taylor, Chris and Gabriel looked at each other, waiting to see who would reply. Taylor said, "It's not your fault he is the way he is, Clifford."

Still smiling, Clifford said, "It took a while for me to convince myself, but I finally did. I know that now, but I still have regrets."

Gabriel said, "There's too much to risk. You are the face of the demons, they turn to you for guidance, to comfort them. What if something goes wrong?"

"It won't. And if it does, there are many others in the Eldership that are capable of taking my place."

Taylor said, "I will protect you."

Clifford nodded. "It's settled then. We recover Sam, and then set a trap for Dionysus, while Gabriel creates a rebellion amongst his people. Should be simple, don't you think?"

"With Super-Angel here," Gabriel said, motioning to Taylor, "it should be a piece of cake."

Twenty-Six

The boy was fully recovered. Remarkable. Nearly eaten by a monstrous gargoyle and he was ready to fight again within hours. The boy stood next to Dionysus, watching him intensely. Dionysus stared right back. Dionysus said, "What do you propose we do, David?"

"Forget Cassandra. The human girl is too valuable to waste on a trade." David's words were cold, uncaring, businesslike.

Dionysus decided to put him to the test. "We can't just abandon one of the New Archangels. What if it were you that was captured, David? What then?"

"I would say the same thing. My life is forfeit compared to carrying out The Plan."

Dionysus was impressed. He detected only truth in the boy's words. Of course, the boy was extremely hard to read, his voice monotone, bland, emotionless, like something out of a thriller movie where the killer is a child sociopath looking to chop his family to bits before snacking on their body parts.

"What if I disagree with you, decide to make the trade?" He was testing him again.

The boy's eyes never left his. "I will support you. But then I have another idea."

Dionysus said, "Go on."

"I lead a mission of the New Archangels. We need to draw the key demon supporters out of the hole they're hiding in, and without the human girl, we don't have any bait. So we start attacking humans. That will surely get their attention."

Dionysus raised his eyebrows and finally blinked twice—he had been staring at David for more than five minutes without moistening his eyes. *Attack humans.* Dionysus had never really considered it. The Plan had always been very specific on the order of events. Defeat the demons—the protectors of the human—and then the rest would be easy. Sure, he had murdered his fair share of humans but only when absolutely necessary for experimental purposes or for some specific reason. But haphazardly killing humans just to get the demons attention? It was madness! It was also genius.

"Okay, David. Your mission is approved. You'll leave as soon as we get Cassandra back. But it will only be you, Lucas, and Cassandra."

"Yes, my lord," David said.

Twenty-Seven

The agreement was specific. The trade would take place halfway down the battlefield. No Archangels could participate, except for Cassandra, of course, who was part of the trade. Christopher, as well as any angels supporting the demons were also prohibited from participating, as Dionysus said, "The filthy traitors are not recognized by the angels as authorized demon parties." Taylor fell into the category of Archangel, according to Gabriel.

She watched the transaction on a large screen, which was fed by a series of cameras that were used to film each and every battle in the Great War for tactical and strategy purposes. The room was filled to capacity, like a sold out movie theater showing the latest *Harry Potter* film. It was mostly demon Elders, and a few dozen other key army personnel.

Gabriel sat on her left and Chris on her right. Sampson was also there. Kiren would participate in the trade as she didn't meet any of the criteria to be excluded—and she had insisted.

The tension level was high. Any number of things could go wrong, which Chris couldn't seem to stop pointing out, like he was trying to prepare himself for the worst. He whispered to Taylor, "What if Cassandra tries something? I don't trust her."

Taylor sighed. She reminded him, "The agreement is that both prisoners must remain bound until they are back in their respective mountains. If they try to release Cassandra early, you're gonna teleport Gabriel and I out there and we will resolve the situation together. Try to breathe, Chris. It's going to be okay, I promise." Taylor was surprised to hear herself making a promise for something she had very little control over. Lately she had been surprised to see herself doing a lot of things; it was as if she were a robot, being controlled remotely by some great inventor.

Chris's cheeks inflated, and then he released the air in a long, slow breath. "Thanks, Taylor."

She nodded and grabbed his hand, gripping it tightly. Her other hand held Gabriel's, but not as firmly. She turned her attention back to the screen, where the first flicker of activity was occurring.

A trio appeared in the distance, walking towards the camera. Using her angel eyes to zoom in on them, Taylor said, "The one in the middle has a sack over her head."

"That was also agreed," Gabriel commented. Taylor remembered that the rest of the agreement included no teleporting, flying, or even running fast. Both parties could only send two escorts, who were required to walk "reasonably slowly" to the meeting place.

A similar trio appeared in the foreground with their backs to the camera. Taylor recognized one of them as Kiren, and knew the curvy one in the middle with the bag over her head was Cassandra. Taylor cringed at the thought that Gabriel was once friends with her. Out of the corner of her eye she glared at him. He didn't notice.

The second escort—another demon—was someone Taylor couldn't recognize, or didn't know.

They proceeded at a similar speed to the approaching party, ensuring that they met at the exact center of the valley, which was marked by a flag, half-white, half-black. The long walk took only eight minutes, but felt like an eternity to Taylor.

As the traders approached each other with their prisoners, the camera zoomed in to show as much detail as possible. Although the camera was capable of picking up sounds—the intermittent chatter of birds chirping for example—neither party spoke. Instead, Kiren and her counterpart simultaneously raised their hands and clasped the prisoner head coverings. With a dramatic flourish, they removed the sacks.

It was Sam alright, and she actually managed to smile. Lighting up the screen, her teeth and lips looked beautiful, in spite of whatever she had been through while captured. Taylor wished she could see more than just the back of Cassandra's head. Her face would likely be contorted into a sneer of sorts, a stark contrast to the vision of goodness and beauty that stood before her. In the purest sense, Sam and Cassandra represented the difference between good and evil, love and hate. *Interesting that they found themselves being traded for each other*, Taylor thought.

With short strides—due to their legs being shackled—each prisoner was pushed forward to the opposite side. Sam's arms were held tightly behind her back, like Cassandra's. Kiren grasped Sam's arm and led her back towards the camera, and safety. The angels did the same with Cassandra, and the parties slowly diverged.

Ten long minutes later, the six bodies had been swallowed up by their respective mountains and the trade had gone off without a hitch. Applause filled the auditorium, but Taylor didn't participate; she, Chris, and Gabriel had already risen and were headed for the door, anxious to welcome Sam.

Knowing that she would initially be taken to the medical wing for a mandatory examination, they caught a transporter there, arriving in less than five minutes. Sam was already there, having likely been teleported as soon as she entered the mountain. Kiren was waiting for them when the exited the transporter. They followed her to the exam room.

Sam, still smiling, sat on a bed, while a shadowy male doctor took a blood sample. Her smile remained wide even when the needle punctured the skin in her arm. Sam said, "Remind me to write a review on Tripadvisor.com, that hotel was one of the worst I've stayed in."

Taylor laughed out loud. Good old Sam. Chris grinned, but it was forced. He was still in concerned-boyfriend mode. He took two long strides and ducked around the doctor to kiss her.

The doctor said, "Just a minute, just a minute, please. I need to check a few more things and then she'll be free to go."

Chris backed off, waiting eagerly, like a dog at the front door just before its owner gets home. Taylor said, "So what did they feed you in that place?"

"Nothing, zip, nil. Not even a complimentary glass of water with some stale bread. And there was certainly no mint on my pillow. In fact, there was no pillow at all," Sam said.

"Angels," Taylor said, "can't live with 'em, can't live without 'em."

Sam laughed. "It's good to be out of that place. It was really scary. I may have screamed a few times, I have to admit."

"That's cool, we won't tell anyone," Taylor joked. "And we'll go straight to the café for some grub after we get out of here."

The doctor said, "You can go eat now. You seem to be perfectly fine, not a scratch on you."

"Thanks, doc," Sam said, hopping off the table.

Chris immediately grabbed her, picking her up and holding her tight. He kissed her a few times. Taylor and Gabriel looked at each other, smirking, for a few minutes, until Taylor finally said, "Uh, this is awkward."

Laughing, Chris said, "Okay, let's go." It was like a huge weight had been lifted from him, both physically and mentally. He had a bounce in his step and a spark in his smile.

Taylor said, "Damn, Chris, I think you were hurt more by the whole kidnapped girlfriend thing than the kidnapped girlfriend was."

Laughing again, Chris said, "I know I look tough, but at heart I'm a big softie."

Sampson met them at the café and the triple-pair were reunited. There was a lot of laughing, more than enough joking, and a fair bit of hugging. Although Taylor enjoyed herself immensely, she couldn't help thinking that it was surely the calm before the storm.

Twenty-Eight

Lucas and Cassandra were on board with the plan. It hadn't been hard to convince them. Take human pain and suffering and add it to Lucas and Cassandra getting to inflict that pain and suffering, and you had a mission that they were interested in. The only sticking point was the chain of command.

"Why will David lead the mission?" Lucas asked.

David glowered at Lucas. Dionysus said, "It was his idea and upon creation of the New Archangels, you each have an equal level of authority. I plan to spread the missions out amongst all of you. This one will be David's."

Cassandra said, "The kid's barely even been on a mission, much less led one."

"You should talk," David spat out. "You were the weak link in the last mission. You're lucky to even be invited on this one."

Cassandra opened her mouth to respond, and Dionysus had a vision of a death match between her and David—which was a very enticing prospect, but not now. Not when he needed as many supporters as possible. So before she could speak, he said, "Enough! The decision is final. Learn to work together. Cassandra screwed up, but it won't happen again. Let's focus on planning the mission."

With that, it was settled. And why shouldn't it be? Dionysus was still the Head of the New Archangel Council, more powerful than czars, than kings, than the damn President of the United States of America.

David said, "I say we target New York City first."

Lucas scoffed. "You can't be serious. There's no way we'll be able to do that without being caught on camera, without being seen by someone who escapes us."

"There will be no survivors," David said between gritted teeth. "We target less populated areas late at night, and we kill swiftly and completely."

"And then we shove it under Clifford's nose so he can get a whiff of how effective his demon army is at protecting the humans," Dionysus said. "New York it is, mission leader."

Lucas opened his mouth like he was about to say something, but then closed it.

Cassandra said, "When do we leave?"

"Immediately," David said.

Dionysus nodded, grinning. "Good. Very good."

PART III

"You say you want a revolution
Well, you know
We all want to change the world
You tell me that it's evolution
Well, you know
We all want to change the world
But when you talk about destruction
Don't you know that you can count me out
Don't you know it's gonna be all right
All right, all right

You say you got a real solution
Well, you know
We'd all love to see the plan
You ask me for a contribution
Well, you know
We're doing what we can
But when you want money
For people with minds that hate
All I can tell is brother you have to wait
Don't you know it's gonna be all right
All right, all right"

The Beatles- "Revolution"
From the B-side of the single "Hey Jude" (1968)

Twenty-Nine

Gabriel was already gone. That fast. Just when they had recovered Samantha, Clifford called a meeting and announced that Gabriel would leave immediately on his mission. Sampson went with him. That was more than an hour ago.

With Taylor's mission on hold for the moment, she didn't know what to do with herself. Sam and Chris had gone back to UT. Sam had homework to catch up on and an exam in a few days. Taylor could have ported with them, but begged off saying that she would hitch a ride with one of her guards. She needed time to be alone. To think. And she figured Sam and Chris would want to be alone, too.

So she wandered around the Lair for a while, trying to get lost. Each time she came to a crossroads, she turned the opposite direction from where her instincts told her to go. It worked, and an hour later she was hopelessly confused as to which way led back to the café, the recreational area, the Elders' Chamber, her room, or any of the other areas she was familiar with.

After making another right and passing by a few unmarked doors, Taylor came to a dead end. A transporter waited to whisk her off somewhere. She boarded the futuristic-looking pod, wondering where she would end up.

It turned out to be a long ride—more than thirty minutes—which probably meant she had managed to get way off track, and was being brought back to civilization. It gave her time to think.

Looking back, the last seven months of her life seemed impossible. It was like her old life had been snuffed out, and in its place a new life created. Moving to the other side of the world—to Russia or China—would be no more different. Besides Sam being her best friend, the only thing that hadn't changed was her. Of course, physically she *had* changed—sprouting wings and spouting orbs of light probably fell into the change category—but her personality was the same. She was the same old Taylor, with no control over the chaos of her mind, direct, a bit on the weird side.

One thing that was very different was having a boyfriend. It wasn't something she was proud of, but she really had no choice in the matter. Despite all Gabriel's imperfections—his temper, his tendency to do stupid things—and because of all of his perfections—his wit, his leadership, his gorgeous face and body—her heart had chosen him, for better or for worse. At first she had been resistant to that choice. She was too young for a soul mate, too young for true love, too young to be a slave to a relationship. So she had rebelled, pushing Gabriel away at times, but like metal to a magnet, she couldn't stay away from him. She couldn't resist him. Finally embracing the relationship, Taylor found that she was able to be herself, independent and uncontrolled, while still being Gabriel's girlfriend. And he respected her for it—liked that about her. For her it was a revelation, and explained a lot about her mother's relationship with her father. A partnership. A promise. To be their own selves while being a fitted pair at the same time. She only hoped that her relationship with Gabriel could one day be as good as her parents' had been.

While her thoughts dwelled on a photograph of her parents she had in her room at home, she felt the transporter slowing. Despite the length of the trip, it had passed by remarkably fast. What would the doors reveal when they opened? Not the UT campus, not her dad mowing their front lawn, not anything normal, that was for sure. Instead, it would be like something out of an adventure movie: dark shapes moving through torch-lit tunnels, carrying fiery swords and bows; subtly glowing angels moving casually amongst the demons; there would be no humans, surely, not even Sam, who was pretending to study but was really making out with a demon.

The doors opened and she saw no one. A rocky alcove. There were two torches. It was not familiar—she had never been to this place before. In the rock wall there was a large, wrought-iron door, domed at the top, medieval by design, with intersecting metal bands forming a cross on its face. There was no handle, no push bar, no knocker. From her experience, Taylor knew that doors like this usually required the flaming touch of a demon to open, for security purposes. Which probably meant there was something cool behind the door, something worth seeing. For once, she wished one of her demon guards were nearby. She glanced behind her, half-expecting to see one lurking in the shadows, watching—always watching—but she saw only the empty transporter.

Three choices: board the transporter and enjoy a half-hour ride back to being lost, sit down and wait for a demon to come by, or pound on the door and hope that someone inside hears her. She sat down to wait.

Less than five minutes later she felt a rumble in her rump, a buzz in her butt. A short vibration beneath her, like the ground was trembling. It stopped. Then started. Then stopped. Then: four or five more shakes of her buttocks. It was like she was sitting on one of those airport auto-massage chairs that was malfunctioning, or maybe functioning perfectly.

She stood up and touched her hand to the door. *Buzz.* Pause. *Buzz.* Whatever was causing the ground to tremble was powerful, very powerful. And it was behind the door. Her curiosity made option three look better and better. So she pounded on the door, a dull, thudding sound that likely didn't project farther than the doorframe.

After a few minutes with no response, she hammered her fists against the iron three more times. *Thud, thud, thud.* "Housekeeping!" she shrilled in a high-pitched voice, more for her own amusement than to get the attention of anyone who might be behind the thick door.

To her surprise, there was a groan and the eight-foot door began creaking open. In a million years, she never would have guessed whose face would pop out from behind the door. "Kiren?" she said.

"Taylor?" Kiren said, mirroring her surprise. "What are you doing here?"

Kiren's spiky hair was neon pink, and looked strange next to her dark skin. She wore a tight black tank-top that accentuated her toned physique. Her skin glistened with sweat.

"I, uh, just kind of wandered in. I'm not even sure where here is."

Kiren smiled. "You're in for a treat then. Follow me."

Taylor followed Kiren through a short tunnel. The end of the path opened into a massive cavern, brightly-lit by dozens of baskets of fire spread throughout the area. The moment Taylor passed from beneath the tunnel ceiling, she saw a large, black shape thundering towards her. The ground beneath her shook-rumbled-vibrated like there was an earthquake, or T-Rex was charging her.

"Look out!" Kiren yelled, diving to the side.

While the warning registered, Taylor didn't heed it, *couldn't* heed it. Her body betrayed her mind once again, ignoring her commands to *Run, dammit, run!* Instead, she just stood there, with the big thing bearing down on her, about to smash her to bits and send her to angel heaven or hell, or wherever it was that angels went when they died—according to legend, they went to the stars. Frozen in place, Taylor squeezed her eyes shut and prepared to go to the stars.

Stripes of wetness roamed over her face, tickling her. Not slobbery, like a big dog, but wispy, the licks felt like she was being kissed by a fairy. She opened her eyes. Upon seeing the face in front of her, she opened her eyes even wider. The scaly oversized head had its mouth open, displaying three sets of razor-sharp teeth. They would have been menacing, if not for the fact that they seemed to be grinning at her. A snakelike tongue continuously flicked from its mouth to taste her face.

Taylor realized that she had regained control of her body, but still she didn't run. Although the gargoyle standing before her had undergone extraordinary changes since she last saw him, his eyes gave him away. Their blackness was so deep that they were literally the absence of light, but unlike the other demon gargoyles she had seen, his eyes sparkled. How they sparkled while still seeming so infinitely black was a mystery that Taylor knew she would never be able to solve.

"Rocky!" she exclaimed. "I've been meaning to come see you, buddy."

The big fellow roared with glee, sounding more like a lion than a dog. He had really grown up fast. The earth groaned under him as he took a step forward, crashing his foot to the dirty cavern floor with a *Boom!* The ground shook. Taylor took a step back and said, "Whoa there, buddy, you're a little bigger than you used to be!"

Rocky cocked his head to the side as if he was trying to understand what she meant. Perhaps in his mind he was still the rambunctious young gargoyle eating out of Taylor's hand. For him, maybe nothing had changed. Taylor said, "Can I go for a ride on you, Rock Star?"

Rocky bucked his head up and down as if answering in the affirmative and simultaneously demonstrating his appreciation for the nickname his friend had just bestowed upon him.

"Okay, here I go!" With an effortless leap, Taylor mounted him, spinning in midair to ensure she was facing forward when she landed. She sat in a natural indentation between his head and wings, which looked tiny relative to the rest of his bulky frame. Rocky let out a happy roar and spun around to face the empty hall. He pawed a foot like a bull and then took off, thundering across the cavern.

Taylor was left breathless for a moment, as the speed of his scamper took her by surprise. She had expected him to lumber along, perhaps reaching a top speed equivalent to that of an elephant, but instead, she felt like they were moving as fast as a galloping horse.

And then they flew.

Against all odds, they flew, as Rocky's fairy wings managed to lift him and Taylor from the ground. They didn't rise quickly, but like a hot air balloon, they gradually moved towards the ceiling. With another roar, Rocky began to twirl through the air, spinning Taylor in a circle again and again.

Taylor laughed gleefully, girlishly, like she hadn't laughed in a long time. Uninhibited. Rocky was showing off for her and she loved it.

Taylor dove from his back and her wings opened naturally, allowing her to settle into a gentle soar. She did a lap around Rocky, who was smiling and trying to keep up with her. She did loops, twists, and somersaults, flying freely—not as part of some training exercise—for the first time since she'd obtained her wings.

Eventually, Rocky grew tired of flying—his wings weren't cut out for long excursions in the air—and he descended slowly to the ground. Taylor followed suit, landing in a crouch in front of him. She ran to him and gave his tree-trunk-like leg a hug. Rocky purred with delight.

Kiren approached cautiously. "That was incredible," she said.

"Yeah, it's amazing how they can fly so well with such little wings," Taylor agreed.

Shaking her head, Kiren said, "No, not that. He didn't freak out when he saw you. That's what's amazing."

Puzzled, Taylor said, "Why should he freak out?"

"Because you're an angel now. His instincts should be telling him to attack you, to hate you, but instead, he seems to *love* you."

"Don't tell Gabriel, he might be jealous," Taylor joked. "It's probably just because he knew me as a human before and still just sees me as his friend." Turning to Rocky, Taylor said, "Isn't that right, buddy?" Rocky roared in agreement.

Kiren said, "Whatever you say. Hey, do you wanna watch him train with me?"

"Sure."

Taylor gave Rocky another hug before following Kiren across the grounds and then up a dozen stone steps onto a raised seating area. Rocky followed them, shaking the earth as he walked. Luckily, he didn't try to pursue them up the staircase, which was barely wide enough for Taylor to squeeze through. Instead, he watched them ascend and sit down, before he plopped down on his hind legs in an attempt to copy them.

Taylor laughed. "You're welcome to sit with us until it's time to train, Rocky." Rocky purred.

Kiren said, "Sorry I didn't invite you to come with me, I didn't plan on coming here."

"Me either, I just ended up here by accident. So why did you come?"

"To be honest, I don't really know. Just to take my mind off things I guess. I'm worried about Sampson, he's always getting into trouble."

"Tell me about it, Gabriel's a walking disaster sometimes. The two of them together scares me, too," Taylor half-joked.

Kiren laughed. "If you're trying to help, you're not," she said lightly.

"Sorry, I guess it's my way of dealing with things. I like to make jokes."

"For me, it helps to watch the gargoyles training. I don't know why."

"I know why," Taylor said, "because they're awesome!"

"Most demons—and angels too, I think—see them as grotesque, an abomination, only to be used in war."

"I'm not most people," Taylor said. "If there's anything my mom taught me, it was to not always follow the popular opinion."

"That's good," Kiren said.

"So things are pretty serious with Sampson, huh?" Taylor asked.

Kiren blushed, her dark cheeks becoming even darker. "Yeah, it is. I've never felt like this about someone."

"I know how that is. Gabriel is my first real boyfriend. It scares me sometimes how strong my feelings for him are. Like I can't control them. Like I'm dependent on him or something. But I've realized I'm not really. I'm still me, as independent as ever. It's nice having someone to love though."

Kiren said, "Thanks, Taylor."

"For what?"

"For being there to talk to. Being a female in the army, I feel like I'm surrounded by guys most of the time. There are more girls than there used to be, but we're still seriously outnumbered. It's just nice to hear that someone else has the same feelings as me."

Taylor laughed. "Sam's in the same boat, although she got in it quite differently. Before Chris, her boyfriend count was about a thousand, with the average length at maybe a week. But now it's like she's married. Weird how things change."

"Yeah," Kiren said. She had a faraway look in her eyes, like she was trying to make sense of how her life had led her to date an angel.

Taylor said, "It's starting."

A giant of a man had walked into the arena. Rocky was already up, running over to him. The man carried a long, black stick. His face was covered by a foliage of dark hair in the form of a bushy beard, long mustache, thick eyebrows, and long bangs. His black hair fell to his shoulders and, when combined with his size, gave him the appearance of a professional wrestler.

"Hey, Gargo!" Taylor yelled.

The big man waved. When she had first struck up her uncanny relationship with Rocky, she had befriended the demon gargoyle master at the same time. Although his mother had named him Barnaby, his ability to communicate with gargoyles had earned him the nickname Gargo.

For the next hour, Gargo put Rocky's skills to the test, using his rod to communicate. He waved, spun, and thrust the rod in various ways, each of which was a new command. Taylor was glad to see that the pole was not used to prod or strike the gargoyles, merely to communicate with them, like sign language.

With pride, the young gargoyle was able to meet every challenge, roaring and smiling at his audience of two with each success. He shot streams of fire at small targets from his gaping mouth; he dodged or blocked anything that Gargo threw at him; he ran and flew through a complex obstacle course meant to increase his agility; and most impressively, he crushed anything in his path, from stone walls to concrete blocks, kicking or shouldering his way through them using only raw power and strength.

When it was all over, Taylor and Kiren stood, clapping and whistling. "Go, Rocky!" Taylor yelled. Rocky beamed, as only a gargoyle with three sets of teeth can. With a final roar, Rocky allowed himself to be shepherded through a huge tunnel that presumably led back to the gargoyle paddocks.

Taylor was energized. Rocky had inspired her. She was ready for her mission.

Thirty

Gabriel checked his watch. Nine-thirty in the morning, local time. Four thousand miles north, and nearly two thousand miles west of the Lair. Only thirty seconds of travel thanks to the demon travelling with them.

The demon said, "I will stay close. Signal if you are ready to move on."

Gabriel nodded but the demon was already gone.

"You ready for this?" Gabriel said.

"Just like old times," Sampson replied.

They walked out from behind the patch of bushes in which the demon had left them. It was a cold morning and they could see their breath with each exhalation. It was vastly different to UT's warm-weather campus or the Lair, each of which were significantly closer to the equator. But they were angels—the cold didn't bother them. Turn up the inner light a notch, risk a little extra body glow, and it was like wearing a thermal coat, wool gloves, and a toboggan hat.

They were in northern Central Park, New York City. The plan was to focus on the places in the world with the highest angel populations. NYC was a natural starting point, boasting over a thousand angels throughout the urban sprawl. Most were married to humans, had families, and lived relatively normal lives, except for the part where their kids attended angel school on the weekends to learn about the evils of demons.

Gabriel's family had lived in New York for a spell, before his dad was transferred southwest for his job. Now his family was in hiding, sheltered by the demons in the Lair, not safe after having been kidnapped by the angels and used as bait. Gabriel didn't want them to have to hide anymore. This mission would help make that happen. The goal: start a rebellion. How? He didn't have a clue, but hoped he would figure it out when the time came.

They walked down a path, heading for Fifth Avenue. The park paths were crowded with runners, dog walkers, and bundled up business men and women walking to another day of meetings, computers, and coffee breaks. Their lives were normal. Gabriel didn't envy them though. He liked his life. Especially now that Taylor was in it.

Using a combination of walking and underground subways, they made their way through the gridlock of swarming sidewalks and busy streets to their destination: an apartment building in the Upper East Side. Gabriel had confirmed with his parents that he still lived there.

The building had security, but not a security desk; the main door was locked, requiring a key to open. A metal intercom with a keypad and speaker was inset in the brick entryway. Gabriel pressed one and then five. He waited.

A man's voice came through the speaker: "Timothy?"

"Guess again," Gabriel said.

"I have no idea," the man said.

"Gabriel Knight and a friend."

"Gabriel Knight? Light-swords and orb-blasters! I surely didn't expect to find you on my front doorstep."

"Can we come in?" Gabriel asked.

"Of course, of course, I will buzz you in. The elevator will automatically take you to the fifth floor only. I am number fifteen, but of course you already know that."

There was a soft hum and a click as the door unlocked. Sampson pulled it open and held it for Gabriel. "Ladies first," he said.

Gabriel punched his friend playfully as he entered first. A minute later they exited the elevator onto a landing with three doors, marked thirteen, fourteen, and fifteen. Gabriel lifted his fist to knock on fifteen, but the door opened before he could complete the motion.

"Gabriel, my boy, it feels like forever since I have seen you," the man inside the door said. He was tall, with a long face, long neck, long torso, long arms, and long legs. Even his fingers looked abnormally long and Gabriel suspected that if his shoes were removed they would reveal three-inch toes as well.

"Uncle Martin!" Gabriel said. "It's been too long." He embraced the man and then turned and said, "Sampson, meet Martin Hargrave. I've known him since I was a very little boy."

Shaking Sampson's hand, Martin said, "Longer than that, although you probably don't remember. I saw you shortly after your birth, Gabriel. Your parents were so proud. You were their first."

Sampson said, "It's a pleasure to meet you. So you're Helena Knight's brother?"

"Alas, no. I am an only child, but both Helena and Theodore became such dear friends to me that the mere restrictions of blood could not stop us from being uncles and aunts to each other's children. But where are my manners, come in, come in, please."

Gabriel followed Martin into the apartment with Sampson behind him. The first thing he heard was the soothing tinkle of light piano music in the background. They entered into a sitting room. An antique couch and four antique chairs provided seating for up to seven guests. A colorful, Asian-inspired rug decorated the open space between the seats. Lovely paintings of historic New

York City adorned the walls. The place was kept meticulously clean. *Good old Uncle Martin*, Gabriel thought. He and his brothers used to drive Martin crazy with the messes they would make when they were visiting.

"Who's Timothy?" Gabriel asked before they sat down.

Martin said, "I thought you were my 10:30 appointment. A young human boy, just learning to play. He must be late."

Sampson said, "Play what?"

"The piano, of course," Martin said.

Gabriel explained: "Martin is a renowned pianist. He's played in concert halls all over the world. But—correct me if I'm wrong, Martin—you have always preferred teaching to playing."

"You're absolutely right, my boy. Playing for hours doesn't do for me what teaching for five minutes can. It's my life work."

The phone rang. Martin strode over to a wall-mounted phone. Before answering it, he said, "Please, please, make yourselves at home."

Gabriel and Sampson sat in two of the chairs while Martin took the call. Lowering his voice, Sampson said, "Will he be able to help us?"

"Trust me, if anyone is plugged into the angel network here, it will be Martin. Before we left, he was the head of the local angel chapter."

"But will he be receptive?"

Gabriel leaned back in his chair, contemplating the question. Then, leaning forward, he said, "Martin was always one of the most caring people I knew. He valued equality, honesty, generosity. He teaches human kids to play the piano. Unless he has completely changed since I last met him, he's our guy."

Sampson nodded as Martin returned. Martin said, "We're in luck, my appointment's been cancelled. I was worried you would have to sit through an hour of rough, beginner playing."

"Great," Gabriel said.

"So, what brings you to the Big Apple? I presume this is not a social call."

"What makes you say that?" Gabriel asked.

"No advance notice, for one. And secondly, when I returned from my phone call a moment ago, the two of you were whispering like a pair of co-conspirators in a bank heist. I'm getting old, but my mind is as sharp as ever, you can't fool me."

Gabriel laughed. "I don't suppose I can. And you are right, of course. We've come to request your help."

"It must be important. Last letter I got from your parents said that you were at the front lines of the War—that's a solid ten hour flight to New York."

"That is where we've come from," Gabriel said, choosing not to mention that they had teleported rather than flown. They needed to ease their way into the subject of their alliance with the demons.

"So you're a fighter, too?" Martin asked Sampson.

"I try, although my girlfriend tends to save my butt half the time," Sampson said chuckling.

"Ahh, your lady is in the force, too. That's good. Long distance relationships are hard." He said it matter-of-factly, from experience. Gabriel knew Martin's story; it was one of love, joy, and ultimately sadness. His wife had been in the angel army, returning home a few times a year, when the soldiers were given leave for holidays. Eventually she had been killed in a battle. Their four kids had been somewhat scarred—as would be expected—by the experience of losing their mother so young. None had joined the army.

Gabriel said, "Uncle, I have a story to tell you, but you might not believe a lot of it. I ask that you try to keep an open mind."

Martin's eyebrows arched when he heard Gabriel's disclaimer and request. "Gabriel, I have always known you to be trustworthy. I will not look for lies in that which is true."

Gabriel was glad that his Uncle wasn't up to date on some of his recent history, which included a spat of lies to various people, including to his own girlfriend on multiple occasions.

"Thanks. This might take a while, but feel free to stop me if you have a question or would like to take a break."

"Out with it, my boy. You've certainly piqued my interest."

With that, Gabriel began from the beginning. He left nothing out and made no effort to hide his own indiscretions. His mission to abduct Taylor, the lies he told her, his effort to escape with her: he laid his soul bare without making excuses for any of it. Occasionally, Martin would sigh and stretch his arms high over his head, as if the story was making his muscles sore. To his credit, however, he didn't interrupt, stopping Gabriel only once to make a cup of tea for the three of them.

When Gabriel reached the part where Sampson rescued him from the angel dungeons, Martin murmured, "Mmmm," and nodded his head. At that point, Sampson went back in time to tell the story of his decision to side with the demons after becoming uncomfortable with things he had heard about Dionysus's ultimate goals.

Finally, Gabriel finished with a flourish as he described Taylor's miraculous evolution, her destruction of six members of the Archangel Council, David's corruption, and the subsequent evolution of the group now calling themselves the New Archangels. At the end of the tale the silence was so complete that you could have heard a teardrop splash on the meticulously polished hardwood floors.

Leaning forward, Martin looked into Gabriel's eyes intensely, and said, "Why exactly are you here, Gabriel?"

"I think you know, Uncle," Gabriel said.

Changing gears, Martin said, "Your poor parents, they must be a mess. David was always such a good kid. And he idolized you."

"They still have hope that he will see the error in his ways, but I have seen the heat of his anger. He is furious with me for betraying the angel cause. Ever since that day on the Warrior's Plateau…he's been different. He's not the brother I once knew."

Switching back to his initial line of thinking, Martin said, "This is not going to be an easy sell, Gabriel, not when decades of belief have been engrained in the angel population. Angels are brought up hating demons, wishing them dead. I mean, you were blinded to what was really going on, too. Dionysus has fooled us all."

"So you believe me," Gabriel said.

"It's not so much that I believe you that I want to believe you. I have always wished there was a way to make peace with the demons, settling things without killing each other. It helps too that I know you. The others will not be so trusting."

"That's where you come in. They know you, they respect you, they trust you. I am hoping that between the three of us, we can convince enough of them to make a real difference."

Frowning, Martin said, "And then what? We all rise up and fight alongside the demons. Most of us aren't in the army because we don't want to be. We want to live a normal life."

Gabriel stood, his hands fisted with energy. "Then you must fight for that normal life. This affects everyone, all of us. The world as we know it is about to be destroyed, to be replaced with an Evil Utopia dreamed up by a madman. Mankind has no idea what is about to hit them, and even if they did, they would be incapable of defending themselves. Who will stand up to defend them? The demons will. Will you? Will you defend the defenseless?" By the time he finished speaking, Gabriel's face was shining with emotion.

Smiling, Martin said, "Of course I will, Gabriel. I was only trying to see if you had what it takes to convince the rest of them. That speech shows me that you do. Bring that same fire with you to the gathering."

"What gathering?"

"The one I'm about to set up for tonight." He looked at his watch. "Look, it's only two o'clock now. You guys can make some lunch while I hit the phones, try to get something scheduled."

Gabriel said, "Thank you, Uncle. Thank you for trusting me."

Thirty-One

There were humans everywhere. Despite having grown up with them and being fathered by one, David's tolerance for humankind was low. Just the smell of them was making him nauseous. The way they walked around talking arrogantly on their cell phones about finalizing their meaningless deals, how they drove expensive cars while playing loud rap music, and their ultimate belief that they were the rulers of the earth, the supreme species: it all made David want to put them on an island—and then blow it up.

Angels should be ruling the world. They should be free to roam the skies, to fill the world with light, to chase away the darkness. Instead, they were forced to hide their true selves. Because of the demons. If the angels moved, the demons were always there with them. Watching. Waiting. Protecting the insolent fools that wandered through their pointless lives without a clue as to their true place in the pecking order. Humans were third, at best. Clearly the angels and demons were above them. And David would probably place dolphins and certain breeds of dogs, like collies for example, ahead of the filthy humans as well.

David wanted to know what it was like to feel the life ebbing from a human, because he, of the superior race, had exercised his authority over the lowly human. Disgusting. Vermin.

He sat on a bench and watched them crawling over everything, like cockroaches. Cassandra was on his right, Lucas on his left. David said, "I wish we could start now."

"Too risky. We have to wait until nightfall," Lucas said.

"I know that," David growled. "I just wish."

Cassandra said, "We could start…"

"Don't encourage him," Lucas warned.

"Shut up! Let her speak. What did you mean by that, dear Cassandra?" David asked, the tone of his voice transitioning seamlessly from sharp and cold, to smooth and buttery. It was a little trick he had learned from the master actor himself, Dionysus.

"I only meant that there are less risky targets we can begin with. Targets that will be easily handled without fear of detection. Like old people, for example. The kind that sit at home and watch soap operas with their cats."

"You're sick," David said. "I like it."

"No, let's just stick to the original plan and wait until dark and then go after a few drunks on the street." Lucas had stood up and was towering over David, who was still seated.

"Disagreeing with the mission leader. Tisk, tisk, Lucas. Your actions could be construed as an act of treason, grounds for imprisonment or even execution."

Lucas backed off and looked at Cassandra for support. She said, "It could look that way, Lucas."

Defeated, he sat back down. A few minutes of silence passed, and then he said, "Fine. But we have to be very careful or the entire mission could be ruined."

David said, "That's a good little bee, follow me." With that, he stood up and marched off. He could hear feet scuffling behind him as his two pawns followed behind like obedient dogs. He vowed never to take orders from either of them again.

David walked and walked, not really caring in which direction he was going, until the streets thinned out, and the foot traffic dwindled. While he walked, he trained his ears to pick up sounds directly behind him. He heard harsh whispers, like an argument. The two love birds were disagreeing about something. Lucas was probably proposing an immediate coup against their leader. His rationale would be that there were two of them and only one of him and that they had seniority and should be running the mission anyway. Cassandra was probably saying that she agreed but that Dionysus would punish them when they returned. He trusted neither of them.

Tuning his super-hearing elsewhere, David ignored his little doggies and focused on finding his first target. *First of many*, he thought. He passed a group of punk kids sitting on a stoop, smoking cigarettes and laughing at an inappropriate joke one of them had made. Probably skipping school. Probably from broken homes where one parent was long gone and the other couldn't care less about what their kids were doing as they worked three jobs and were more concerned with putting food on the table. They were good targets, but would have to wait until night. They might have guns, and while David didn't fear such arcane human weapons, they made a lot of noise and would draw attention.

A few more blocks and the neighborhood got even older, more rundown. Sidewalks crumbled, buildings chipped and rotted, mailboxes were covered in graffiti. An old man was sitting on his front step reading a newspaper. No witnesses nearby. Perfect.

David approached him confidently, like he knew exactly where he was going, what he was doing. "Hello there, sir. How are you today?" David said politely.

Without looking up from his paper, the bald guy said, "Keep on movin', son. Whatever you're sellin', I ain't buyin'."

A quick flare of heat bubbled into David's head. *How dare the filthy, insolent human ignore his superior like that!? Breathe, breathe*, he told himself. The anger subsided and David managed to maintain his polite expression, his cool tone. "Thank you, sir, but we're actually not selling anything. We're giving."

Finally, the man looked up, probably because David had said *we* and he was curious to see who else was with him. He glanced at Lucas and Cassandra, who had caught up, his gaze lingering on Cassandra, wandering up and down her curving body. David thought the old pervert might actually lick his lips. Instead, he said, "So you're Jehovah's Witnesses then? I'm still not buyin'."

"Wrong again, sir. We are here to present you with a prize you have won."

"I didn't enter no contest," the guy said gruffly. Then, changing his tone, he said, "What prize?"

When he said it, David knew the man was as good as theirs—a dead man walking. "Maybe your wife did," David said, taking a guess that the guy was married. "And it's a cash prize."

Upon hearing the word cash, the man's eyes gleamed, but his mouth was still skeptical, cocked to the side like he was chewing on the inside of his mouth. "How much cash?"

"Unfortunately, you did not win the grand prize of ten thousand dollars, some lady in Brooklyn did. Oh, you should have seen her face, the surprise, the delight. Some days I just love my job!" David was laying it on so thick that he almost threw up in his own mouth.

"How much cash?" the guy repeated. The skepticism had washed completely from his face, and every muscle was tensed, as if focused on the tiny piece of information related to what else?—money!

"Like I said, you didn't win the first prize, but you did get second, sir, which is quite an accomplishment. I mean second out of all those thousands of entrants, it's something you should really be proud of…"

"How much!?" the man growled, truly believing his life was about to be changed.

"Five thousand dollars," David said proudly.

The old guy's jaw dropped to his knees. "Five…," he trailed off. Suddenly snapping his mouth shut like a mousetrap, he said, "Give it to me."

David reached in his pocket and extracted the clip of crisp hundred dollar bills that they would be using and reusing to set traps for their victims, and started to hand it to the man. Just before the bills reached his outstretched hand, David pulled back sharply. "Wait, I totally forgot. My gosh, I can't believe I….Of course, we need to verify some information, to make sure we're giving the money to the right person."

The man's face fell, like he already knew that there had been some mistake, that the money was meant for someone two houses down, someone more deserving than him.

David said, "Okay, first question: Do you live at 45…"

The man's eyes lit up. "45 Berkeley Street?" he said.

"Yes. Berkeley Street. Number 45. That's your place?" David said, motioning behind the man.

"Yes, my place. Well, mine and my wife's."

"Okay," David said. "As long as you can confirm that you live here, then you're the winner. Do you have a rental agreement or even a phone bill that proves you are living here? You know, something that we can come inside and take a look at?" David marveled at his innate ability to lie so smoothly, to invite himself into the man's home and yet make it feel like it was the right thing for the guy to do.

"Yes, yes. Come inside, please. My wife takes care of all the finances; she'll be able to show you something."

Although the man looked creaky, old, arthritic, he practically leapt up the stairs and shot through the door, yelling, "Marta! We have company! Get out the bill register!"

For the first time since they left the bench, David turned around to look at his followers. He smiled at them. It was time. Their expressions were indifferent, but he sensed a challenge beneath their casual stares. Perhaps

Lucas had won the argument. He would be ready for them.

David led the way up the stairs and into the man's home. Once Cassandra and Lucas were inside, he closed and locked the door.

His sword released a dull glow when he unsheathed it. There would be no screams to hear. Day or night didn't matter.

Thirty-Two

After watching Little Rocky—who was now Big Rocky—train for an hour, Kiren and Taylor grabbed a bite to eat. They talked nonstop the entire time. It was good getting to know Kiren. They seemed to click on many different levels. The conversation had drifted to family when Taylor's cell phone rang.

"Hello?" she answered.

"Clifford here. I've called a meeting. It's time to begin your mission. My office—ten minutes."

"I'm with Kiren," Taylor said.

"Bring her, too," he said.

She hung up and Taylor relayed the information to Kiren. They hurriedly finished their lunch and five minutes later were on a transporter to the tunnel wing that housed the Elders' offices. Clifford's was the last one. The door opened before they reached it.

"You're late," Sam joked.

Taylor said, "Have you been assigned to this mission, too?"

Sam laughed and said, "After doing time in angel prison, I think I would prefer a few weeks of R&R, but definitely put my name down for the next one."

The three girls entered the office, in which Chris already sat, facing Clifford. Sam had been invited because even if she wasn't, Chris would tell her everything immediately after anyway. And Clifford liked her.

Although Taylor had been in Clifford's office several times before, for some reason she had never really looked around much. After spending time with Kiren, she felt contemplative. Her eyes scanned her surroundings, looking for clues that might give her some insight into who the head of the demon Elders really was.

Like most places in the Lair, the room was dark, lit only by a dozen candles. It smelled of dust and old book pages, which made sense because there were wall-to-wall bookshelves on three sides. Each shelf had a thin layer of dust marred only by gentle scratches where books had been removed. There was clutter everywhere; evidently Clifford never threw anything out. A bronze world globe on one shelf, a model ship in a bottle on another. There were no photos or artwork.

The warm brown desk separating Clifford from Taylor and her friends was the only clean surface. It was currently being used only as a rest for Clifford's folded hands, and a support for Sam to lean her elbows on.

Taylor realized the others had already started talking. Clifford was saying, "…no word yet, but they haven't been gone long. We expect to hear from them in the next couple of hours."

Taylor intuited that it was Gabriel and Sampson he was referring to. She wasn't sure whether no news was good news.

Clifford said, "Shall we talk about your mission?"

"Do you still have this crazy idea that you are going to participate in it?" Chris asked.

Clifford smiled. "I know what you're thinking. Old Clifford has lost his head, he's having a midlife crisis and wants to do something adventurous."

Chris said, "That's exactly what I was thinking."

"Well, you're wrong. For one, I am way past the middle of my life, so if anything, it would be a late-life crisis." He paused to laugh at his own joke. Then he said, "Second, without me, you have no mission. You have no bait. It would be like throwing a hook in the water and hoping to catch a fish."

"There are other ways, sir. Dionysus is probably dying to get his hands on Taylor, too. She could be the bait."

"Not anymore. Now that she's become an angel—and an unpredictable one at that—and he has managed to evolve his New Archangels, he has no need for her. No, he wants me more than anyone else. I am going to do this."

Taylor said, "Okay, Clifford. We'll do whatever you ask of us."

Clifford sighed. "I know you will. And I know I will be in good hands—the very best actually. That's another reason I feel this is a risk worth taking. Is everyone with me?"

The question was directed at both Chris and Kiren, but Clifford's eyes never left Chris's.

Kiren immediately agreed, but Chris just stared back at him, as if he was trying to use telepathy to change Clifford's mind. After thirty seconds, Sam said, "Of course the stubborn one agrees too, don't you?"

Finally breaking his stare, Chris said, "Yes, but I do so under strong advice to pursue another course of action."

"Noted," Clifford said rigidly. "Now, for the plan." He rubbed his hands together rapidly.

For the next forty-five minutes, Clifford explained his proposed plan. Chris made recommendations for improvements several times, each of which Clifford readily accepted, but the overall nature of the plan remained unchanged. Clifford would contact Dionysus under the guise that he was tired of fighting and that he wanted to face him once and for all. Although Taylor didn't believe

Dionysus would go for what felt like the oldest trick in the book, Clifford assured her he would be able to convince his angel counterpart. Once the fight started, Taylor, Chris, and Kiren would rush in to help him kill Dionysus. They fully expected Dionysus to have plenty of backup, in the form of the New Archangels, but at least he would be temporarily exposed and they would have a chance to take him out. Chris and Kiren would try to hold off the Archangels while Taylor went after Dionysus.

Once every last detail had been agreed, Clifford adjourned the meeting and promised to contact them once the timing had been set. The foursome left together, hoping to find an open pool table so they could waste away the day.

Thirty-Three

Unbelievable. It was a call that Dionysus had always hoped to receive, but never expected to. For years Dionysus had tried to lure Clifford out, but he had always declined, using important words like leadership and duty as excuses for his cowardice. While he knew his demon opponent was spineless, he also knew that he wasn't stupid. Which meant that this would be a trap. Clifford was playing on his pride and lust for revenge in an attempt to get him out in the open. But Dionysus was fine with that, because it would force Clifford out into the open as well.

He finally had a chance to cut the head off the demons, and he wasn't about to waste it just because of some pathetic demon trap. After all, he would have three of his New Archangels with him. He considered calling the other three back to Headquarters, but decided against it. With David and the other two assaulting New York and Dionysus killing off the head of the demon Elders, his enemies would be stretched too thin.

He had taken the call in his room, where he had been admiring himself in the mirror. He turned his attention back to his naked reflection—his evolved perfection. The time of the humans had passed; the time of the demons had passed; even the time of the angels had passed; the Archangel Evolution had begun, and it wouldn't end until they ruled the earth.

Thirty-Four

Gabriel checked his watch again, for the tenth time that afternoon. 4:30—another ten minutes had passed, slowly.

After they had raided Martin's refrigerator—building triple decker sandwiches with roast beef, ham, turkey, and all the salad fixings they could possibly want—Gabriel and Sampson had listened to Martin work the phones. At one point he had three phones going at once, a feat that even the most capable executive assistant would be in awe of.

Anytime Gabriel tried to ask how it was going, Martin said, "Later, later, my boy," and shoved another bite of sandwich into his mouth before dialing another number.

At around 4:45, Martin hung up one last phone and said, "It's done."

Gabriel had long since finished his lunch and had resorted to picking rye seeds out of his teeth with a toothpick to pass the time. Sampson chose to spread out on the couch and read a classical music magazine for about two minutes before passing out with the reading material on his face. His light snoring buzzed the pages with each exhalation.

Gabriel shook his friend, who said, "What? What?" as he scrambled back into a sitting position, the periodical flapping wildly to the floor.

"What's the plan?" Gabriel asked.

Martin said, "Midnight. It's the earliest I could get. Babysitters have to be lined up, night-workers need to call in sick, arrangements must be made."

"That's fine. Who?"

Martin smiled. "You did come to the right place, Gabriel. About seventy-five percent of the adult angel population in New York will probably be there. That's New York state, not city."

Now it was Gabriel who was smiling, ear to ear. Sampson, still groggy, was blinking rapidly as if trying to come back to reality from some dream world that continued to flash before his eyes. Gabriel said, "Uncle, you're a miracle worker."

Martin said, "No, Gabriel. This was nothing. The real miracle needs to happen tonight."

Gabriel nodded solemnly. "It will, Uncle. It has to."

Thirty-Five

Two strokes and the lucky prize winner and his wife were dead. The geezer was rummaging through an old file cabinet, presumably looking for proof of residence, when he was killed. The wife had been making some tea. Neither made a sound—David caught them well before they hit the floor. It was professional, precise, easy. And it was fun—for David anyway. In fact, he enjoyed it immensely. The other two just watched like a couple of useless piles of crap.

On the way out, David said over his shoulder, "Lucas—call 9-1-1. We need to report a crime."

"Do it yourself," Lucas retorted.

David stopped, still inside the old guy's apartment. Here it came. The coup de` etat. Turning around slowly, David said, "Must I remind you of the chain of command and the penalties for not following it?"

"Screw the chain of command," Lucas said. "We've got our own rules. It's based on seniority, so I'm in charge, with Cassie second."

David's eyes narrowed. Although the two standing before him had evolved, like him, they were messing with destiny. And everyone knows you can't mess with destiny. As a distraction, David started to say, "I suppose we could work something—" and then with incredible speed of hand—faster than any pickpocket, or card-hiding cheat gambler, or magician with a renowned disappearing act—he extracted his sword and backhanded it at Lucas, who stood a few feet away.

Lucas reacted quickly, grabbing his own sword hilt, but it was too late. David's sword pierced the skin on Lucas's left breast, leaving only the silver hilt in view at the front—David assumed at least half the blade-end of the weapon was now protruding from Lucas's back. By the time the blade had pierced his once-upon-a-time master, David had already moved in its wake; he was now close enough to grab the handle once again.

When he pulled, however, the sword only retracted about an inch before stopping. Not skin, nor organs, nor even bone would be capable of holding fast to an angel sword, so David looked around his dying—or maybe already dead—opponent, to see what might be causing the problem.

He saw the sword coming and ducked. Cassandra's blade snipped a lock of wavy hair from his head. With nothing supporting his body, Lucas collapsed to the ground, leaving David exposed. In the split-second before Cassandra attacked again, he could see the reason for his stuck sword. The clever Cassandra had bent the blade to the side, flush with Lucas's back, in an L-shape. And angel swords could not be bent easily. She was strong—incredibly strong. And fast.

She leapt at him, whipping her sword around like freaking Zorro. Somehow David managed to dodge each attempted killing stroke. Wanting to end the fight early, Cassandra thrust wildly for his heart—but David was expecting the maneuver. Even before she had fully committed herself, he sensed what she was about to do and purposely left himself exposed to just such an attempt. When she outstretched her arm to stab him, he spun gracefully, allowing the tip of Cassandra's weapon to barely cut a tatter of cloth from the side of his coat. As he spun, he moved towards her, getting inside the range of her sword strokes.

With all the power he could muster, David let loose a booming punch to her face. The blow—which was infused with the power of light—sent a shock through him, and presumably her as well, as it threw her across the room. She smashed against the far wall, and crumpled in a heap on top of the bloody carcass of victim number one, the old guy.

David was already moving.

In one deft motion, he wrenched Lucas's sword from its sheath, hopped over him, and took his first stride towards Cassandra, who was pulling herself up awkwardly. She had lost her weapon when she flailed through the air. Spotting it on the worn carpet, she rushed to it, grabbing the handle to raise it. It didn't move. David's heel was jammed down hard on the broad side, holding it firmly in place.

Cassandra froze.

David smiled.

She said, "David…don't. If you don't, I will obey you forever. I will be your slave, and you will be my master."

"Talk is cheap," David snarled, bringing his blade down across her neck. The two thuds that followed were like music to his ears.

Thirty-Six

"Eight ball, corner pocket," Taylor said. A firm tap, a clink, and a plunk, and it was over.

"Nice shot, Tay," Sam said. "When did you get good at pool?"

Taylor shrugged. "I guess it has to do with the angel thing. Better vision, better hand-eye coordination, that kind of thing." She and Kiren had won three in a row thanks to Taylor's streak of not missing a shot. Chris and Sam—not used to losing—were struggling to get even one ball in.

Chris's phone rang. "It's Clifford," he said, and suddenly all eyes were on him. And ears too—listening to his side of the conversation and straining to hear the other side through the muffled speaker on his ear.

"Yes, sir. I understand……..Of course………That will not be a problem, sir. Thank you." Chris, who had been focused on something on the ground—his own feet, or a speck of dirt perhaps—looked up to see six eyeballs boring into his. "He did it," Chris said. "Clifford is fighting Dionysus tomorrow night, one on one. Of course, they both know it's a trap, but both think their trap will be more effective. I guess that's up to us."

"We'll do it for Clifford," Kiren said.

"No," Chris said, "we're doing it for the entire world."

Sam said, "I don't care if you do it for the haunting ghost of Elvis, just do it."

Taylor said, "Personally, I'm doing it for all of monkeydom. The poor little guys just want to swing from the trees, eat bananas, and throw their own poop at tourists. Who am I to deny them that?" Managing to keep a straight face during her monologue, Taylor finally cracked a smile when Sam snorted while trying to hold in a laugh. Then they all laughed together. Kiren snickered, Chris chortled, Sam giggled through the hand clamped over her mouth, and Taylor chuckled. And Taylor was glad. A little pre-mission-that-might-end-in-death laughter was good for them. Everything had been too serious lately. Way too serious.

When the last of the laughs had passed, Taylor said, "So when do we start the mission to save the marsupials?"

which started a whole new round of laughter. When they finally managed to wipe away the tears, catch their breaths, and hold onto their heaving stomachs, Taylor said, "Sorry, sorry, I couldn't help myself."

In between deep breaths, Chris said, "It's going down tomorrow at midnight. Dionysus chose the location: the Warrior's Plateau. It's like he wants to prove that he can defeat us where Taylor hurt him the most."

Kiren said, "But isn't there a—"

"Battle?" Chris said. "Yes. Coincidentally the armies are scheduled to fight a rare midnight battle tomorrow as well. Neither side has requested to cancel, so it's still on. While their leaders are doing battle, the armies will be waging war, possibly for the final time."

Chris's words were serious, ominous, and yet Taylor couldn't seem to keep a straight face. Cracking a smile, she said, "For the monkeys?"

Chris laughed. "If you say so."

"I do."

Sam said, "Taylor, given you are killing us every game anyway, do you want to go for a walk? Around UT maybe?"

The thought of UT, of college, of girls and guys carrying books and backpacks around, to class, to the library, suddenly gave Taylor the desire to be there. "Sure, let's go," she said.

Chris said, "You'll take your guards with you?" He phrased it like a question, but Taylor knew it was really a command.

"Yes, Dad," Taylor joked.

Sam giggled and grabbed Taylor's hand, pulling her towards the door. As soon as she could, Taylor shook her friend's hand away. "We can walk and talk, but none of that girly crap," Taylor said.

"We'll see," Sam said, smirking.

Taylor located one of her guards and told him what they wanted to do. He spoke sharply into his headset and half a dozen other demons were by their side in a matter of minutes. They made their way to the teleport room, and soon were back in their dorm room.

"When you leave your dorm, we'll stay close," the demon guard said, before teleporting away.

"I want to kill Dionysus and end the War just so I can get rid of those guys," Taylor said.

"I think it's kind of cool, like you are famous and have your own entourage," Sam said.

"Based on that comment, I think it was really meant to be you who evolved into an angel."

"Yeah right, Tay. I don't think I could lift a sword, much less fight with one."

They left the room and marched down seven flights of stairs because the elevator was broken again. Once outside, Taylor tried to ignore the shadowy escorts that tracked their every move.

Neither of the girls really led, but somehow they walked together, in the same direction, turning at the same times, no question about where they were heading. Except neither of them really knew where they were going. At least Taylor didn't. While they walked, they talked.

"Sometimes it feels like all of this is just a dream," Sam said.

"Yeah, and you're not the one with wings."

"Do you think it might be?"

"Try pinching yourself," Taylor advised.

A moment later, Sam yelped, "Oww!"

Taylor laughed. "That was my reaction when I did it. Definitely not a dream. That trick works every time in dreams."

"Will our lives ever be the same?"

"Do you want them to be?"

There was silence for a moment while Sam thought about it. "Sort of, I guess. Not having to worry about your best friend and boyfriend dying, not being kidnapped and forced to live with the rats…"

"There were rats?" Taylor interrupted. "How did you cope with that?"

"I think not having a mirror or makeup was worse," Sam joked, or at least Taylor hoped she was joking but feared she wasn't.

Taylor said, "I think once the War is over, things will sort of go back to being the same. I mean, there will still be the absolutely unbelievable crazy things, like me and my boyfriend having wings, your boyfriend lighting candles with his finger, and Gabriel and I one day giving birth to a gargoyle, but—"

"You're already thinking about having kids with Gabriel?" Sam asked incredulously.

"Sam—you've known me for how long? Our entire lives. I was kidding. In any case, it will be you and Chris who are having little demon babies. You'll have to fireproof the whole house and white picket fence."

Sam laughed and said, "And who knows what Kiren and Sampson will have. It will be the first half-demon, half-angel offspring. A new species perhaps. So what you're saying is that things will never really be the same?"

"Not exactly the same, no. But all the worry about friends dying may go away, and that's really the only bad thing, isn't it?"

"I guess so," Sam said.

"We will win tomorrow," Taylor said.

"I know you will, Tay. I believe in you more than anyone else."

"You're nuts."

"No, really, Taylor. Gabriel and Chris are strong, capable, determined. But you're all those things, too. And more so. I still trust you above all other people."

"I said no girly, mushy stuff!"

"No, you never said mushy, just girly. In any case, I'm going to have to insist just this once." Sam put her arm around Taylor's shoulder and squeezed. Taylor started to shrug her off, but then stopped. She knew Sam needed it, and she probably did too. Putting her arm around Sam, she squeezed back and they walked across campus, supporting each other the way they had their whole lives.

Thirty-Seven

The hall was filling up. Angels poured in from three separate entrances, filing down the aisles to the first unfilled row and then moving to the center of each row in an orderly fashion. They left no seats unused.

The hall was really an old movie theater that had been purchased years ago as the angel population had grown. Martin had explained it all on the way over, while driving with one hand and talking to someone on the phone with the other. Evidently the place had been quite popular fifty years earlier when it showed the latest movies starring actors and actresses like John Wayne, Sean Connery, Julie Andrews, and Audrey Hepburn. When business declined, it eventually changed management and was converted into a two dollar cinema, showing movies that had been out for a few months already. When the Angel Council of New York, under Martin's name, made an offer to buy the old theater for three times the value, the owner readily agreed. The walls between the six screens had been torn down and a much larger single hall was built. It was used to hold regularly scheduled Council meetings.

Today's meeting was a rare emergency meeting, and the hall was buzzing with speculation as to why the assembly might have been called. Despite the late hour, five minutes to midnight, all eyes were open wide, focused, interested. Gabriel sat in a chair on a raised stage. He was next to Martin, who sat next to eleven other angels—each were leaders of the local Angel Council, of which all other angels living in New York were members.

On Martin's advice, none of the other leaders had been briefed on the purpose of the meeting. He believed the best approach was to try to get popular support from the members first, and in that way force the leaders, who represented the members, to support their cause too.

Sampson sat in the first row and was expected to provide testimony to the truthfulness of Gabriel's words.

Gabriel tried to look calm, confident, although he was acutely aware of the many interested eyes looking at him from the crowd. They wouldn't be used to seeing a thirteenth angel sitting in a position of honor, especially not one so young. Although he managed to sit still, inside he was squirming in his seat, nervous.

Once every seat had been filled and the latecomers had taken a standing position in the back, Martin stood. He looked even taller than usual. He wore a striped button-down shirt and a polka-dot bow tie. He stood at a podium in the center of the stage. The microphone carried his voice to the outer reaches of the expansive room: "Friends, leaders of the Council, and guests, thank you for coming on such short notice. Most all of you know me, and many of you know me quite well, and I hope you believe I am of such a character that I would not call such a quick and ill-planned meeting if it were not to discuss matters of the utmost importance."

While Martin spoke, Gabriel watched the crowd, gauging reactions. When he said the word *guests* most eyes flicked over to him for a moment, before moving back to the speaker. Most heads were nodding when Martin spoke of his relationship with them. Nothing negative—so far.

Martin continued: "Tonight I have a message of deceit, one that will be difficult to receive, to believe, to conceive, even under the best of circumstances. And instead, we are under the worst of circumstances as you will find out soon, making the message infinitely harder to discern as truth. I implore you all to open your ears, your hearts, to see the truth behind this message."

Gabriel was impressed with how his uncle could work the room. As he spoke, he swept his arms and eyes across the grand hall, almost beckoning each angel in attendance to come to him. The angels leaned in, hanging on his every word, as if he were a prophet presenting the meaning of life. Clearly, he had experience. Gabriel had none. He had commanded troops before, but that was from a position of power, to those who were trained to obey him. Now he would be speaking from an inferior position, to ears that had no reason to take him seriously. In fact, they had every reason not to listen. Five decades of knowledge would defy his every word.

His uncle had told him to present his message with the same passion that he had used to defend himself in Martin's living room. Gabriel hoped he would be able to do just that when the time came.

Abruptly, Martin said, "While I have heard the fullness of the story you are about to hear, it would be better told by one who has lived it, participated in it. I present to you—Gabriel Knight. Some of you may know him already."

The crowd applauded as Gabriel rose to his feet, but he suspected it was for the departing speaker, not for him.

He walked into the spotlight that was focused on the podium, cringing as the light hit him, as if the bright rays had caused him physical pain. It was the first time in his life that he felt threatened by the power of light. In this case, the only danger was that it illuminated him.

He tried to find his words as he scanned the audience, looking for a friendly face. Instead, all he received were intense stares. Not angry, but focused. He took a couple of deep breaths, trying to calm his hammering heart.

It seemed like he had been standing there, unspeaking, for at least five minutes. But the crowd hadn't grown restless yet, so it had probably only been about ten seconds. He began, his words clear and determined, and he marveled at the firmness of his voice, unsure of where the steadiness came from when he was quavering on the inside. He wondered if he was even the one speaking, or if Martin had stood to relieve him.

"I echo Martin's words of thanks to you all for coming tonight." A reference to Martin—Gabriel's heart leapt as he realized he was the one speaking. And he was off to a good start!

"The words I bring are hard for me to impart. Because I was brought up like many of you. Taught well, trained well. I was a scrub in the army, and then Junior Special Missions Leader, and finally, Leader of the Special Missions Corps." There were a few murmurs in the crowd. Whispers. The Special Missions Corps was known to be reserved for only the most talented angels. He was building his credibility. Another one of Martin's ideas.

When the audience quieted down, Gabriel continued: "Yes, I did well for myself, was on the fast track to the top...but I was deceived." More murmuring. "I've made many mistakes in my life. I will tell you the biggest of them tonight in the hope that you can learn from me."

Gabriel could tell the audience was captivated, hanging on his every word, their eyes on him, their ears tilted towards the podium. After a quick request to allow him to finish his entire story without interruption, Gabriel began. Like he had with Martin, he started from the beginning. The more details the better, he and Martin had agreed. Details would make his story believable, credible.

For the better part of two hours he plodded along, telling his tale. When he arrived at the present, to his current mission, he said, "I am not here to persuade you to join the demons in the fight against Dionysus. I am only here to give you the facts, to finally tell the truth that has been hidden for years, to allow you all to make an informed decision. I'm happy to take questions at this time."

Silence. One beat, two, and then: Chaos.

The room erupted in a disorganized smattering of discussion amongst peers, questions and comments shouted from the room, and a mixture of applause and boos. Gabriel stood stock-still, unsure of how to regain control of the restless crowd. Thankfully, Martin shouldered him aside gently and shouted, "ORDER! ORDER!"

There was a gradual dulling of the noise and then the clamoring voices stopped altogether. Martin said, "Please, friends, we know that was a lot to hear, and it is late, but this must proceed in an organized fashion. Please raise your hands with questions."

At least a hundred hands shot up, more than a few of them from the leaders sitting on the stage. Martin pointed to a middle-aged woman sitting near Sampson in the front. "Yes, Ms. Baker, what is your question?"

The woman stood and said, "Why should we take one man's word over years of history?"

Before Martin or Gabriel could respond, Sampson stood. "If I may," he said to Martin.

"Yes, please, come forward," Martin said.

Sampson leapt casually onto the stage and wedged himself in between Gabriel and Martin so he could speak into the microphone. "Friends," he said, "it is not only one angel's words, but many, including mine. I have seen the treachery at the uppermost levels of angel leadership. I was in the army. I heard things that caused me to question my beliefs and eventually to move over to the demons. What I have seen since then would tie your stomachs in knots, would make you cringe. Dionysus has corrupted us all, although most of us aren't even aware of it. We send our children, our friends, our families off to war. A war that is being fought for all the wrong reasons, against the wrong enemy. There are many others like me, who chose to question the status quo. They couldn't be here today because they are fighting against their brothers, their sisters. Not because they want to, but because they have to, because it's the right thing to do." Sampson finished strongly, stepping away from the stand amidst a small dose of applause.

Gabriel had never seen the level of intensity, of passion, of leadership that was being shown by his best friend. Duly impressed, he shook Sampson's hand firmly before he stepped down and retook his seat.

Gabriel said, "Next question?"

A house of a man stood up on the stage—one of the Council leaders. Despite not having a microphone, his voice thundered through the hall, like he was a god shouting down from the clouds, as if he were Zeus himself. "I don't care if you have a thousand witnesses. We need proof! What acts of treachery has Dionysus committed? I have seen nothing, only a man who has strived to protect humankind from the greatest force of evil the world has ever seen—the demons!"

Gabriel started to answer, wanted to answer, to rebuke the ignorant fool, to put him in his place, to outline the evils that had occurred under Dionysus's reign, but Martin, probably realizing the rise in Gabriel's blood pressure, stepped in front of him and said, "There will be proof, very soon, but for now you will have to rely on the testimony of our witnesses."

The house shook his head and sat down, muttering, "You won't get my vote without proof."

Martin said, "Other questions?"

Another hundred hands. Martin said, "Yes, Professor Strambaugh, in the eighth row."

A white-haired man with an impressive comb-over stood. "Why are all the witnesses of such a youthful age?

If there was true corruption in the angel ranks, I would expect there to be others of greater *experience* that would be aware of it."

Gabriel smiled. He had been waiting for this question and thus, had saved his secret weapon for this very moment. Not even Martin knew what was about to happen.

"Thank you, Professor. A valid point, one that will soon be rectified. I'd like to invite the guests onto the stage." Gabriel extended an inviting arm to the side of the auditorium.

A family of three angels made their way down the aisle: a dad, a mom, and a child who was perhaps seven- or eight-years-old. A gasp came from the audience as many recognized the guest speakers. Martin was smiling. Gabriel said, "Thanks for coming, Mom, Dad, Peter."

Helena Knight hugged her son and then took a wide, commanding stance across the podium. Theodore Knight shook Gabriel's hand and stood to the side, allowing his wife to speak. Gabriel put an arm around his younger brother, Peter, who was looking at his feet, clearly embarrassed to be in front of so many angels.

"Every word my son has spoken tonight is true," Helena said forcefully. As she spoke, Gabriel watched the crowd for reactions. They seemed to be mesmerized. Sensing movement to the side, Gabriel glanced over at the Council leaders. Half were hanging on every word, and the other half were engaged in tense discussion. The house-sized angel seemed to be leading the whispery conversation.

Helena continued: "A few months ago I was sitting in the same place as you are now. I would never have believed the fantastical story that you have heard tonight. As far as I knew, my eldest son, Gabriel, and his best friend, Sampson, were young men serving in an army that was protecting humankind, protecting my husband, our way of life, everything that I hold dear. Then Dionysus's hit squad entered my home without invitation, abused my family, abducted us, and used us as a lure to recapture Gabriel, who had made the hardest decision of his life, the rightest decision of his life: to join the demons. I was rescued, along with my family, by Gabriel and a convoy of angels and demons alike, fighting alongside each other for the truth. Since then we have been sheltered, fed, and protected by the demons, who are not—I can assure you—the enemy."

Helena paused, taking a deep breath. Gabriel was so proud of his mother, but was frustrated by the five or six Council leaders who were ignoring her speech. He was not surprised when the house stood and spoke.

"No proof I tell you! For all we know, these angels have been abducted and brainwashed by the demons to be used to set a trap for us all. Without proof, your testimony is useless."

Heads in the crowd nodded and a few angels yelled, "Yeah!" or "Give us proof!"

Gabriel knew they were in trouble. With half the Council leaders against them, they would likely lose the remaining leaders, which would put them at a big disadvantage when trying to convince the rest of the members.

That's when a miracle occurred. A miracle mired in tragedy.

Thirty-Eight

There was no need to dispose of the bodies. Once dead, Lucas's and Cassandra's bodies turned to light, flashing away into oblivion. David didn't believe they went to the stars like the legends said. They were just gone. Which was good. Because they had been annoying him. Things were much easier when it was just his opinion that mattered.

He left the human bodies to rot. Eventually some neighbor would smell something, or a relative would come to visit them, or the mailman would realize they never collected their letters from the box. The cops would be called and an investigation would begin. David would be long gone by then.

He stepped outside and a brisk wind hit his face. To his left was an empty sidewalk. To his right the gang of punks were still laughing and smoking on the stoop. *Screw it*, he thought. Nightfall was too far off, he wanted some action now.

He approached the one in the middle, a big black guy with lots of bling bling. The others looked at him with respect; he was probably the leader.

"What joo want, fool?" the guy said.

David was tempted to shut him up the fun way, but thought better of it, and said, "What are you sellin'?"

"I ain't sellin' nothin', man. You some white cracker undercover cop or somethin' comin' up in here with them rags on?" A couple of the other guys had stood up, flanking the leader, who remained seated.

Before reaching his hand into his coat, David said, "I'm going to show you some money and you tell me whether undercover cops would be carrying this kind of dough." Slowly, David extracted the billfold from his pocket, making a point of showing it to them as he removed it.

The leader jumped up and shouted, "Put that away, dude, what joo tryin' to do, get us all arrested, man?"

David was surprised by the reaction but obediently slipped the cash back into his coat pocket.

"What joo lookin' for?" the leader said.

"Whatever you got. My boss just wants whatever I can get him," David lied smoothly.

"Who's yo' boss?"

"No names, please."

"Follow me," the leader said. He snapped his fingers and the two guys that were already standing each grabbed one of David's arms and led him down the block. The leader followed behind. David cringed at the humans' touch, even though there were a few layers of clothing between them and his skin. The urge to lash out at them rose up, but David swallowed and forced it back down. *Be smart*, he thought.

The guys turned right down an alley and led him behind a dumpster. David waited patiently for the leader to catch up. When they were all there, he said, "I'm sorry, but I might have lied to you." The trio frowned, confused, and started to grab him, but they were too slow. He drove his right forearm into the left guy's skull, hearing it crack beneath the force, and then launched a wicked right-footed kick at the right guy. His heel connected solidly with the guy's chin, which snapped upwards violently. Both men went down hard.

The leader backed away, pleading for his life. "Please, man, why joo doin' this?" David knew the guy was acting, trying to distract him, to buy time. With a practiced precision, his hand went for his pocket, and he whipped out a large handgun, aiming it at David's head. "Die," he said as he pulled the trigger.

David was already unsheathing his sword when the trigger was pulled. The bullet left the muzzle when he slashed upwards. Two tiny pings sounded from the hard asphalt at his feet. The leader looked down to see what had made the sound. When he saw the two halves of the bullet rolling at David's feet, he looked up at him with wide eyes. "Who the hell are you?" he said.

"Death," David said before slashing his sword.

The man's scream would surely bring the rest of his gang running. He took two more swipes, one at each of the downed bodyguards, finishing them off before the first of the gang members rounded the corner.

Their toy guns were already drawn.

David smiled.

Thirty-Nine

Darkness fell and the killing continued.

After the gang, David had reveled in the beauty of human death. Perhaps he had lingered for too long. Perhaps a few witnesses had come around. He couldn't leave witnesses so he used his sword again and again until he heard the police sirens.

With no other option, he spread his wings and took to the sky. A guy in an approaching TV van might have spotted him, but he couldn't risk going back.

He flew a few miles and then landed on an apartment building where a lady was clipping wet linens to a line. She screamed. He liked the sound and wanted to hear it again, but didn't have time so he quickly put an end to the noise. Her whites were no longer white.

From there he entered the apartment building from the roof and methodically picked his way along the corridors, entering apartments uninvited and ending lives. Pleasure. Pure pleasure.

More sirens. Someone had tipped off the cops. He leapt from a window, smashing through the glass because it wasn't open. He flew. Saw a man with a camera taking a picture. But he didn't care. What was the stupid photographer gonna do? David was invincible, untouchable, and soon he would rule the world, along with Dionysus of course. But for the moment he was the king.

As dusk fell, David knew that more than one hundred had fallen to his sword. That would get the angels' attention. That was the plan, after all. He had done well. Dionysus would reward him. Dionysus would understand why Lucas and Cassandra had to be dealt with swiftly and harshly.

The sun was gone and David was flying home just when the mission was supposed to begin. Dionysus would be surprised to see him home early. Surprised, but pleased.

David smiled. It had been a good day.

Forty

An angel burst into the hall, shouting something that Gabriel couldn't understand. All heads turned to see what all the commotion was about. Martin said into the microphone, "Jason, what is it, what's the matter?"

"New York is under attack!" Jason yelled, still running down the aisle.

Gabriel later found out that Jason was a reporter for the *Times*. He often worked the late shift to help the paper meet its deadlines.

"Under attack by whom?" Martin demanded.

Reaching the stage, Jason leapt up and spoke directly to Martin and into the microphone at the same time. His voice echoed throughout the hall, bouncing off the walls hollowly and spinning across the rows. "By an angel—or at least one angel," he said, sounding like he wasn't even sure if he believed his own statement.

"Tell us," Martin prompted.

As if finally realizing he was not only speaking to Martin, but to a large audience, Jason's head jerked to face the crowd. His eyes were wild, scared. "I've been following a breaking story all day. There's a homicidal maniac rampaging across the city, slashing, cutting, piercing, stabbing. Killing. Killing people. All dead, all of them. They never had a chance. He's bold. And getting bolder. Killing more openly. Not afraid of being seen."

Jason paused to take a breath, and immediately the house stood up. "Another witness—a member of the Council, yes, but still no proof. Angels don't attack humans...ever. We are their protectors. It is probably just a human killing other humans."

Jason said, "It's *not* a human. I have proof, I do." He lowered his head and lifted a strap over it. Only then did Gabriel notice the camera hanging from his neck. A nice camera, an expensive camera, a camera full of proof. The proof they needed.

"I have photographs," Jason said. He pressed a button on his camera and Gabriel looked over his shoulder while Martin leaned in. A photo flashed on the digital screen. Gabriel noticed the wings right away. The angel was flying—buildings could be seen around him. Jason cycled to the next photo. Dead bodies—and lots of them. Slashed, torn, bloody. All dead. Next photo: more bodies, massacred. Looked like gang members; they had the same tattoo on their forearms. Tough guys, hardened by tough lives, not easily killed. It would take another gang—or a New Archangel. Another photo of the angel, this time zoomed in closer.

Gabriel shuddered. It was him. Not him, but looked like him. David. David was the homicidal maniac angel terrorizing the city. "Oh no," he breathed.

Jason looked back at him. "Do you know this angel?" His words sounded accusing as they projected through the speakers and out into the hall.

Gabriel said, "He's my brother, David. Dionysus's apprentice."

Footsteps boomed across the wooden stage. The house was approaching. "Let me see that," he growled, pulling the camera away from the reporter. A few seconds of silence as he cycled through the photos. "Proof...," he said, almost to himself. "I'll be damned," he whispered. As silent as the hall had become, Gabriel had no doubt that the giant angel's mutterings could be heard at the very back of the auditorium.

Looking up, the house's eyes were intense and serious. "We have to act fast. Nothing like this has ever happened," he said.

Gabriel said, "I know. That's what I've been trying to tell you all. Will you help me?"

The house nodded and then turned towards the rest of the Council leaders. "Who's with me?"

One by one they raised their fists in agreement. Gabriel's shoulders slumped. His mission was essentially over. With the support of the leaders, the members' agreement would shortly follow. And with New York on his side—along with the photographic evidence—the other major angel hubs would soon join the cause, too. London, Paris, Tokyo, L.A.: Thousands of angels would come together, united, to fight against a dictator, the angel version of Hitler or Hussein.

Gabriel should feel happy, but he didn't. He felt cold, lifeless, lost, defeated. His thoughts swirled aimlessly. *His brother. His brother. His brother. David. Not David. Not anymore. David was not David, not really.*

PART IV

"Another shot before we kiss the other side
Tonight, yeah baby
I'm on the edge of something final we call life tonight
Alright, alright

Pull on your shades 'cause I'll be dancing in the flames
Tonight, yeah baby
It doesn't hurt 'cause everybody knows my name tonight
Alright, alright

It's hard to feel the rush
To push the dangerous
I'm gonna run right to, to the edge with you
Where we can both fall over in love

I'm on the edge of glory
And I'm hanging on a moment of truth
Out on the edge of glory
And I'm hanging on a moment with you
I'm on the edge"

Lady Gaga- "Edge of Glory"
From the album *Born This Way (2011)*

Forty-One

A final hug and it was time. Sam looked at her seriously. "Don't get yourself killed, alright?"

Taylor said, "I'll be fine, I always have been."

"I know."

Taylor watched awkwardly as Chris embraced his girlfriend. As much as she hated to admit it, she missed Gabriel. She wished he was coming on the mission.

Earlier, she and Kiren had met with Clifford for an update on Gabriel's and Sampson's mission. He wouldn't tell them much, except to say that it was going extremely well and that their boyfriends were safe. She wondered why he was being so tight-lipped. The only thing she could come up with was that he didn't want to distract her from her own mission. *As long as Gabriel was okay*, she thought.

Taylor had spent the previous day hanging out with Sam. It was fun, like the old days—before serious boyfriends and wars. They ate ice cream and laughed. They went shopping, which Taylor normally hated, but enjoyed this time. They shot pool. While sharing a mushroom pizza for dinner, they reminisced about high school, back when times were simpler. For the first time in a few weeks, they both slept in their own beds alone, talking late into the night about everything and nothing. It was what Taylor needed.

Now she was focused on what she hoped would be the end of the Great War. She didn't know how to defeat Dionysus, but she knew she was capable. And she knew she would have Chris and Kiren with her, two of the most dependable friends she had ever had. Good friends, true friends.

It was time.

The mission team left together, walking side by side down the familiar tunnel, onto the transporter, and into the other familiar tunnel that led to the teleport room. Once inside, the threesome held hands. Chris said, "Ready?"

"Are you sure Rocky can't come along?" Taylor asked.

Chris laughed. "I don't think he would do too well on a stealth mission. Each of his legs weighs about a ton."

"I've seen him tiptoe; he can be quieter than you might think."

Chris said, "Maybe next time."

"I hope there isn't a next time," Taylor said.

Kiren said, "You say that now, but trust me, you'll miss it once it's gone."

Taylor knew she was right but didn't want to admit it. "Okay, ready," she said instead.

Twisting-turning-melting-spinning—the trio moved through a strange vortex. Taylor closed her eyes so she wouldn't get dizzy. When the motion stopped, she reopened them to a different world. The fiery torches had been replaced by the shining sun; the rocky walls were no more—she could see for miles in all directions, her view obstructed only by the twin mountain ranges that rose up on either side of the valley; the heavy, cavernous air had changed to fresh, sweet air, which she gulped at greedily.

Taylor's team was sitting in the uppermost branches of a pine tree that had grown high above one of the mountain peaks. The fresh smell of pine needles filled her nostrils, like the scent in a room just after a real Christmas tree had been erected.

"A tree, huh?" Taylor said.

"We look after our angel friends," Chris said. "Given you have wings like a bird, we thought you might prefer to nest in a tree. It's not our thing, but…"

"A ledge would have been just fine," Taylor said, smirking. The demons in the Lair were constantly teasing their angel guests, calling them various bird names, like robin, or sparrow. They shied away from using the term *pigeon*, which was considered derogatory by the angels. They also shied away from using grander bird names, like eagle or kingfisher, as the point was to get under the angels' skin, not compliment them. It was all in good fun and the angels certainly didn't back down, using nicknames like nightcrawler and hyena to describe their darker allies.

From the top of the tree, Taylor could see the Warrior's Plateau, the site of the fight between Clifford and Dionysus. The fight wasn't scheduled to start for hours, but they had arrived early to set up surveillance. They assumed the angels would do the same, so they had left two hours earlier than they would normally, to ensure they were the first ones on site. The stakes couldn't be higher, and they wanted to grab every advantage they could.

"How's Sam?" Chris asked.

"You should know, she's your girlfriend," Taylor said.

"Right. Do you always tell Gabriel exactly how you're feeling?"

"Sampson and I tell each other everything," Kiren interjected.

Taylor said, "Really? I think we hide our true feelings sometimes. I do it mostly because I don't want him to worry about me and hover over me like a concerned parent."

"He just does it because he loves you," Kiren said.

"I know, but it gets annoying."

Chris said, "I do it sometimes, too, because I'm expected to act tough and macho, but—"

"You're really just a big softie inside," Taylor finished. "I know, I know, you've said it before. What's your point?"

"My point is that I think Sam tries to act tough sometimes when I'm forced to put myself in dangerous situations. I'd like to know how she's really feeling."

Taylor said, "She's so scared she might pee herself. That's the truth. Now don't think about it or you're not gonna be able to do what you need to do."

Chris laughed. "You have a way with words, Taylor."

Something caught Taylor's eye. Turning her head to the left sharply, she discovered it was actually some*one*. An angel, given away by his dull glow, picked his way along the mountainside. *No, not just one angel, four.* Three glowing figures trailed behind the first, moving silently across the wooded slopes. Unless they happened to look up they wouldn't see their watchers.

Taylor whispered, "We've got company," and pointed below. Chris and Kiren peered through the branches.

Chris hissed, "The New Archangels: Johanna, Sarah, Percy, and…"

"David," Taylor said. Suddenly she was glad that Gabriel wasn't on the mission with them. While he knew his brother was dangerous, he also desperately wanted to talk to him, to reason with him, to make him understand. If he were here, he might try something stupid. And today needed to be a stupid-free day.

"They're setting up surveillance, too," Chris said. "I'm glad we got here earlier."

Taylor nodded. "They're missing Lucas and Cassandra," she noted.

Kiren said, "Maybe Dionysus doesn't trust them after the last time. Lucas nearly got killed and Cassandra was captured."

Chris shook his head. "They're too powerful to leave behind. If they're alive, they'll be here."

Taylor felt her fists squeeze tight. She almost hoped they *would* show up.

Forty-Two

Organizing a thousand angels had taken several hours and by the time they had finished, dawn was rising in the east. Not that they could tell—the hall had no windows or skylights.

Gabriel was satisfied with the plans that had been made. Two hundred angels had volunteered for city watch. They would disperse throughout the most densely populated areas of New York City, creating city protection units, or CPUs, communicating by cell phone in the event that one of the New Archangels began attacking humans again. In the short-term, Gabriel hoped they could prevent any further deaths until a more structured system could be developed.

Sampson would travel by teleport with a convoy of angel leaders—including Martin—to spread the truth about what Dionysus had really been planning. They would hit the five cities with the highest angel populations. Assuming the cooperation of the members of each local angel Council, CPUs would be set up in each city, and the remaining angels, if willing, would be sent to the Lair to join the demon army. Gabriel, and the approximately 800 other New York angels, would go immediately to the Lair to begin mustering for the battle scheduled for that night.

Gabriel yawned as weariness hit him. He rubbed his eyes and then blinked a few times to keep them open. "Surely the leader of the rebellion doesn't get tired," Sampson said, approaching him from the side.

"I'm just the messenger," Gabriel said. "And messengers get tired."

Sampson clapped a hand on his shoulder. "Whatever you are, well done. You're a great leader."

"I couldn't have done it without you, man. The way you spoke was impressive, but don't let it go to your head. Honestly though, I'm not sure either of us could have done it without Jason showing up at the last minute with the horrible news."

Martin joined the conversation. He said, "Dionysus didn't realize that his little human killing mission would help to start a rebellion."

Gabriel shook his head. He was still shocked that it was his brother who had done the killing. It was all over the news: radio, television, and print. The public had been advised by local police to travel in groups in well-lit areas and to keep doors locked at all times. Luckily, no other reporters—other than Jason—had been able to capture David flying away from the crime scenes. Jason wouldn't submit the pictures to the *Times*, although several witnesses had claimed to have seen a winged man soaring through the air. None were being taken seriously yet by police, as each of their stories were quite different and ranged from little green men from Mars to masked and caped superheroes. The word *angel* hadn't been used by anyone yet, although *serial killer* had been used several times.

"When do you leave?" Gabriel asked Martin.

"In a few minutes. At Robert's request, one of your demon friends is doing a few practice teleports so the leaders can get a feel for it before they're taken halfway around the world in the blink of an eye."

Gabriel laughed. It was bizarre to see demons walking amongst the throngs of angels. He had found out that the house-like angel that had been their biggest opponent during the meeting was named Robert, and that since seeing the photographs he had become their staunchest supporter. He would be going with Martin to convince others to support the cause.

Sampson said, "We'll move from city to city as quickly as possible so we can get back in time for the battle tonight."

"Okay," Gabriel said. "Speaking of which, I should get going to arrange things on the demon side."

Gabriel shook both of his friends' hands, holding Martin's for an extra second as he said, "Thank you, Martin. Your help will save many lives today."

Martin just nodded, but the emotion in his eyes conveyed far more meaning than words ever could. Respect, admiration, brotherhood, truth, and light were all reflected in his dark pupils.

Gabriel turned and looked for the demon who would be coordinating the teleports to the Lair. He spotted the dark, mohawked guy chatting with two female demons. Gabriel had heard he was quite the ladies' man. "Jeremy, are you ready to start?" Gabriel said.

"Sure, boss," he said, winking at one of the demons, who immediately blushed.

"You don't have to call me *boss*," Gabriel said.

"Okay, boss," Jeremy said. The other female demon laughed like it was the funniest thing she had ever heard.

Gabriel said, "What's the best way to approach this, a mass teleport?"

"Bad idea, boss. You see, while it can be done, there is a high risk of something logistical going wrong on the other end. The last thing you want are 800 angels appearing in the wrong place in the Lair. There would be mass panic, with demons thinking they were under attack."

"Okay, then how do we do it?"

Jeremy ran one hand over his mohawk while playing with his earing with his other hand. "I propose using the standard method, via the teleport room. The room can only fit 20 bodies at a time, plus the escort, so that's 40 trips. But if we organize things well on the receiving end, we can get each group out of the room and into the tunnel in less than a minute, so we should be able to transport everyone in less than an hour."

"Okay," Gabriel said. "Let's do it."

"Righteous," Jeremy said.

Gabriel went first, with Jeremy and a few other demons. Two seconds later, they arrived thousands of miles away, deep inside the Lair.

Gabriel said, "Recruit as many angels and demons as you can to welcome the incoming angels to the Lair. Take all of them to get food first and then to the armory. I will address them after they have been fitted for armor and armed."

"Will do, boss," Jeremy said.

With the arrangements made, Gabriel took off down the hall, reaching the outer security door a second later. The door opened for him and he entered. The five minute transporter ride felt slow. Gabriel was eager to see Taylor, to tell her the good news.

Exiting the transporter, Gabriel's heart jumped slightly in his chest. He was as giddy as a school boy and suddenly he felt ridiculous. "What is wrong with you?" he said to himself. He had only been apart from Taylor for a day and yet he was acting like he had gone off to war months ago. Speaking to himself once more, he said, "Get a grip on yourself, man."

He stopped to take a deep breath. His heart stopped wobbling around in his chest. *Good*, he thought. First he checked the room she usually stayed in when she was visiting the Lair. Knock, knock. No answer. Next he went to Sam's room but she wasn't there either. Pool hall, demon café, gargoyle paddocks: no, no, no.

Finally, Gabriel caught a transporter to the Elders' wing, to which he had full access. Clifford's office door was open so he walked in, rapping lightly on the door as he passed it.

The old demon looked up from beneath dark, bushy eyebrows, his black eyes speckled with the reflecting light from the lit candles that lined the walls.

"Gabriel! Welcome back," Clifford said warmly. "And congratulations are in order I believe."

Gabriel smiled and said, "I had a lot of help. Sampson, Martin, my mother, and…." Gabriel's smile dissipated.

"And evil," Clifford finished. "You can only control what you can control, Gabriel. If the whole universe bent to your will this would have been over long, long ago, for better or for worse."

Gabriel said, "I want to build my anger, harness it, use it to fight….But I can't. I can't. Whenever I do, I just get sad. He was….is so young." Gabriel realized his fists were clenched tightly at his sides, his knuckles white from the tension. They were beginning to ache. He saw Clifford's eyes flick to his fists and then back to his face.

"Those fists look pretty angry," Clifford said.

"Yes, but not at my brother. At Dionysus, Lucas, whoever else was involved in corrupting him." Suddenly remembering why he had come, Gabriel said, "Taylor—where is she?"

"On her mission."

"But I thought it was scheduled for tonight, I was hoping to see her."

"Early surveillance. Don't worry, she's with Chris and Kiren."

"I'm not worried, I just wanted to wish her luck." Gabriel was tempted to request to be included on her mission, but held his tongue. He already knew the response he would get and wasn't in the mood to hear Clifford talk about legends and rebellions and the chosen one. He was just a damn angel. An angel who had done a lot of stupid things. No one special.

Clifford said, "You can go with her if you want."

Gabriel's head spun. That was the last thing he expected to hear come out of Clifford's mouth. *Go with her.*

It sounded so good. He looked at his hands, trying to understand. His eyes snapped back to Clifford's. The old demon's eyes were sparkling—tongues of flame danced across the obsidian orbs. Except this time it wasn't from the reflection of the candles. His eyes were actually engulfed in real flames. Gabriel jumped back in his chair and teetered for a moment, before grabbing the desk in front of him to prevent himself from falling backwards.

"Ho ho ho," Clifford laughed, as his eyes returned to normal. "I haven't used that party trick in a long time considering all of my parties are with demons who would think nothing of it."

Gabriel stared at the old man like he was crazy. He had never seen this side of him. "You're in a good mood," Gabriel said.

"And why shouldn't I be? Tonight we end the War."

Clifford's words were so honest, so determined, so matter-of-fact, that Gabriel couldn't help thinking they must be true, like the old demon had been blessed with clairvoyance.

Despite every bone, tendon, and muscle in his body shuddering with excitement at the prospect of accompanying Taylor on her mission, Gabriel found himself saying, "I'll lead the army. If that's okay with you, of course."

Clifford laughed again, deep and throaty. "You already know what I think. You have your orders. Go, Gabriel. Meet your destiny."

Gabriel stood and left. The word *destiny* rang through his ears and he tried to block it out, but couldn't. He couldn't ignore the authority behind Clifford's words. It felt like Clifford had become the master of the universe, and he a puppet, certain to perform exactly as Clifford desired him to. It was comforting, in a way. Like he couldn't fail, even if he did something stupid. To his surprise, he swelled with courage, with confidence, with determination.

He would lead the first ever full angel-demon army. And he would be victorious.

Forty-Three

She couldn't bear to wait in the Lair so she went back to campus, to her dorm room. Dusk had come and gone and she had stared at the ceiling, seeing nothing. Instead, still-pictures cycled through her mind. None of her visions were from the past, none of them real; rather, they were from a future not yet decided.

Squeezing her eyes tightly shut, Samantha tried to remember all the good times, tried to conjure up images of true memories, good memories, happy memories. To her frustration, her visions of the future continued their endless cycling.

There was one with Taylor soaring through the air, headed for battle, her helmet shiny and bright. That one was impossible though, the battle would occur at night, no shining, no brightness.

Another showed Chris's mouth wide open, as he took a blow on the shoulder from an attacking angel. She could almost hear his pained scream torturing the quiet of the night.

Next there was a vision of Gabriel, hopelessly outnumbered and clanging swords with three angels simultaneously.

Stop, stop, stop, "Stop!" she finally yelled. Unintentionally, her thoughts had spilled from her mouth, breaking free of her skull. "It will be okay," she said to herself. She checked the clock: Eight o'clock, four hours to go.

Unable to wait any longer, Sam left, looking for a distraction. She was vaguely aware of the dark shapes that followed her across campus—her loyal protectors. She worried that if they were protecting her, they couldn't be helping to fight in the battle. She was having trouble breathing, trouble thinking clearly: the effects of anxiety, stress. Desperately, she searched for a distraction.

Moving past the library, she headed for the center of campus. Her mind continued working overtime, and not in a good way. She envisioned Chris bleeding, yelling for help, black liquid streaming from his head. Gabriel tried to come to him, but staggered, unable to maintain his balance. He was bleeding too, the bright, white fluid washing over his arms much faster than she thought possible. And then she saw Taylor, her wings hanging uselessly from her back, tattered and mangled. Fighting another angel; losing her sword; pierced by her enemy; collapsing.

"Sam... Sam!"

"Wh...what?" Samantha said, startled out of her trance by a familiar voice. She turned, searching for the source of her name.

First she saw the tall, skinny guy with glasses. The voice had been a girl's, probably hadn't come from the guy unless puberty had been particularly unkind to him. Next to him: a tiny girl with no more meat on her than a Chihuahua.

"Marla?" Sam said. "What are you doing here?"

"I go to school here, remember," Marla said, laughing. "Jenkins does too."

"Good one, honey," Jenkins said, squeezing his girlfriend's hand.

"Right, sorry. I was kind of thinking about something," Sam explained.

"We called your name about ten times," Marla said.

"Really? I only heard it twice."

"Must have been some pretty intense thinking," Jenkins said.

"Yeah, I guess it was," Sam said.

Marla eyed her strangely, as if something on Sam's face was communicating with her. "Hey, do you want to hang out with us tonight? We were thinking of having a pizza and movies night."

Sam smiled for the first time in hours. Her mouth felt stiff, like it wasn't used to such a foreign expression. "Actually, Marla, that would be perfect," she said.

Forty-Four

Thirty minutes to go. Taylor was still in the tree, still with Chris and Kiren, still scoping out the area surrounding the Warrior's Plateau. She stepped down to a lower branch and stood up, stretching her legs. Everything hurt from a long day spent stationary. Her legs and arms ached, her back was stiff and sore, and her butt throbbed where the thin branch had been pressing up against it.

Earlier, the enemy angel foursome had passed below them and moved a half-mile further down the mountain range, eventually entering a hidden cave situated high above the valley, which would likely provide a good view of the site of the Clifford vs. Dionysus fight. Surely they weren't there just to watch, like a pay-per-view boxing match. They were there to kill Clifford and to protect Dionysus. A trap, albeit one that was expected. *At least they knew where the enemy was*, Taylor thought. As far as they knew, their presence remained a secret.

In addition to loosening her knotted muscles and tight joints, Taylor prepared mentally for what lay ahead. *No monkeys*, she thought. No monkeys, no ice cream, no nutty thoughts about banjos or accordions or harpsichords or harmonicas. Or leaping clowns or dancing leprechauns either. She needed to focus. Tonight she would let her instincts have free reign—to do whatever was required. To make good choices. To make fast choices. To live or die as was necessary for the greater good.

She hoped it turned out to be *to live*.

Weapons had been selected, armor had been fitted, assignments had been communicated, and introductions had been made. The army was ready. The fact that there had been no major disagreements or fighting between the two races was a testament to the quality and professionalism of the angels and demons involved.

In the large cavern used for mustering the demon forces, Gabriel stood atop a large boulder that had been rolled out for the occasion. His breath caught when he looked out upon the army. There were angels and demons standing alongside each other, some even talking and laughing and joking. Like old friends. Like they had never been enemies. It was something he had wished for when he set out on his mission, but never really expected to happen—at least not fully, not like what he was seeing now.

Over the course of the day, the number of angels teleporting into the Lair had increased, as Martin, Sampson, and their team of New York Council leaders had been successful in drawing other major cities to the cause. By the afternoon they were targeting less densely populated areas using mass communication methods like e-mail and text message. Angels from across the globe were able to call a central number to arrange pick up by a friendly demon who would teleport them back to the Lair.

The force standing in front of him was one united. Although the angel and demon units had been separated due to differences in fighting style and ability, they were one cohesive group, with the same goals and spirit. As was their nature, the angel units were in tight formations, organized, and although this contrasted with the demon units, which were clustered haphazardly with no apparent structure, somehow they seemed to fit together, almost complimenting each other.

Gabriel glanced at his watch: 11:45. Showtime. He raised a fist in the air and a diligent demon sounded a loud horn throughout the cave. The chatter immediately died down to a few whispers and then a deep and penetrating silence. Any nerves that Gabriel had had when he addressed the gathering of angels in New York were long gone. He was in his element. The confidence he had felt after speaking to Clifford earlier had persisted. He knew it would carry him through the next few hours.

Without hesitation, Gabriel began his address: "Clifford wanted to be here. Many of you know the head of the Eldership of the demons to be a kind man, a caring man, a gentle man. Others of you don't really know him, and until today likely believed him to be a tyrant, a true demon from the depths of Hell, sent to destroy the earth. I can assure you all today that I know Clifford, and he is fully the former. The latter description of Clifford is a myth, a lie concocted by Dionysus to further his cause—a cause which would have the human race enslaved for his own evil purposes. And so I say again, Clifford wanted to be here.

"I say that because I want you all to know the kind of man he is. One who supports his people. Not just the demons, but all who are united in the same cause. Sadly, he couldn't be here today. But not because he's not fighting, too. On the contrary, Clifford will be locked in the greatest fight the earth has ever seen, against the most powerful dictator ever. He is fighting his own fight while we fight ours. He is with us in spirit.

"I spoke to Clifford earlier today and there was no doubt in his mind that with our two races united, we would be victorious. Seeing you here today, I now know that he was right. None can stop a force united under a noble cause. That I believe—must believe—and I want you to believe it, too. That belief will carry us through the night. Do you believe?"

There was a moment of near-silence as Gabriel's question echoed off the walls, hanging in the air like a puff of smoke—*believe believe believe*—until it escaped through a crevice or a crack in the rocky walls. Then someone yelled, "Yeah!" And then another, and another, until the air was filled with a cacophony of cheers, yells, and whistles.

Gabriel couldn't help but to bask in the spirit of the moment, allowing the army to whip themselves into a frenzy, almost like a football team in the locker room just before taking the field. When the noise level reached what Gabriel believed to be its maximum level, he spread his arms and gently bobbed his open hands up and down, signaling the need for quiet once more.

Abruptly, the noise subsided, but not fully. Although no one was speaking, there was an intangible noise in the air, as if the energy of the moment caused sound waves to float above their heads, giving voice to the atmosphere.

Gabriel said, "We shall have no mercy for those who oppose us, as we fight not for ourselves, but for those who cannot hope to defend themselves. But remember, if our brothers and sisters lay down their arms and surrender, we shall show mercy, for they have been deceived too, like us." A quick glance at his watch: 11:50. It was time.

"Go with honor, go with pride, go with power!" As Gabriel said *power*, two things happened simultaneously: The angel/demon forces erupted into cheers, once again filling the cave with a deafening roar, and the massive iron gate began to crank open behind him.

Before the night was out, he would drink the blood of his father. The brute who had once called him a fool was now an old man. But he was still young, strong—and getting stronger. Dionysus smiled. It was time.

Leaving the angel stronghold without an escort for the first time in his life, he shot from a portal that had opened above him. Tonight he had nothing to fear; tonight he was invincible.

He was walking into a trap, most likely, but he trusted his New Archangels to defeat any force who might oppose him. And then he would kill his old man, Clifford—he who had caused him so much pain and anger over the years. *Revenge would be sweet*, he thought, as the world rushed by beneath the powerful strokes of his wings.

He landed on the Warrior's Plateau. Death was near. He could sense it.

"He's there," Taylor said.

Chris said, "Clifford will follow soon. Be ready."

Taylor gritted her teeth, adrenaline rushing through her body. Suddenly she had to pee. *No*, she thought. *No peeing, no monkeys, no ice cream.* She slapped herself hard across the cheek. It stung, but the pain overwhelmed her need to urinate.

Chris looked at her strangely.

Taylor ignored him, continuing to watch the plateau. A fire leapt up at the near side of the space, directly opposite where Dionysus stood waiting. The fire raged for a few seconds and then disappeared into the dark of night. In its place stood Clifford, holding a long, black staff.

Directing her angel ears at the plateau, Taylor heard Dionysus say, "I didn't think you would show up, old man."

Clifford said nothing, but began a slow and purposeful walk towards his adversary.

Kiren, who was watching the cave where the New Archangels had taken shelter, said, "No movement from the birds yet."

Dionysus mimicked Clifford and moved forward, extracting a bright sword from his belt as they neared. It was happening so fast, Taylor barely had time to think about what she would do when it was time to act. *That was good*, she thought. *Less thinking, more instincts.*

And then Dionysus was violently slashing his sword towards the demon leader, their friend. Taylor had always thought of Clifford as old, like a grandfather. Slow moving and fragile. Sometimes she forgot he was even a demon. Not now.

The man moved with demon-quickness, sliding to his left and blocking the barrage of blows from Dionysus's lightning-quick blade. The clangs of metal on metal shrieked through the black of night. The first round was over with Dionysus the aggressor and Clifford the successful defender. They backed off, eyeing each other.

A horn sounded in the distance. The battle had begun and abruptly Taylor's thoughts went to Gabriel.

Gabriel led the army onto the battlefield. Not in their midst or behind them, like some puppeteer who never really got his hands dirty, Gabriel walked ahead of them, more at the front than those on the front lines.

He had no fear, no concern for his own life. Like so many battles he had been in before, he thought only of victory. Defeat was a term used to describe his enemies' futures, foreign to his own life.

His finely tuned angel ears picked up a slight sound, like a pin dropping to the floor. Only there was no pin, no floor. From the corner of his eye he saw it: a flash of a bright sword, a flare of fire from a burning staff. The sound had come from another fight. Dionysus versus Clifford. Evil versus Good.

He swiveled his head forward again, trying to focus on the gleaming, marching angel army headed towards him. Instead his thoughts fell naturally to Taylor. First to her looks: her face, her hair, her smile. Then her personality: beautiful and funny and kind and courageous. The horn had already sounded when he realized that his feet had stopped moving.

The battle had begun.

Forty-Five

"The birds are on the move!" Kiren said.

Gabriel's face melted from Taylor's mind as she snapped her head to the right to see four bright angels soaring above the trees. Their direction was clear: the Warrior's Plateau. There was no doubt that Clifford was their target.

"As planned," Taylor said.

Kiren leapt on her back as she spread her wings. Chris disappeared.

Taking a deep breath, Taylor threw herself off the branch, freefalling for a few seconds to gain momentum before allowing her wings to catch a gust of wind and propel her and her rider forwards and up. They gained altitude rapidly, moving on an angle, not towards their enemy, but at a spot that their enemy would reach in a few seconds, like a defending football player rushing down the field to stop a ball carrier streaking down the sideline.

One second, two seconds, three. Taylor watched the nearest Archangel in her peripheral vision; she was coming closer, closer, not noticing Taylor's approach yet. Taylor thought her name was Johanna. She felt Kiren's hands tighten on her shoulders as she prepared to leap from her back.

Just when she thought she would collide with Johanna without her even noticing her presence, Johanna's eyes twitched to the left, widening as she saw that Taylor was nearly on top of her. Kiren let out a scream as she launched herself from Taylor's back. Johanna swerved rapidly to the right and it looked like Kiren would miss her target, but then she disappeared in mid-leap, suddenly reappearing on Johanna's back, using a pinpoint teleport to clear the remaining distance she needed.

There was an explosion of fire and Taylor saw Johanna start to fall from the sky, burning from head to toe. Kiren remained on her back, landing quick rabbit punches onto her head and shoulders. Johanna screamed in agony.

With the noisy attack on Johanna, the initial element of surprise was expended, and the other three New Archangels reacted to Taylor's presence. They veered to the left, honing in on Taylor's flight path. Immediately she recognized David, and her heart skipped a beat. He looked so much like Gabriel. He was the first to attack.

ʕʔ

Although the horn had sounded only for a moment, it continued to ring through Gabriel's head, helping to clear his muddled thoughts for the first time since they marched out on the battlefield. He had no thoughts of Taylor, or of Clifford, or of destiny, or of victory. Also for the first time, he took a look at his opponents on the other side of the field. That's when he saw the varied expressions on their faces.

Unlike the faces on his men and women—hard, determined, ready—the faces across from him were different. Some were hard, angry, but not in preparation for battle. Angry for another reason. Angry because they saw so many angels rising against them—all traitors in their minds. Other faces were surprised, and some even appeared scared, or unsure of themselves. Not in a million years would they expect an angel force of such magnitude to join the demons in opposition. The last expression Gabriel saw was sadness, as if the thought of fighting—and possibly killing—so many of their brothers and sisters caused them great anguish. Maybe they weren't all evil, weren't all lost causes. Just confused, like he had been.

Gabriel knew what he had to do.

He stopped, raising his open hands to signal for his troops to follow suit. There were some on both sides who had already begun running, faces full of rage, hearts set on killing, on destroying. When Gabriel stopped, both sides stopped. Somehow he knew they would.

He spoke, his voice loud and clear. "Angel brothers, angel sisters. You have been deceived!" He pronounced each word slowly and crisply to ensure their meaning was clear. "Dionysus has a plan, but it's not what you think. He would have you all think him a humanitarian, but he is not. He wants to enslave humankind, destroy their right to choose, take their freedom. He is a liar!"

Gabriel paused, waiting for a reaction. The angel army began murmuring, low and rumbling, some speaking to each other and others to whoever might be listening. "You're the liar!" a large angel on the front lines yelled.

"All lies!" yelled another. "Demons are scum!"

Gabriel shook his head. "No! You have it wrong, backwards. These angels behind me have heard the truth, have seen evidence of the truth, and now they believe. Will you listen to what they have to say? Will you listen to their message?"

A group of five or six bulky angels broke from their ranks and approached Gabriel. Their hands were open and arms extended, a sign of peace. Gabriel's heart leapt in his chest. The impossible suddenly seemed possible. No more blood spilled, no more death, no more fighting.

Three of the angels led the way, two following close behind. When they were within two steps of coming face to face with Gabriel, they stopped. "We will listen," the angel in the middle said calmly. His words were friendly, honest. "And so will my friends," he said, moving to the side to create an opening for the two angels in the rear.

As the hole opened up, Gabriel caught a glint of steel as two blades were thrust at his chest.

※

A basketball-sized orb shot from David's hands. It would be an easy block, just an initial volley. Taylor fired her own orb to seek and destroy the incoming missile. Prior to impact, however, David's orb split into three, one meeting Taylor's and exploding violently. The other two danced around the explosion and reformed into a larger orb. It was too late, she was too surprised. The orb contacted her chest, sending blades of pain through her entire body and throwing her backwards through the air.

As she fell, she tried to block out the pain and regain control, but found that her wings refused to obey her commands, like when she was first learning to fly. She spiraled out of control, holding her breath as she prepared to crash onto the hard earth. And then Chris was there, holding her hand. Twisting-spinning-funneling: They reappeared on the Warrior's Plateau, where Chris set Taylor onto her feet.

Only problem: She couldn't feel her legs. They collapsed, knees buckling. Her brain commanded her arms to break her fall, but they ignored her, flopping like rubber, as useless as dead fish. She smashed face first onto the dust.

Chris knelt beside her. "Are you alright?" he asked.

Before she understood his question, she heard the fierce twanging of steel beyond him. Looking around his shadowy form, she saw Dionysus whirling his sword like a baton, recklessly pushing Clifford back towards the edge of the cliff. The old demon wielded his staff with skill, blocking each blow with precision, careful to ensure he didn't lose a finger in the process.

"I'm fine," Taylor lied. "Help Clifford."

Chris nodded and left her. Every cell in her brain struggled to regain control of her muscles, but it was as if she were paralyzed from the neck down, only able to twist her head from side to side.

Pinned to the ground, Taylor was aware of a presence approaching behind her. She closed her eyes, not wanting to see Death.

❦

Although his body had relaxed, his mind had not. Realizing the danger, Gabriel's mind forced his torso to bend backwards, forced his hands to the ground. As if in slow motion, Gabriel saw the twin swords slide past above him with barely an inch to spare.

His quick mind was already three moves ahead, and his body obeyed. Kicking upwards heavily he caught each of his assailants in the head with a boot while springing back and away to safety. Vertical again, he saw that his maneuver had knocked the angels to the earth and dislodged their swords. While they struggled to regain their feet, Gabriel drew his own sword and rushed to them, picking up one of their swords as he passed it. With a deft flick of each wrist, Gabriel pointed the blades to each angel's neck.

Under ordinary circumstances Gabriel would have killed them immediately. It wasn't that he was coldhearted or enjoyed killing; rather, it was the law of war. Kill or be killed. No mercy. No second chances. And yet he paused, watching his adversaries carefully. The three angels that had escorted the two assassins made no move to help their fallen comrades. The downed angels' eyes were wide with terror, convinced that their last breaths were moments away, maybe less. Gabriel realized that this was a life-changing moment. Kill them and he could carry on the tradition of war, a tradition started by Dionysus. Spare them and perhaps things could change.

It was a risk.

If he didn't kill them, one of them might kill him or someone he loved. His destiny seemed to hang on the very edges of the swords he wielded.

With a sigh, he retracted the swords, tossing one to the ground next to its twin and returning his own to its scabbard. He said, "We do not wish to kill anyone. Please, let us speak as equals. Allow us to share our message of peace."

He extended a hand to one of the attackers. "Please, my brother, take it."

Hesitantly, the angel extended a hand as if Gabriel's touch might burn him or send an electric shock through his body. Instead, Gabriel grasped his hand firmly and pulled him to his feet. Then he did the same for the other angel. "My brothers," he said to them. "I have a remarkable story to tell you. Can you convince the rest of them to listen?" He gestured to the army standing behind them.

Instead of responding, one angel said, "Why did you show us mercy when we would not have done the same for you?"

Gabriel said, "Brother, my every instinct would have had me slit your throat. But I am tired of the killing. So tired. And I realized that the instincts I have to kill are borne of the lies of our leaders. This I can prove. That is why these angels are with me today."

Satisfied, the angel said, "We will listen. I will try to convince the others."

"Thank you, brother," Gabriel said. He motioned to his unit leaders, one of whom was Sampson. When they approached, he said to Sampson, "Make peace with these angels. Gather together in the Lair. Anyone from either side who is unwilling to make peace should be bound and guarded. Is that agreed?" He looked to both sides for confirmation.

One of the opposing angels said, "We can live with that."

Gabriel's angel and demon unit leaders nodded. Speaking for all of them, Sampson said, "We agree."

Gabriel said, "Good. Now I must go. There is something I must attend to before it is too late." Before anyone could question him he sprang into the night, his wings spreading wide and propelling him off to the east, where flashes and blazes could be seen against the dark of the horizon.

ʃɀ

Someone shook her shoulder. "Taylor, Taylor—are you hurt?" a voice said. It didn't sound like Death.

Taylor opened her eyes and blinked to clear her vision. Kiren knelt beside her, her eyebrows tense and concerned. Taylor said, "I can't move my body."

"He must have hit you with a paralyzer. It will wear off soon."

"Go," Taylor said. "Help Chris, help Clifford."

Like Chris had done before, Kiren sprang to her feet and ran in the direction of the battle. On one side of Kiren's running body, Taylor saw Dionysus bearing down on Clifford, who appeared to be tiring, his staff moving somewhat slower. On the other side, Chris was encircled by the remaining three New Archangels. Johanna was nowhere to be seen—evidently Kiren had finished her off.

Taylor knew Kiren had a choice to make. Help Clifford or help Chris. They both needed it desperately. What they really needed was a miracle.

And they got one.

A magnificent creature swooped down from above, landing behind Dionysus with a thump. At first Taylor thought it was David, moving to gang up on the demon leader. But she could still see Chris fighting three New Archangels, one of whom was David. Unless he had learned to clone or split himself into two, the fourth angel could only be one person: Gabriel!

From across the plateau, Taylor heard Gabriel say, "Let's end this now."

Dionysus, who had been on the verge of breaking through Clifford's defenses, whirled around just as Clifford tripped and fell back, landing dangerously close to the edge of the cliff. His staff clattered from his hands and bounced over the edge, disappearing into oblivion.

Taylor felt a twitch. Not a crazy, I-can't-stop-my-face-from-spasming kind of twitch, but a slight movement of her left foot. She wasn't sure if it was an aftershock from the paralyzing orb that had struck her, but it was something. Looking down at her shoe, she concentrated hard, trying to get it to move again. Nothing.

She heard a scream to her right and twisted her head to identify the source. Dionysus had leapt at Gabriel, wielding his heavy sword as easily as a feather, aiming his powerful strokes at Gabriel's head, heart, and lower abdomen. Gabriel parried each blow with ease, dancing around like a prize winning fighter. With each deflected blow, Dionysus's anger grew. His body glowed brighter and brighter as he sucked the light from the firmament, trying to overmatch his opponent.

Taylor feared for Gabriel. She remembered how he had struggled against Cassandra in her evolved state. This time, however, he was not struggling. It was as if he himself had evolved, like he was different, somehow. With the grace of a ballet dancer, he spun and flipped and parried around the plateau, defending himself, and generally making Dionysus's extraordinary ability look rather ordinary.

He even had time to taunt the angel leader. "Is that all you got, old man? C'mon!"

Hearing Gabriel's words, Dionysus shrieked with fury and redoubled his efforts. Gabriel was ready. He ducked under the first powerful stroke and simultaneously stabbed upwards, into the belly of his enemy. With a sickening scraping sound, Gabriel's blade slid between the flaps of metal armor, through the skin, and into his opponent's innards.

Another twitch. Taylor's right foot this time. She looked down, hoping to see her feet dancing a silent jig.

Instead, when her vision passed by her arm, she noticed her right hand. It was balled into a fist. She remembered clearly that it had been open when she had fallen. Her body was coming back to life.

She strained at the invisible bonds that held her to the ground, picturing ropes snapping and chains breaking. It worked.

She sat up. Her arms and legs were tingling, like they had all fallen asleep in unison. Sharp prickles of pain lanced along her joints, as if there were a thousand Liliputians jabbing her with tiny swords. Gritting her teeth, she blocked out the fierce pain and struggled to her feet.

Gabriel was standing over Dionysus, a foot placed firmly on his chest. Dionysus was laughing, madly, maniacally, as if he had lost all understanding of where he was, what was about to happen to him. Something white bubbled from his lips as he laughed; it was bright in the darkness. Blood. From his internal injuries.

Gabriel thrust his sword downwards, through Dionysus's heart. The crazed laughing stopped. He lay still. Dead, maybe—hopefully.

Possibly sensing Taylor's watchful eyes, Gabriel turned sharply to his left. They made eye contact. She started to run towards him and then remembered the others. Her attention had been so focused on her boyfriend's battle and her own struggle with her disobedient body, that she had been ignoring the other fights.

For a second she wondered whether the remaining New Archangels had been somehow connected to Dionysus's life force. A strange memory popped into her head of a book she had read as a child. It was about an evil magician who controlled an army of demented clowns. Eventually the magician was destroyed, and his murderous clowns crumbled to pieces, as if they had never existed. Would the same happen to the New Archangels now that their leader had been destroyed? Somehow she knew it wouldn't.

The fight was far from over.

Now she scanned the plateau until she found Chris and Kiren, fighting for their lives along the cliff's edge. Each had their hands full with one of the New Archangels. They were losing. Maybe about to lose. So much for the deranged magician story.

Something was missing. No, not some*thing*—some*one*. David, the third New Archangel. Taylor frantically looked for the boy, sensing Death was on the loose. Gabriel saw the change in her expression and turned to follow her gaze. They spotted him at the same time.

He was shaking with rage, towering over Clifford, who was on his back, weaponless, defenseless. Just as Taylor started to run for them, Gabriel yelled, "Noo!" and headed in the same direction.

They were too late. Far too late.

Forty-Six

Taylor stopped when David plunged his sword into Clifford's chest. Gabriel, however, kept running, charging, like a bull seeking a red cape. David, who continued to hold his blade in Clifford's body, didn't see his brother coming. Running at full angel speed, Gabriel slammed into him, pulling David off the demon leader and slinging him to the rocky earth. David's hands had been tight on his sword's hilt and it was wrenched from Clifford's frame during the collision.

Taylor glanced to her right. Chris and Kiren were swordless, having been defeated by Sarah and Percy. The New Archangels would show no mercy.

Her eyes flashed back to Gabriel. Her heart dropped in her chest when she saw him. Staggering, falling: Gabriel was on his back, David advancing.

David's sword was ripe with shining fluid from his victim.

Chris and Kiren were about to die. Gabriel, too.

Her entire world was about to be destroyed, annihilated, eradicated, like rats by an exterminator.

Fire, pain, heat, and power seared through her veins. Her skin blazed with light. She had done nothing. Her body had done everything. Her vision went black, and then she saw it. A slithering black snake of impossible size, dripping fangs, coarse skin, blood-red eyes. Evil in those eyes. Death in that stare. Closing in on its prey—coming for her.

Taylor had a sword but she tossed it aside. *No*, she thought, *how can I kill Death without my weapon?* But her arm wouldn't obey her, wouldn't retrieve the sword. Instead, she saw herself glowing in the dark, getting brighter and brighter. Through her clothes she could see the tattoo on her ankle, on the inside of her wrist; they glowed the brightest of all. She peered over her left shoulder and caught a glimpse of her first tattoo—the snake's head was as bright as the sun. And then she exploded. Or so it seemed, such was the intensity of the pain, of the light, of the impact on her body. All went quiet and dark. When she opened her eyes the snake was gone. Instinct told her that it was gone for good—really dead this time.

Vision returned to her. She didn't know how much time had passed, but saw that David had not yet killed Gabriel; Chris and Kiren were still alive. Although the vision had seemed to last for at least a minute, in real time it must have been as short as a blink of an eye, maybe less. Her body was still changing, performing, out of control. The fire-pain-heat-power sensation escalated and she saw her clothes begin to burn away, but not all over. On her ankle, the outline of a snake strung up on a sword appeared; on the inside of her wrist there was a blazing set of angel wings. And although she couldn't see it, she knew that the large snake etched into her back and shoulder had burst from its shroud, piercing the night with the intensity of the sun.

No, no, no, no! she thought. It was about to happen. The explosion. Everything destroyed, except for her. Not the snake this time, but Gabriel and Chris and Kiren—the New Archangels, too, which was good, but not at the expense of her friends. There had to be another way. But if there was, her body wouldn't allow it.

She screamed as her body was racked with tortured agony and all went white. Whiter than white—the absence of darkness. And then her life went black.

Forty-Seven

She didn't open her eyes. Didn't want to open them. Didn't want to see—maybe ever again. Blind to the truth she might be happy.

"Taylor, Taylor," the perfect voice said. Oh the sweetness of the voice, the love in its tone. Gabriel's voice. Her heart leapt. Maybe she had died along with everyone and was about to be reunited with him, with her friends. But then she remembered Samantha and misery swept over her mind, her heart, her soul. She pictured Sam crying, mourning the loss of her boyfriend, her best friend. Taylor felt like crying, too.

The voice again: "Taylor, Taylor." A gentle touch on her shoulder accompanied the voice. She was scared to open her eyes but she did. Gabriel was looking at her, frowning. "Are you okay?" he said.

Taylor thought the question was dumb. "If dead is okay, then I'm great," she said.

Gabriel laughed. Taylor couldn't help but to think how rude it was for one dead person to laugh at the death of another. He said, "You're not dead."

"Gabriel, it's good that we get to keep seeing each other, but I'm not going to be one of those stupid ghosts like Bruce Willis in *The Sixth Sense* that don't realize they're dead. I am going to try my best to accept it and move on with my life—well, not my life, but my death I guess."

Gabriel said, "Sit up, hero-girl. You're as far from death as anyone on this plateau."

Despite her mind's objections, Taylor allowed Gabriel to lift her into a sitting position. She scanned the area around her. First she saw Chris and Kiren, rising to their feet, walking towards her. They didn't seem to be dead. She noticed the wetness on Gabriel's arm. "Are you...?" she said.

"Hurt? Yes, but it's only a flesh wound. I'll be just fine."

Nodding, Taylor continued her gaze, looking for the New Archangels, for Dionysus, but they were gone. "Where?" she said.

Gabriel said, "A blast of light resonated out from you, in a circle. They were vaporized, just the New Archangels."

"But how?"

"We may never know, Taylor. I'm not sure it matters."

"David?" Taylor asked.

"His body is still there, but he might be dead."

"But why didn't he vaporize like the rest of them."

"Look for yourself," he said.

Taylor rolled over, allowing her head to face the direction where she had last seen David. His body was flush with the earth, pinned flat, as if some invisible force was pushing on his back. A bubble surrounded him, bursting with light from the edges, cradling him, protecting him.

"But how?" Taylor asked.

Before Gabriel could reply, the lifeless form within the force field reanimated, pushing slowly to his feet. The bubble changed its shape to allow him to stand while remaining within its borders. David's back was to them.

He turned.

When he saw them looking at him he spoke. "Death lives," he said simply.

Gabriel's voice cut through the still of the night. "It's over, David. No more."

He laughed, loud and shrill. "Not over. Never over," he said.

"No, David. The angels and demons are at peace. The War is over."

David's eyes were like steel, cold and hard. He was speaking to Gabriel, but staring at Taylor. Penetrating.

She felt him in her head.

The War has just begun, Taylor heard him say. Gabriel couldn't hear him. Not from wherever David was speaking. As if through some evolved channel of communication, David's message filled Taylor's mind. She shivered.

David didn't respond verbally to his brother. Instead, he crouched, and then pushed off from the ground, his wings extending within the confines of the glimmering circle of light, which followed him through the sky like a starburst.

Gabriel started to pull away from Taylor, to follow his brother, presumably. "No, Gabriel!" Taylor yelled.

Gabriel stopped, looked back. Looked forward and up again, watching his brother grow smaller and smaller until he disappeared like a firefly in the night. Made a decision. Turned and walked back to Taylor.

"Why did you stop me?" he said.

"He would have killed you," Taylor replied bluntly.

"I could have talked to him, reasoned with him, convinced him."

Taylor wanted to agree with him, to lie to him, to tell him his brother was still somewhere within the evolved angel. But she couldn't lie. Not anymore. There had been too many lies already. In their relationship, in their lives. "He's too far gone," she said instead.

Gabriel winced, like she had slapped him in the face, but then nodded. "I know," he said.

"He spoke to me."

Gabriel's head tilted to the side, his eyebrows narrowing. Her words probably seemed senseless, like she had been injured worse than he thought.

Taylor said, "When you told him the War was over, he didn't respond to you, not verbally, but I heard him in my head. Telepathically…or something."

In another life, in another time, perhaps he wouldn't have believed her. But he did without question. He said, "What did he say?"

"*The War has just begun*," she quoted.

Gabriel's frown remained. "He'll never stop, will he?"

Taylor shook her head. Then she remembered. "What about Clifford?"

Gabriel's head jerked up as if he had forgotten about the fallen demon leader too. Without a word, they scrambled to their feet, meeting Chris and Kiren as they ran to where Clifford was last seen. He was still on his back, still on the ground, still bleeding from the wound administered by David. Eyes closed, mouth dusty, beard crusted with crumbs of dirt and sand.

The fastest of the four, Taylor reached his side first. Touching his arm, she said, "Clifford?"

There was so much blood, more than she had ever seen. The wound was wicked and deep. She didn't expect a response.

"Uhhhh," he croaked, his lips parting slightly. His eyes slitted open. "My dear," he whispered.

"Clifford, we're gonna save you," Taylor said as the others approached, kneeling in a circle around their dying leader.

Clifford's eyes never left Taylor's. "No you won't," Clifford said. Taylor was about to argue, but Clifford said, "Shhh. You have done well, young angel. You have done much, much more than we could ever have asked of you. I am so thankful to have lived long enough to meet you. It has been a privilege, Taylor, but now I must go to meet my father in the land of the dead."

Tears flowed freely from Taylor's eyes; they felt hot and fierce on her cheeks. She tried to speak but couldn't. Instead, she gripped the old demon's hands with both of hers, hoping that some of her life would leak into him.

Clifford turned to Chris. "Young demon, long shall your name be remembered amongst your people. Seek honor in all that you do."

"I will," Chris said, his eyes misty.

To Kiren, Clifford said, "You are quite a woman, my dear." Kiren's eyes were already overflowing, her sobs choking her.

Lastly, he gazed at Gabriel. "You have fulfilled your destiny, my angel friend. I knew you would."

Gabriel's tears dripped from his lips as he said, "It was your destiny too, my king."

Clifford smiled and then died, his last breath taken while he was in a moment of true happiness. The foursome—two angels, two demons—huddled over their fallen leader reverently for ten minutes, arms around each other in comfort.

Gabriel finally said, "Let us make a pact now—that we will honor Clifford's memory by always fighting to maintain the peace that has been made between angels and demons today."

"Peace?" Taylor said hollowly. The word sounded foreign to her.

Gabriel said, "We did it, Taylor. There will be no more fighting."

Taylor didn't comprehend how it was possible, how it could be over—the Great War. But she knew his words were true, despite what David had said to her. "I will help however I can," she said solemnly.

Chris said, "As will I."

Kiren nodded, still unable to speak.

Gabriel said, "Let's get Clifford home."

Forty-Eight

They teleported all together, arriving seconds later in Clifford's empty office. Chris and Kiren left with Clifford's body, which was already turning to ash. They wanted to ensure the ashes could be collected and preserved for the funeral.

Taylor and Gabriel were alone.

Gabriel sighed forcefully.

"What?" Taylor asked.

"I dunno, I'm just tired I guess. Emotionally more than physically."

"I know what you mean. I can't believe Clifford's gone."

"Yeah, and David, too."

Taylor put her arms around Gabriel's neck, rested her head on his chest. His heart was thumping loud and quick, like he had just sprinted. "Gabriel...David is messed up inside. It is no one's fault."

Gabriel sighed again. He didn't answer. Instead, he said, "Taylor, you were amazing today. I don't know how you did it, defeating the Archangels while protecting us."

Taylor laughed. "I don't know either. My body just does things—I'm glad it does—although sometimes I wish I could control it."

Gabriel smiled. "Maybe you're just meant to be that way."

"Maybe."

He squeezed her tightly. She felt warm, safe—partly because of him, but mostly because of herself. Her mom would have been proud. She was herself. Strong, independent, capable. Not pretending to be someone else like so many others. She heard a voice in her head, not David this time—her mom: *When you find true love, the love that you can't live without, the love that fills you with joy, you hold onto that love until the day you die.*

Taylor squeezed Gabriel back. She promised herself never to let him go.

Gabriel looked down at her, kissed her forehead. Normally Taylor would find such a kiss to be condescending, but this time it felt loving, tender.

"I should address the troops," Gabriel said.

"What happened, anyway?" Taylor asked.

"We stopped fighting," Gabriel said. "There was no more killing, no more war. I told them all to stop, and they stopped. I don't really know how it happened."

"Clifford was right," Taylor said.

"Oh don't you start," Gabriel said, pushing her away. "I'm just an angel, nothing more."

"Maybe so," Taylor said, "but you're special."

"You mean short-bus special?" Gabriel said, using the same joke Taylor had when he had referred to her as *special*. It seemed like a long, long time ago.

"That's *exactly* what I meant," Taylor joked.

"Let's go, angel-girl."

Taylor put her arm around him and he did the same. They followed the long hallway out of the Elders' Chambers and boarded the waiting transporter. They switched transporters twice as they made their way to the large cavern where Gabriel had first assembled the troops. The Lair was like a ghost town, deserted and quiet.

A final passageway and a heavy wooden door lay ahead of them. Behind it they could hear the drone of voices. Gabriel hauled the door open, spilling torchlight into the tunnel.

Taylor let Gabriel enter first. The spectacle in the cavern was like nothing she had ever seen. From behind him, she could see thousands of shapes, some light, some dark, all smiling. When Taylor and Gabriel entered, every man and woman raised an arm. The demon hands held flames, the angel hands held light. Taylor's breath caught as the room was filled with fiery, flickering, glowing, *sparkling* beauty.

A cheer rose up, starting mild and professional and then raucous and filled with whistles and catcalls. Taylor laughed. *Probably par for the course for a merry gathering of angels and demons*, she thought. The crowd parted in front of them and they passed through like celebrities. For a final time, Taylor squeezed a flap of arm skin between her thumb and forefinger. Her nerve ending fired, sending the pain to her brain. She didn't cry out, loving the reality-confirming pain more than anything. *It was no dream—never was.* This was her life.

A stage had been erected. Sampson met them on the platform and gave Gabriel, and then Taylor a hug. "Well done," he said.

"You, too," Taylor said.

Kiren appeared at Sampson's side, clutching his hand. She wiped a tear from her cheek.

"It's done?" Taylor asked.

Kiren nodded. Clifford's ashes had been collected.

Suddenly, Chris appeared with Samantha, who rushed to Taylor, hugging her fiercely. "Thank God," she said. "I was so worried, even after Chris said you were fine."

"A piece of cake," Taylor said.

Sam released her, a shocked look crossing her face. "Here I am, all worried about you, and you're thinking about your stomach."

Taylor laughed. "You should be an actress," she said. "I actually thought you were worried."

"You should have seen me an hour ago, I was a mess. Marla and Jennings found me wandering the campus like a blind mouse trapped in a maze. You should have seen their faces when Chris teleported into their dorm room while we were watching a movie. I'm not sure how we're going to explain that one!"

The reunited group of friends laughed effortlessly. Taylor stopped laughing first and took a moment to just watch their faces. No hint of stress or strain clouded any of them. Taylor hated to break up the party, but she had to tell Sam the news.

"Sam, there's something I have to tell you."

Her friend's smile faded. She nodded. "Taylor—Chris told me about Clifford. I'm overcompensating with the jokes. I'm not sure how I'm going to deal with it, but I really don't want to right now. I'm really gonna miss—" She choked on the last word and brushed a tear from each eye.

"I will, too," Taylor said. "We all will." She put her arm around her friend.

Gabriel said, "Everyone's waiting. We'd better get the party started. Taylor, will you say a few words?"

Taylor looked at her boyfriend's dark eyes. She hated public speaking and was afraid that her words wouldn't come out the way she wanted. She had to trust Gabriel. Finally, he had earned her trust back. She shook her head.

"No, you are our leader. Clifford would want you to speak. I want you to speak. Say what's in my heart."

Gabriel's eyes widened. "Taylor, I don't know…"

"Yes, Gabriel. Yes, you do. Speak for me, speak for your family, speak for Clifford, speak for yourself, speak for all of us." Taylor's words felt right even as she spoke them. Her gut confirmed it.

Gabriel's lips tightened, but he moved to the podium at the center of the stage. Taylor followed him, as did Sam, Chris, Sampson, and Kiren. Six friends, three races, a plethora of relationships—all united.

At the microphone, Gabriel paused, scanning the crowd, which had grown uncannily quiet. He spoke, his voice starting as a low rumble, but growing bolder with each word, each syllable.

"Angels…demons…and humans," he started. "Friends, former enemies, brothers, sisters, patriots, and traitors…We…have….WON!" he roared. The crowd erupted in frenzied applause. He raised his arms in the air, silencing the masses. "The Great War, which we now know was started under false pretenses, is over. There will be no more bloodshed. Not today, and if we stick together, not ever again!" More cheers.

Taylor grinned. Gabriel was magnetic, like her mother had been. She was proud of him.

"We must stick together, for we have learned that it only takes one to start a war. We lost a great man today. He was a demon, but I would not hesitate to call him my friend, my brother. We should honor Clifford by keeping the peace that he fought and died to bring about." Gabriel paused. The audience leaned forward, anticipating his powerful words.

His wings burst from his back, arching over his head, shining magnificently. "My wings are white!" he declared. "But they would be no less beautiful if they were black! There is no dark or light, only shades of gray. We are all human inside, all different, all good, all bad. All human," he repeated. "None better, none worse. All equal."

Taylor's skin tingled. Not with evolution, like before, but with excitement, with wonder, like listening to a brilliant vocalist hit a high note. He was speaking for her. Her thoughts, her feelings, and her beliefs had received a voice from Gabriel. Like she could never have provided on her own.

"Look at me," Gabriel continued. "I did horrible things. Horrible. But I made up for them. Look at me now. If anyone is a shade of gray, it's me. Let's all be gray together. What do you say?"

The crowd cheered. Screams of "Yes!" rose through the cavern, echoing in the hollow space.

Taylor felt alive.

Forty-Nine

Two months had come and gone like a fast car on the highway. Between attending classes, studying, and visiting the Lair, Taylor had very little time to think.

But now it was all over: her freshman year, final exams, the signing of the Great War Abolition Act by the new angel and demon leaders, Clifford's funeral. It had been a busy time, full of emotions—both happy and sad.

A new colony of angels and demons had been organized, with their primary goal being to protect humanity. Those who volunteered to be part of the colony would infiltrate all manner of human organizations, from hospitals, to political parties, to law enforcement agencies, in the hopes of being able to heal the injured, protect the innocent, and diffuse political tensions. They would be secret messengers of peace.

A special task force had been created to search for David Knight, the last living Archangel besides Taylor. They hadn't heard from him. No communications, no threats, no violence against angels or demons or humans. And so they hunted for him, not knowing which continent he might be on.

Gabriel seemed happy, but at the same time, Taylor knew he was troubled. She knew he felt responsible for unleashing the monster that his brother had become. No matter how many times she tried to convince him it was the result of some mutant gene in David's DNA combined with the mental games played by Dionysus, he wouldn't forgive himself, obsessing over his brother and where he might be, what he might do. He lay awake at night, staring at the ceiling. Even when he was able to drift off, he was never restful, twitching in his sleep.

For the last eight weeks, Taylor had worried about him. When the time had passed without event, he got better, happier. He still worried, but obtained some level of peace. It helped that he had so many responsibilities. After all, he had a colony to run! Gabriel had been unanimously voted as head of the new Demonangel Colony, of which all of Taylor's friends were now members.

Taylor would join eventually. After college perhaps. Taylor and Sam had agreed to wait. But now Taylor was ready for a break. Ready for normal.

She leapt from the cliff, allowing gravity to take her on a free-fall, her stomach lurching magnificently up and down, right and left. Just before being dashed to a thousand pieces on the rocks below, Taylor's wings burst from her back, caught the wind, and pushed her higher, skimming the treetops as she rose. *Yeah, normal was good*, she thought as the sun hit her face. *Okay, maybe not the normal that most people have, but normal for an angel.* "I'm an angel!" Taylor yelled as she soared over the mountaintops.

"I *thought* there was something different about you," Gabriel said, coming up behind her.

Chris appeared in the air in front of them. He said, "Being a demon ain't so bad either."

Wingless, he began to drop. Taylor saw Sam's head pop over his shoulder. "Don't forget the humans!" she yelled. Before hitting the ground, they disappeared, reappearing moments later on a tree branch below.

A flash of white buzzed over their heads. Sampson said, "Woohoo!"

A dark shape glanced back as they passed. Kiren said, "Woohoo!" She was clinging to her boyfriend's neck.

"An angel together with a demon…weird," Gabriel said. "I never thought I would see the day."

"Clifford did," Taylor said. "He knew it all along."

"You're probably right. He always seemed to be a step ahead."

"Try two," Taylor said. "Race me back to the Lair?"

"Give me a head start, ten seconds."

"Wimp," Taylor joked.

"You're an archangel!"

"Okay, angel-boy. See you at the finish."

Gabriel took off and Taylor counted to five before racing after him. Her boyfriend *was* the head of the new Demonangel Colony, after all, and ten seconds was a long head start.

She passed him halfway to the Lair, but stopped to let him catch up. Instead of passing her, he flew into her arms. They embraced, enjoying the moment, spinning through the air, the freedom of being alive, the act of being in love.

Taylor hoped it would last.

Enjoy a BONUS CHAPTER at:
http://davidestesbooks.blogspot.com/p/archangel-evolution-bonus-chapter.html

Discover other books by David Estes at:
http://davidestesbooks.blogspot.com

The Evolution Trilogy
Book One—Angel Evolution
Book Two—Demon Evolution
Book Three—Archangel Evolution

About the Author

After growing up in Pittsburgh, Pennsylvania, David Estes moved to Sydney, Australia where he lives with his wife Adele. When he's not writing, he's enjoying the sun and surf at Manly Beach.

Made in the USA
Charleston, SC
01 February 2013